ABBOT POND

ABBOT POND

STEVE HOBBS

www.hobbspond.com

ISBN-13: 9780999317730
ISBN-10: 0999317730

Library of Congress Control Number: 2021905652

Hatchet Mountain Press
Manchester, NH

For Raish,
who never really left us . . .

CONTENTS

Rachel stepped from the car and swore into the wind. The cold and the snow sobered her a little, but her thoughts still weren't clear. She kept the door open, and the inside lights spilled onto the dark street around her. Too bad nothing else worked.

She took a sip from her plastic cup and placed it on top of the Camry. The street was narrow and barren with no houses or even streetlights, just skyscraping trees and uncut bushes. Rachel wanted to kick the side of her father's car or maybe just scream. Mainly, she just wanted to go back. She wasn't so angry at her mother anymore. She never really was.

The falling snow mixed with a cold rain and she was shivering. She only wore a light sweatshirt and jeans. No jacket or boots. Hardly winter clothes. The trip had been so impromptu she barely had time to pick up the booze. Now, she was stuck in the middle of nowhere with a crappy car that wouldn't run.

Should she call them? What would it hurt to swallow her pride and let them know she needed them? She did need them.

A car approached slowly and stopped beside her.

The passenger side window lowered, and a welcome blast of heat crossed her face.

Hopefully, this guy could help her.

CHAPTER ONE

ABBOT POND

His father stood on the deck, holding his big coffee cup with steam trailing upward from it. He wore work boots, of course, Dockers, and a dark-hooded sweat suit covered with white chlorine stains. He rested against the snow-covered railing and stared across the giant silver dollar of a pond behind them. Occasionally, he sipped from the cup, but he focused on the ice sheet in front of him, probably thinking about Ryan. Everyone thought about Ryan when they were on the deck.

Freddie opened the door and stepped outside. "Does Mom know you're here?"

Jack Morgan's face was lined and kind of raw, but his smirk was impish. "I've got a key."

A blanket of cold and snow enveloped Freddie, and he shivered. Abbot Pond was one of the largest ponds in Maine and one of the coldest. He nodded toward the door, and they both trudged inside. Freddie poured some water from the dispenser on the front of the big refrigerator and sipped from it. Freddie only ever drank water.

"Your mother's sending us to Bangor," his dad said. "We're picking up Danny."

Danny Cole had stayed with them multiple times over the last few years. His parents took turns going to jail, usually for drugs or for stealing money to buy drugs, and he was often without a home. Freddie's mother sometimes took in fosters, and some of the kids were fun, but not him. Danny wasn't a bad kid, but he liked to sit in the room and just sort of exist. He was like a skinny, long-haired piece of furniture that got moved around from time to time.

"Why do you think he did it?" Freddie asked. "Took the pills, I mean."

Jack sat at the oak table, nibbling on a bagel. He generally came off as a rascal—not too serious, the lively partner to Freddie's very thoughtful mother—but he was the one who Freddie went to for real answers. "Danny is not a happy boy."

Freddie sat in one of the heavy chairs across from his father and nodded. The overhead fan was on, though it was early winter, and it made a *thud-thud* sound as it spun endlessly. A round mirror hung on the wall behind Jack, and Freddie stared into it, examining his brown face and dark hair. He straightened it a little and thought he looked okay. He was seeing Sophie later, and he had to look good.

"*You're* happy though, aren't you?"

Freddie smiled. "You know I am."

"It's not such a silly question," his father said. "Your mom can be hard, and I'm in and out of the house."

His parents weren't technically married any more. In fact, they were now twice divorced, and a recent reconciliation was not working out. Jack stayed in one of the rentals in Camden while he repaired the damage left from some young tenants. Young tenants were always the worst.

"You'll be back," Freddie said. "You always are."

His father flashed the smile again, and his blue eyes danced with humor. "Damn right I will be."

"Let me go get my stuff," Freddie said. "I'll be right back."

He lifted his sturdy frame from the seat and hurried through the ornate living room. The room was the largest in the cottage, and the furniture was high end, though he knew his mother had gotten a deal. The wooden floors were polished, and an electric fireplace sat at the center of the far wall. A huge picture book rested atop the glass coffee table no one ever regarded, and a few bookshelves with hardcover copies of classic books lined the wall. The television was small, and they had only switched to cable this year. A few framed photos, mostly of Ryan, were scattered across the wall by the stairs. The room was never dusty and always smelled of wood polish.

Freddie ran up the stairs to his room and grabbed his jacket from the edge of the bed. His room was neat enough, but nothing like the rest of the house. He cleaned it once a week and vacuumed the low carpet whenever it felt too crunchy. His room was small, but he had a great view of the pond from his window. A thin diagonal line of frozen moisture had formed on the outside of his window. From the outside, the window probably looked cracked.

The room was painted in basic blue and was dotted with country music posters. Other than his largest poster, the one with George Strait holding a guitar in front of thousands of fans at some stadium, the posters were generally girl singers in shorts or skirts, looking very down-home. His current favorite was a singer named Kelsea Ballerini, though that was subject to change on a frequent basis.

He grabbed his cell off the desk and texted Sophie. *Have to go to Bangor to get Danny.*

She must have been waiting, because her response was immediate. *Ok. I'll see you later. Did you have the dream again?*

Freddie's dreams were always an adventure. He generally dreamt in Spanish, but he no longer remembered the language, and he rarely recognized anyone from his dreamworld. He never saw his parents or Sophie or any of the kids from the team. Lately, he'd been dreaming about an old lady standing over him as he slept. She would point angrily at him, waving a crooked finger, yelling one word at him. Freddie remembered the word and even knew how to spell it. *Aleveso.*

He wrote, *Yeah, she's really pissed at me.*

He grabbed his jacket and a baseball cap from a shelf while he waited. Sophie texted a lot, so he assumed she was talking with her friends while she waited to hear from him. He'd had a few girlfriends over the last few years, and she was his favorite. He imagined they looked like an odd pairing with his dark features and stocky build matched against her fair skin and bright blond hair. He liked spending time with her; though he didn't kid himself that she was perfect or anything. Neither of them were.

The phone buzzed, and he read her message. *Don't worry. I'll protect you.*

His father honked the truck horn. He put the phone into his inside coat pocket and stepped into the hallway. The door to the room across from him, Ryan's old room, was open a crack. Freddie couldn't remember a time when the door wasn't closed and locked. He pushed against the heavy door, and it opened a little more. He flipped on the light switch by the door.

He felt like an intruder, but he had to make sure everything was all right. Ryan's bed was neatly made, and his baseball stuff patiently waited on a shelf by the bed. A cardboard box filled with Legos lay against the wall. Ryan's *Star Wars* toys and a half-solved Rubik's Cube sat on a small desk in the corner of the room.

The wood floor smelled freshly cleaned. He decided that his mother must have cleaned the room earlier and hadn't quite closed the door. He shook away the sadness and hurried down the stairs.

CHAPTER TWO

The Lakeside

Sophie Lindstrom turned the key and popped open the trunk to the brown Audi. She grabbed a handful of spokes and pulled until the rest of the wheelchair was visible. She wrestled with it briefly until it came loose, and she plopped it down and snapped it open in one neat move. Sophie shivered as she wheeled it past the passenger door and waited for Parker to climb out. She pushed her hands into the pockets of her tight J Brand skinny jeans and impatiently tapped her foot.

Parker Bradley wasn't dressed as fashionably as Sophie—no jacket and wearing baggy Levi's that masked her skinny legs. She sort of glided her butt across the dark aluminum bar and fell into the chair, her legs flopping uselessly as she dropped. Sophie remembered when those legs were toned and strong, but that was a different time. The rest of her was strong though, and she was still prettier than Sophie. Sophie felt a little envious of her friend, as odd as that sounded. Parker Bradley was not someone to feel sorry for.

They crossed the parking lot toward the welcoming doors of Lakeside Residence. The Lakeside was technically less than half a mile from Freddie's house, but that was across water. By car, it could take half an hour or more to reach it, depending on traffic. She knew Freddie could swim it in twenty minutes, and he'd skated across it in even less time. The water was so close to the Lakeside's backyard that the owners installed iron fencing to keep wayward patients from falling in.

The building was old but solid, two stories high, and as long as a football field. Originally, it had been the largest house in town and had belonged to a rich couple. They didn't have children, so, when they were gone, their estate turned it into a small hospital that burned down in the 60s, and it wasn't rebuilt until the 1980s, when Alzheimer's was becoming a thing. Whoever owned the place made a killing now. People were always moving in.

Parker stopped, stuck on a jutting river of ice, and tried different angles to roll over the obstacle. Her tiny, bare arms knotted with surprisingly large bumps as she rolled to and fro. Parker's face tightened, and she had her *I can do it* look firmly on display. But Sophie was cold; her cute blue blazer was not designed for October in Abbot Pond, so she grabbed the handgrips behind Parker's shoulder, tipped the wheelchair backward slightly and rolled her friend over the ice. Parker bounced in her seat.

Her friend turned her head and glared. "I could have done it, Sophie."

"I know, but I'm frickin' freezing out here. Can we just go in?"

The oak double door was under a light wooden canopy. Sophie tapped a wheelchair button on the post nearest the entrance, and the doors opened inward. Parker waited as Sophie banged the dirt and sludge from her brown boots onto a welcome mat then tapped another wheelchair button and a second set of doors opened. The foyer was warm, almost hot, and old-time music played. Maybe Frank Sinatra?

A smiling middle-aged woman who always recognized them waved from the sign-in desk. Betty usually wore a blue shirt with a white sweater, even in the summer. Her hair was dark but looked a little touched up to hide some grey. Sophie didn't want to go grey.

"Hello, ladies," Betty said. "Who are you here to see today?"

Sophie said, "No one in particular today. Maybe we'll check on Nancy?"

Betty sadly shook her head, and Sophie's heart stopped beating for just a second. She and Parker shared a quick look, then Parker signed them into the logbook, which she had pulled from the desk to her lap.

Sophie thought about sweet, old Nancy for a moment then nodded to herself, shaking away the grief. "How is her family taking it?"

"They haven't been in yet," Betty said. "Honestly, I've only met them a few times."

The girls approached the north wing entrance, and Parker tapped 5-5-5 onto a keypad by the entrance. The keypad was about the only evidence of the twenty-first century in the building. A framed poster of Clark Gable hung in the common room, and most of the movies were taped from some cowboy channel. The most popular CD in the wing was Bing Crosby's *Greatest Hits*. None of the residents had ever heard of Katie Perry.

The keypad beeped, and the door unlocked. Sophie slowly opened the door into the carpeted hallway. Parker rolled in fast and tight, Sophie right behind her, hoping to close the door before the Sentry spotted them.

The Sentry was a woman named Lucy Diamond. She was grey and wrinkled now and mostly wore sweats, but Sophie had seen photos of her from the 1950s, and she had been a stunner. Sometimes, in black and white, she was dressed as a nurse, but usually, she wore some dark dress, and one photo on her dresser had her dazzling in a bright one-piece bathing suit, chasing a small boy into the sea. Sophie doubted Lucy remembered much of that these days.

Lucy stood in front of them, upset. Her blue sweatshirt had a circular stain atop her right breast. It looked like Jell-O or, possibly, cranberry sauce. "You're late. I called for you hours ago."

They only stopped to make sure the door was closed and locked, then they continued down the hallway into the entertainment room. Patients filled three blue couches that sat near an old TV displaying a black and white cowboy show. Only a few were actually watching the program. Most of the residents were sleeping. Some were drooling.

A tall redheaded kid wearing a white shirt and white pants approached them. His pale skin highlighted the dark lines under his eyes. His smile was big and infectious. He pushed a mop and bucket and looked distracted.

"Hey, Sammy," Parker said. "When did you start working here?"

Sammy Burns was a year older than the girls, and he had been a starter on the varsity basketball team every year he had played. He was a cute guy and was one of the nicer jocks. Not as nice as Freddie, but respectful. Sophie was almost sure Parker had dated him before the accident. She knew not to ask.

He looked really fit, like he'd really hit the gym these last few months. He still didn't look as good as Freddie, who barely worked out any more. Freddie had some good genes—good Colombian genes.

"I've been here a while. Turns out, I have to pay my way through school, so I work here on the weekends."

Parker asked, "What's the bucket for? The Whizzer?"

"Mr. Auburn? No, he doesn't do that anymore. He just sort of sleeps now."

Sophie knew what that meant. Everybody in this place had their own thing. Lucy was the sentry, Mr. Auburn peed on the floor, and Nancy moved furniture around. When their thing stopped, whatever it was, and the sleeping started, that meant they were getting ready to move on. The girls had been volunteering for almost a year now, and they had seen the process ten or twelve times. Alzheimer's was a terrible disease.

"Did someone else pee on the floor?" Sophie asked.

"No. I'm cleaning Mrs. Grayson's room. Someone made a mess in there."

"Nancy's room? What happened?" Parker asked.

He shrugged. "I don't know. A pitcher of water was dumped on the floor, and broken glass is everywhere."

"We'll help you," Sophie said then stopped to text Freddie. *Pick up Danny yet? Have him join us tonight.*

Her cell tried to send the message, and she watched a circle on the screen spin frantically. Eventually, her phone sent her an error message. Wi-Fi was terrible in this place. She decided to resend it when she got back to the car.

She put the cell in her pocket and followed Sammy past the dining room into the living section. Another old TV and more couches adorned the center of the room, and the patients' living quarters wrapped around them. A table rested near the TV area, and a young woman was talking with a patient. They were both crying.

Most of the rooms had a glass-encased shelf built into the wall near the door usually displaying photos of the patient in more lucid times or recent pictures of children or grandchildren. Nancy's case was empty. Sophie knew the poor woman had lived in town her entire life, but she was practically abandoned now.

Nancy's room was a good one though, which meant it was expensive. It was light-colored and had two medium-sized corner windows that kept the room illuminated until mid-afternoon. It was one of only a few single occupancies in the home and was probably larger than the doubles.

Sophie glanced through one of the windows and saw snow flurrying onto the ground. Sophie recognized the print of Nancy's comforter from the old Jordan Marsh, and her dresser was genuine oak. Lucy had apparently loved art, as paintings hung everywhere. No old photos of Lucy existed here either, only paintings from a different time. They were mostly dark in mood and color, and the people in them looked unhappy and cold.

"This explains the glass." Parker had stopped near the entrance to the bathroom—one of the only uncarpeted areas in the room—and a broken frame lay at her feet.

Glass was everywhere, and Sophie briefly worried about Parker getting a flat tire. She knew Parker's wheels didn't work that way, but she always thought about such things. Freddie always told her she was overprotective when it came to Parker.

A broom rested in the corner, and Sophie tried to sweep the shards, but the water made it difficult for the bristles to catch the glass. She sighed.

"Let me try with the mop," Sammy said. "I've done it before."

"Okay. What about that pile of clothes on her bed? Are they clean?"

Sammy nodded.

Parker asked, "You're sure? I'm not handling the dirty clothes again."

"I'm sure."

Sophie pushed some of the clothes closer to the edge, so Parker could grab some, and the girls began folding. Most of the clothes were old and stained, but every now and then, there was a gem—an old dress that looked like it was from the 60s and some nice blouses. Useless to Nancy now, just things that might end up going to charity or being thrown away.

"Do you have some little people living here?" Parker held up toddler pants.

"How did baby clothes get in there, Sammy?"

Sammy looked up and frowned. "We get some weird stuff mixed into the laundry. Someone must have changed their kid and left his pants here."

They heard a crash, and, after a moment, the intercom interrupted the old music. A woman's voice asked for Sammy to go to the kitchen.

He rolled his eyes at the girls and grabbed the broom. "Can you finish mopping for me, Sophie? Somebody dropped a plate."

She smiled and nodded.

Parker said, "Well, it's never boring when we come here."

CHAPTER THREE

DANNY'S BACK

"Is that the idiot?" Richard stood at his desk, peering over Freddie's shoulder.

They were at the cubicle closest to the showroom. Morgan Nissan was one of the largest dealerships in mid-coast Maine, and it consumed most of his mother's time. His dad usually handled the rentals, unless it was time for hardball. Then it was all her.

Freddie turned and saw his father standing by a new Rogue, talking to someone. He squinted and saw Danny sitting in the driver's seat, his hands on the wheel. They both laughed like a couple of kids. Danny looked gaunt, even from a distance.

"He's not an idiot, Richard. He's just had a hard time."

Richard's real name was Ricardo Correa, but he thought he sold more cars with a less Puerto Rican first name. He was tall and middle aged but very energetic and was Freddie's go-to guy on all things Hispanic. Freddie knew his mother disapproved of their friendship, but they got along pretty good. Anyway, it was just a work friendship, and Ricardo was the top seller. He wasn't getting fired any time soon.

"My brother got run over by a Buick twenty years ago. Life is rare and precious," Richard added. "To not appreciate such things make you an idiot."

Freddie watched as Danny climbed from the car and stumbled. He was tall and lanky to begin with, but he was definitely having trouble with his legs. He seemed ready to falter with each step, and his head bounced as though his neck was a spring. He just looked gawky.

"He walks like an idiot as well. Is he retarded?"

Freddie shook his head. "The doctor thinks it's a side effect from the overdose and from being dead for a while. I guess that messes with your head. He's got some memory problems too."

"His clothes don't fit either. Looks like he's wearing a small tent."

"My dad's taking him out later for some clothes that fit."

Richard sat and dug through his top drawer. "Someone gave me their card. A tailor."

He was always well dressed and felt that was key to his sales success.

"That's okay. They're just going to Walmart."

Richard shuddered. "A man should wear clothes that makes him glide."

"You're probably right. I wanted to talk about the old lady."

This got Richard's attention, and his eyes narrowed. "She has returned?"

Freddie nodded. "She yells at me and points and says, *'Aleveso.'*"

"*Aleveso.* You know what that means?"

"Yeah. I think it means to be a traitor or treacherous."

Richard rubbed his chin. "So, you think she believes you have done something terrible, maybe to your people?"

His friend was aware of Freddie's guilt over his good life. "I guess."

"You can't worry so much about these things, Freddie. We are a festive people."

Freddie smiled.

"Anyway, maybe she isn't yelling *at* you so much as she might be warning you about *someone*, perhaps a friend."

"I think some customers need your help by the Pathfinders," his mother's voice said.

Freddie turned and smiled at Maureen Morgan. She was tall and stocky, and white streaks now accented her flame-red hair, but she was still the beautiful woman who rescued him from the streets of Bogota. She forced a smile at him as she faced Richard, who was already on his feet and heading for the door. He smirked and nodded at Freddie as he dashed for safety.

"I may have to let him go one day, Freddie," she said. "How will you feel about me firing your friend?"

Freddie shrugged. They'd had this conversation before.

They approached the showroom watching Jack and Danny. For some reason, Jack lay on the floor beneath an Altima, trying to look up into the engine. His big head made it a tight squeeze between the floor and his skull. Danny laughed with an infectious snort. Freddie couldn't remember a time Danny had laughed like that. Maybe being dead gave him a new perspective.

"He seems happy," his mother said. "Has he been like this all morning?"

"Yeah, he's definitely weirder than usual."

"Jackie Morgan, you get up out of there. You look ridiculous."

Jack bounced up, pretending to bonk his head on the side of the car. The two of them laughed again. He saluted. "Yes, ma'am."

She shook her head and turned to the scrawny teenager beside him. "How are you, Danny?"

Danny stopped laughing and locked eyes with her. He wiped his long dark hair from his wide brown eyes. His cheekbones looked as if they might burst through his pale skin. Freddie couldn't imagine being that skinny.

Danny hugged her. "It's so good to see you."

Maureen looked surprised and stepped away, holding his hand. "It's good to see you as well."

Jack said, "Doc says he's okay for school, but he might be a little behind his class. His memory's a little screwy."

"School is very important," she said. "Very important."

Danny said, "I agree. I'm looking forward to it and to Freddie showing me around."

Maureen said, "Well, Jackie will take you shopping for some clothes, and Freddie can help out here. You two can catch up back at the house, all right?"

Danny looked disappointed, but he nodded.

Freddie couldn't imagine why the kid wanted to hang out. It's not like they were buddies or anything. They went days without talking many times.

"Maybe we can do something tonight, Freddie?" he asked.

"I'm supposed to go bowling with Sophie, but she says you can come along."

Danny smiled and clapped once.

Sophie's out of her mind, he thought.

CHAPTER FOUR

BOWLING BRAWL

Lakefront Candlepin Lanes wasn't anywhere near Abbot Pond, which was not a lake. Sophie knew everyone called it a lake because it was so big, but it wasn't a lake. Even if it was, they were a few miles from the developed part of town, closer to Camden and the Atlantic Ocean than they were to the pond. She guessed everyone just liked to say they lived by a lake. Only the rich kids lived on the lake.

Arnie, the bowling alley's owner, was an older and small-statured man with a scarred-up face from being a boxer a million years ago. He would let Parker wheel close to the line to roll her ball. The other bowling alley in town used the big balls, and they wouldn't let her anywhere near the floor. They said the wheels would scuff the wax.

She sat across from Freddie, who was taking score. He didn't like the automatic scoring, because he always liked to do the math on everything. They watched Danny try to roll, but his arm kept jerking, and the ball would spin into the gutter. It was already halfway through the first string, and he'd probably knocked over five pins so far. He wasn't frustrated though. In fact, he seemed quite pleased.

Danny wore jeans and a grey sweatshirt, and he seemed to absolutely swim in them. Sophie wanted to buy him a burger or something. How could his parents have treated him this way?

Danny returned to the table and sat by Freddie. "My arm's not doing what it's supposed to."

Freddie said, "You just need to practice."

"You're right, Freddie. I just gotta work on my game."

Danny had treated for the drinks and fries. Apparently, Freddie's father had given Danny an advance on some work they would be doing at one of the rentals.

He can't roll a ball, but Freddie's dad wants him to help hang sheet rock, she thought. Still, it was good Danny wanted to try. That was a good step.

Parker wore her same leg-hiding jeans from before, but she had changed into a comfortable UMO t-shirt. Her hair was tied back, and she looked serious. She rolled to the line and set her brake. Leaning to her right, she spun the baseball-sized ball straight down the lane. She got about half of the skinny pins, which was good for her. She waited for her ball and rolled it again, hitting one more pin.

Danny clapped. "You're doing really good, Parker."

Sophie stood up primly and approached the balls. She wore wide-leg crop J. Crews and a tight, tucked-in blue-and-white striped shirt. She felt Freddie watching as she stood at the lane, bouncing the ball from hand to hand. She knew he liked the way she dressed.

She leveled eight pins and picked up the spare, which isn't easy in candlepin.

Freddie high-fived her when she returned then took a sip from his water bottle. "Nice pick up, Soph."

"Thanks. I'm getting pretty good."

He smiled. "You always pretend you're not good at sports and then you beat everyone. It's okay to be good at stuff."

"My mother might disagree with that statement. I guess that makes me kinda downplay things."

She sat down and looked at Parker. She was engaged in some deep conversation with poor Danny as he nodded excitedly. It was hard to make out their conversation over the sounds of pins hitting the deck and the murmuring crowd of kids. Lakefront was a popular hangout.

Parker reached back and flattened her hand against the middle part of her back. Danny's smile faded briefly but then returned. She wondered if he was on some mood-altering drug or something, because he sure seemed giddy. Freddie would know.

"What are you talking about?" she asked.

Parker looked at her. "I was telling him about the accident."

Freddie frowned. "It's been a couple of years now."

Danny asked, "Does it bother you to talk about it?"

"No, not really. I mean, I try not to think about it, but it's there, you know? It's perfectly normal for people to ask me about it. It's kind of weird you're asking me now and not last winter when you were here."

Danny said, "My memory's kinda cloudy. I'm sorry if I didn't say anything then."

Some kids sat at the lane beside them and called to Freddie. They were football players, but Sophie didn't know all of them. The tallest one, a big blonde kid, was Derek Matthews, and he and Freddie were friends. When Freddie left the team, Derek was voted team captain. They didn't hang out that much anymore, and she hoped that wasn't because of her. If she was being honest, she was glad they had drifted apart. Derek was no Freddie Morgan.

Derek walked over. "How you guys doing? Didn't see your Mustang in the parking lot, Freddie."

"We took Sophie's car," Freddie said. "You guys on a team outing?"

Derek nodded. "You gotta build a team mentality, that's what the coach says."

Freddie regarded the guys and tilted his head. "What are you feeding these guys?"

Derek chortled. "Coach has us lifting every day. We're moving away from finesse and more toward smashmouth."

"I guess," Freddie said suspiciously.

Sophie doubted those kids could get that big that fast with extra weightlifting. There was only one way to get that size in only a few months.

Derek looked at Sophie. "Can I borrow your guy for a minute? I want to pick his brain a little."

"Sure, that shouldn't take too long."

She watched them head toward the pool tables. Derek leaned against one of them and talked with his hands chopping the air in front of him. Freddie laughed about something, and then Derek laughed too. She thought this conversation might take a while, and it was Freddie's turn to roll. She sipped her Diet Coke and faced Parker and Danny. He was kneeling beside her.

"What are you guys doing?"

Parker had a weird look on her face. "He wants to feel the spot."

"Excuse me?"

Her friend turned a slight shade of pink. "On my back, where … where I got hurt."

"Is that bad?" Danny asked. "I just wanted to feel it."

"You won't feel anything, knucklehead, and neither will I. But go ahead."

Danny put his hand on her shoulder and slowly slid his palm to the midpoint of her back. Sophie wondered if this was some kind of come-on or something, but Danny seemed so innocent. Parker didn't seem to mind, other than obviously thinking he was kind of odd. Sophie shared that opinion.

He held his hand there for a moment then twisted his wrist.

Parker jerked in her chair and pushed away his arm. Her eyes widened, and she shook her head. "What did you do, you spaz?"

Danny stood and looked embarrassed. "Did I hurt you?"

"No. It was a kind of shock. It was weird."

Sophie didn't have time to say anything.

The widest of the football players stood beside the table wearing cargo shorts, though it was early winter, and a t-shirt with a beer bottle picture. His hair was buzzed to the skull. A weird grin was locked across his mouth. "I think it's cute when people fall in love. Even when it's a couple of freaks."

Danny turned to face the guy. "I don't think Parker's a freak. I think she's smart."

Sophie stood up. "Is there a problem, Michael Gillette?"

"I just like it when cripples find happiness, that's all."

Parker didn't seem to be paying too much attention. She was feeling her back and making faces. What had Danny done to her?

Freddie rushed over, of course, and he looked pissed—always the protector, the white knight. He stomped in front of the boy. "What's going on?"

Mike wasn't too intimidated. "Cripples, I like. But I'm not too fond of *wetbacks*."

"You're calling me a wetback, scrub? Do you even know what that means?"

Mike stepped forward, and Freddie sidestepped, his left foot a little in front of his right. He was dancing, sort of, but didn't seem aware.

Sophie wanted to break it up, but she didn't want to get in his way. She'd seen him fight before.

"I'm not afraid of you, Morgan," Mike said. "Not anymore. You're not so tough."

Freddie said, "We don't have to do this, Gillette. Whatever *supplements* you're taking don't change who you are on the inside."

Mike rushed at Freddie and, for a second, pushed him backward. Freddie looked a little surprised, but then he took control and shoved the guy forward. They faced each other, and Mike threw a haymaker. Freddie was so quick for a big guy, he just stepped away from the punch and threw some jabs. Mike put his hands down for a second, and Freddie levelled him with a hook to the side of his head.

Derek appeared from wherever he'd been hiding and yelled at Mike, who was awake but laying at Freddie's feet. "What are you doing, Mike? You can't be out starting fights. That's not what we're about!"

Mike focused on his captain and nodded, rubbing his temple.

The alley was weirdly silent, everyone having stopped to watch the fight.

Arnie's voice came from the speakers. "Freddie, tell that guy to stop laying on my floor and get back to bowling."

Mike struggled to his feet as the noise of wooden balls smashing into pins resumed.

Derek said, "I don't know what you did, but I need you to apologize to my friends."

Mike looked embarrassed. "I'm sorry, Freddie. You're right. I don't know what a wetback is. I just heard it in a movie once." Mike extended his hand, and Freddie shook it.

Derek exchanged a look with Freddie, and both headed to their tables.

Sophie examined his hands for cuts or bruises, but they looked all right. His face looked good too. "Are you all right?" she asked.

"Yeah, I'm fine. Mike's gotten real strong lately."

"He hasn't gotten any smarter though."

Freddie nodded.

Danny hadn't moved from his spot in front of Parker. "That was exciting."

Sophie looked at Parker, who wasn't paying attention and stared at the floor. Sophie looked down but didn't see anything. Maybe one of Mike's teeth was down there.

"Parker, are you okay?" she asked.

"It's my foot."

Parker's foot was twitching side to side.

CHAPTER FIVE

4 Chamberlain Lane

Jack pulled onto the gravel driveway and stopped at the house. He angled the black Silverado XLT so the lights would hit the cabin's side door. The area was so dark that it seemed like the blackness absorbed the car's headlights, like a black hole eating any light around it. He used to love reading those science books to the kids—first to Ryan and then, a few years later, to Freddie.

This was one of the older rentals and needed a lot of work. For one, he had to replace the whole roof in the spring. The wooden front steps were a little rotten, and he didn't even want to think about the boiler. He was only here to check the locks. Vagrants liked houses like this, and the teenagers threw parties in the deep-woods houses sometimes. Did Maureen have to own every rental in Knox County?

"Why don't you stay in the car?" he suggested.

Danny was already out and heading toward the steps. "It's better if we're together."

The kid walked a little straighter today, but his arms would be sore. They were both dressed in work boots, jeans, and sweatshirts. The pair had hung a lot of sheetrock at the rental on Goodwin Lane, and Jack hadn't gone easy on him. Danny wasn't that strong, but he kept trying, and he learned how to handle the nail gun okay. He wasn't like Freddie. When Freddie used to help, he could hammer a nail with one strike. He didn't need a gun. But Freddie was helping Maureen now, and he had a head for numbers. It made sense that the boy didn't do this kind of work much anymore.

"Okay," he said. "Together."

He climbed the steps and checked the door. The wood around the jamb was splintered, and the door wasn't quite closed. Adrenaline flooded his body, but he quickly suppressed it, remembering he had been in bad situations before.

Jack looked at the kid beside him and pushed open the door. The house was dark and silent yet warm. Someone had left on the heat. He reached for the light switch and flicked on the kitchen light. The bulb was dim, but it was enough to see the beer cans on the floor of the main room. Otherwise, the kitchen seemed okay. The stove looked clean, and the refrigerator hummed. The living room had been the party zone.

Jack mumbled to himself and entered the living room. He yanked on a pull-down chain for the overhead light and more dim light spilled out. The room smelled faintly of puke, and the carpet seemed to have a few new stains. New holes and little spatter marks he thought might be more tossed cookie dotted the off-white walls, and a side window was cracked.

"Don't touch nothing."

"You think it was some teenagers out partying?" Danny asked, his voice echoing in the empty house. He didn't sound scared, just maybe excited.

Jack had seen it before. "Probably. There aren't too many other houses on the street, and only one of them is occupied."

"Should we call the police?"

Jack didn't like calling the cops. Some of them knew him a little too well. "Maybe, but let's look around first."

He stuck his head into the bathroom. The vomit scent was stronger there, and wet spots surrounded the toilet. He knew who'd clean this mess—good old Jack, that's who. Maureen wouldn't even bat an eye. She'd say that was his area, and he would have to get on it. That was his job.

The house was so small they'd pretty much seen everything except the bedroom. That was pristine, as though the teenagers hadn't given it any consideration. Thank God for small miracles. He'd just done the drywall a few weeks ago and didn't feel like doing it again. Maybe they left it clean out of respect? Hardly likely.

Danny stood beside him. The kid didn't seem to understand the danger of all this. He just looked kind of blank, like he was learning as he went.

"Is there a basement?" Danny asked.

Jack was thinking the same thing. "Yeah. The entrance is through the kitchen."

They retraced their steps and found the basement door beside the fridge. Jack had a thought and opened the refrigerator. It was empty except for three cans of PBR. He grabbed one of the brews and closed the door. "None for you, son. You're too young."

Danny grinned. "You're funny."

They stood in the kitchen as he gulped the beer. Finished, he carefully put the can on top of the refrigerator. "Let's have a look. I go first."

He opened the basement door and felt the cool air push against him. He enjoyed that, but the smell of burnt oil spoiled the moment. The light worked, but it flickered bright then dark, which reminded him too much of one of those horror movies he watched sometimes on the television. Hopefully, he wasn't leading them straight into some kind of machete attack. He looked back at the kid; he seemed to be grinning, like it was all a big joke to him.

The only thing that should be down there was the boiler, and it was still humming. He turned to climb the stairs, but Danny blocked his way.

Danny pointed toward the burner. Breath clouds floated from his mouth as he spoke. "Something's over there."

Jack looked again. "Nothing's over there."

Danny shook his head. "I see almost everything. Something *is* over there."

"If you see everything, why don't you tell what I'm not seeing?"

Danny remained silent.

"Well, hell. I'll go look."

"Together, remember?"

Jack nodded as he pulled out his cellphone. He fumbled for a minute before he found the flashlight app Freddie had installed. He pointed it toward the burner, and, sure enough, something seemed kind of stuck in the corner just behind it—something big.

He held his breath and stepped forward. Each step became more clarifying. From a distance, he thought it was a pile of blankets, then maybe it was a pile of clothes but, pretty quickly, he knew what it was. He'd spent time in a desert during the first Gulf War. He knew it was a dead body from the smell of decomposition, which was worse than the oil smell. Someone had stuck the body there and covered it with a blanket. An arm protruded from the blanket, and its fingers were almost pointing straight at him, accusing him of something. "Go back upstairs, Danny. You can't see this."

Danny just moved ahead of him.

"Don't touch anything, Danny. Step back."

Danny lifted the blanket and stared into the open eyes of what had been a horrified young man. Terror was clearly etched across what was left of his beaten face. That, and something else. Maybe disappointment? The dead kid didn't seem much older than Danny.

Jack aimed the light onto the stiff's face and saw a thick patch of red hair. He looked familiar. One of Freddie's friends?

Danny put his hands on the dead boy's face and frowned. "He's really dead, isn't he?"

Jack nodded and took Danny's arm. He led him from the horrifying sight. He was going to say something comforting, but he tripped on a tiny divot in the cement floor and hit the ground. He was still holding Danny's arm, so the kid fell with him. He sat up and groaned. He wanted another beer.

Danny climbed to his feet. "Are you okay, Mr. Morgan?"

Jack rubbed his right wrist, which was burning. "No, I think I might have sprained my wrist."

The kid grabbed Jack's hand—a little too hard apparently—and it burned even more. He yanked it back. "Just leave it alone, Danny. You're making it worse."

Danny apologized and helped him to his feet.

He spotted his cellphone on the floor, still in flashlight mode, and grabbed it. "Come on."

They climbed the stairs and returned to the kitchen.

"I'm gonna have another beer first, and then I'm calling the cops."

"Who do you think that was?"

Jack wasn't ready to guess. "I'm not sure."

Danny's face was animated. "Do you think someone did that to him? Like, it wasn't an accident?"

Jack nodded. "It sure looks suspicious."

He swilled the beer down and felt his nerves settle just a little bit. He grabbed his cellphone and dialed 9-1-1.

A friendly sounding woman answered on the first ring and asked him what the emergency was.

He didn't want to say too much over the phone, so he just told her there'd been a break-in, and he'd found a body.

She asked him the address.

"Four Chamberlain Drive. It's near the big cell tower."

She asked his name and wanted him to stay on the line, but he didn't feel like talking. "I'll be here when everybody gets here."

Danny stood beside the stove, excitedly rubbing his hands together. "I wasn't expecting this when we got here. It's like an adventure."

Jack slowly rubbed his own hands together and realized his wrist felt fine. At least there was that bit of good news. Everything else was just a mess.

CHAPTER SIX

WHAT WOULD RYAN WANT?

"Blunt force trauma to the head," Jack said. "Someone took a pipe to him."

Freddie stood in the center of the living room and tried to take it in. His parents sat on the large sofa, matter-of-factly telling him about a corpse in the basement of one of Camden properties, like it was something that happened every day. Murders didn't happen around Abbot Pond. You had to go to New Hope to find stuff like that.

"Do the cops have any idea who the guy was?"

Jack, still wearing work clothes and boots, had some blue-grey dust covering parts of his shirt. Normally, his mother would be all over him about making a mess on her couch. But not this time. Things were too serious.

His father scrunched his face and took a quick sip of his beer. "I think he might be that redheaded kid you played basketball with. I couldn't quite tell, because his face was, um, distorted."

Freddie felt his pulse race. "Sam Burns. You think it was Sammy?"

His father nodded.

His mother hadn't said much since he'd gotten home, other than telling him they had some news. She looked a little shaken—a rarity for her—and maybe even a little older. She knew a lot of the kids from her days as a middle-school teacher. She'd quit when Ryan drowned, but she was still friendly with a lot of parents and their kids. "Did you mention that to the police, Jackie?"

Jack shook his head. "They'll figure it out, I'm sure, but I won't mention that the stiff in our basement might be someone my son knows. Let's keep Freddie out of it as long as we can."

"I'm not afraid to talk to the police," Freddie said. "They need our cooperation."

"All I know is what I see on CNN. Some cops don't like Spanish kids," his father said.

"That's absurd. He'll have to talk to them sooner or later."

"Right. And it'll be later."

Freddie typed a quick text to Sophie. *Big news over here. Are you still up?*

Her parents didn't usually let them go out too late on a school night, but Sophie had talked them into letting her attend a school play earlier in the evening. She would be busy babysitting Belle on Friday, and Saturday was the big event for the Randall family, so Thursday night had been a go. *Guys and Dolls* seemed a little old school for him, but the girls all dressed kind of retro sexy, and most of the kids could sing pretty good. Sophie had held his hand from the beginning until the end, and it had been great, even though their hands had gotten a little sweaty. She had worn jeans and an expensive-looking white sweater and had on one of her mother's gold necklaces. She had looked like she should have been the star of a play, not Tracy Heathers. And their kiss good night was still the top thing on his mind, even after hearing that his buddy Sam might be the guy beaten to death in one of their properties. How could a kiss seem as important as that?

"Why don't you go check on Danny," his mother suggested. "He went upstairs a while ago."

"Was he really upset?" Freddie asked.

Jack squirmed in his seat as he searched for the right words. "He seemed interested that there was a murder."

"But he didn't seem really sympathetic about the whole thing?"

"I don't know. I can't completely read his feelings."

"You go check on Danny. Jack, go get some blankets, and you can sleep on the couch tonight."

Jack sounded giddy. "I'm staying over tonight?"

"It's too late to be driving around," Freddie's mom said. "Besides, you've been drinking."

Jack winked at Freddie and bounded toward the bathroom where the blankets were stored.

Freddie smiled as he watched his father dance across the floor. This might be a big thing, he knew, and he really wanted his dad back in the house. He wanted his family back to normal.

Freddie took the stairs two at a time, his hand on the heavy railing, and stopped outside Ryan's door. The light was on, and the door was half open. He looked in and saw Danny sitting on the floor in front of Ryan's desk, reading an old comic book, like he belonged here. What was he doing in here? No one was allowed in here.

"What are you doing?"

Danny looked up, smiling. "Reading. I'm probably too old, but I still like *Archie*."

"You're not supposed to be in here. And where did you get that comic book?"

Danny looked confused. "Why can't I come in here?"

Freddie was losing patience "You know this room is off limits. We tell you every time."

"You know I can't remember stuff, Freddie. Your mom really doesn't let anyone in Ryan's old room?"

"It's off limits."

The door creaked open, and Freddie's worst fear was realized—his mother had discovered them, and she was shocked. This was not a good night for her. Why couldn't Danny just be a normal kid?

His mother wiped back some greying red hairs and squinted at them, as if she couldn't believe what she was seeing. She was trying to play it cool, he could tell, but her hands trembled. "Freddie, could you please explain to me why you two are having a wonderful time in Ryan's room."

Danny stood up, the comic book still in his hand. "I'm sorry, Mrs. Morgan. I didn't realize I couldn't come in here."

"Wasn't the door locked?"

"I opened it," he said, as if that explained everything.

"The door was open the other morning too," Freddie said, "before Danny got here. I think I need to look at the lock."

"Well, we have rules, Danny," Maureen explained. "This room is usually locked."

"Why?"

Freddie realized he was holding his breath. What was Danny thinking? Just apologize and get out of the room fast.

"Excuse me?" she asked.

Danny caught her eye and smiled that stupid, goofy smile of his. "I mean, I didn't know Ryan or anything, but he had a lot of cool stuff in this room, and he seems like he was a good kid."

Maureen sat on Ryan's bed, her finger tracing some invisible picture on the blue comforter, and looked at Freddie. "I've been blessed with wonderful children."

"What was he like?"

His mother didn't answer at first.

Freddie wondered what her answer would be. He used to ask about Ryan more, but she never wanted to discuss it, and she seemed so sad. Jack had told him funny stories about Ryan playing hide and seek. No one could ever find Ryan when he hid, but he always knew where Jack was. He liked word searches, and he loved putting puzzles together. And he was really good at math, just like Freddie. He could do his times table when he was in second grade.

Maureen said, "He was a real good boy who deserved more than what he got."

Freddie's phone, still in his hand, buzzed, and he glanced discretely at the screen. *What's going on?*

He put the phone in his pocket and surveyed the room. Danny hadn't really hurt anything, as far as he could tell. The room was still clean, the *Star Wars* thing and the completed Rubik's Cube were still on Ryan's desk, and the bed was made. He had just found a comic book and wanted to read it. What had Danny done that was so wrong?

"I'm sorry if I made you so sad, Mrs. Morgan. I like the feeling in here."

She nodded slightly but didn't look up.

"I just think he wouldn't mind sharing his stuff. I mean, that's the feeling I get. I don't know. What do you think? What would Ryan want?"

Freddie wasn't sure, but she might have been crying. He sat beside her and rubbed her shoulder like he used to when he was a kid and wanted her to be happy. She had so much trouble being happy back then. And now, here's Danny pushing all her buttons. His blood boiled as he contemplated ringing the kid's scrawny neck. He glared at Danny.

She looked at Freddie and must have read his mind. "Danny's just pointing out the obvious, isn't he?"

Freddie frowned but didn't say anything.

Maureen rubbed Freddie's cheek, approached Danny and hugged him for just a second. "He'd say we should share his stuff, that's what he would say."

Jack was there to put his arm around her. How long had he been there?

"Why don't we let this be your room while you're here, Danny. You can sleep in here and not have to listen to your, um, to Freddie snore." Maureen didn't wait for an answer. She took Jack's hand, and they left the room, their footsteps echoing back as they descended the wooden staircase.

Freddie heard them whispering in the living room but couldn't make out the words. They didn't sound mad.

Freddie said, maybe not to Danny, "What just happened?"

CHAPTER SEVEN

Searching for Rachel Randall

Mr. Randall was tall and silver haired. He shook when he spoke to the crowd, as though he wanted to be somewhere far away—probably with his daughter. Parker couldn't blame him if this was true. Who wants to drive to some town two states away and thank people for looking for his only daughter's body? She wondered if he was as old as he looked.

Just a few years ago, she had been a searcher on the third anniversary of Rachel's disappearance. She had climbed through the snow and slush, planting little flags in the ground to indicate someone had searched another piece of the grid. Her legs had been strong then, and she never seemed to get tired. Now, she manned the coffee and hot chocolate table and was stuck in her chair. She felt exhausted.

The sky was dark grey, and snow fell steadily. It had snowed like this on every one of these anniversaries. Parker didn't read too much into that because it always snowed a lot around Abbot Pond in the winter. Maybe it meant more though. If it was a sign, she didn't really understand.

Danny helped hand out the drinks; although he seemed to have trouble telling the difference between hot chocolate and coffee. Two black dispensers were plugged into a generator—each clearly marked—by the table, and his only job was to pass out the right drink to people. For God's sake, they looked and smelled different. But here he was, handing little Belle St. Cyr a black coffee. She sniffed it and wrinkled her little nose.

"Wrong again," Parker said. "Ten-year-olds don't need coffee."

The table sat at the side of the narrow street. The road was closed, and the local authorities were busing in the searchers. Sophie and Freddie were out of sight on the other side of the street. Dozens of people walked beside the road, hoping for some overlooked six-year-old clue to jump out from the snow and present itself. She'd attended enough of these searches to know how it would turn out—no new clues.

Belle was a cutie, for sure. Her hair was almost blond, and her eyes were blue. When she smiled, which was often, her dimples rounded out and made her face even prettier. "I drink coffee sometimes. It's okay."

She scampered to one of her big brothers, and they headed toward the Townsend family's field. A lot of theories had poor Rachel finding the field in the dark and thinking it would lead to a house or something. But it was just an empty property. The Townsends didn't live there anymore, and it was only a field because they paid someone to clear it every year.

Parker was bundled up pretty good, and a thick blanket covered her legs. Her feeling down there was spotty, so she usually overcompensated when she was outside in bad weather. No need to catch frostbite or gangrene or whatever nasty infection could cause them to amputate her legs. For some reason, she was terrified something would happen and they would cut off her useless legs just about a week before some scientist discovered a cure. Everyone else would be walking, but she would stay in her damn wheelchair forever.

"You do this every year?" Danny asked.

Parker didn't bother to tell him that he had been here last year. There wasn't a point. "Every year since poor Rachel disappeared."

"All they ever found was her car?"

She nodded. "Her parents' car, I guess. The door was open, and her ID was still in her purse. There was a cup half-filled with cheap wine sitting on the roof."

Danny was wearing jeans and a heavy sweatshirt, with no hat. His ears were red. He seemed oblivious to the weather, like it didn't affect him like it affected everyone else. Brain damage was a weird thing. They *were* a pair of freaks.

"It's quite a puzzle."

Parker nodded. "It's a big thing on the internet. People have some crazy theories."

A medium-sized man wearing a heavy winter jacket and a Patriots Elvis cap approached the table, carrying one of those little flags the searchers were using. His glasses had a small line centered across each lens.

"Hey, Dr. Hollis," Parker said.

He smiled broadly. "How's the future Dr. Bradley doing today? Are your feet still acting up?"

"I'm fine. They're still trembling a little, but they seem to be settling down. I guess you were right—it was nothing."

Danny handed him a cup.

"What's this?"

Parker shook her head. "He doesn't know."

"Well, thank you, Danny. I appreciate the"—He paused to take a sip— "hot chocolate. I love cocoa."

"Do you come every year?" Danny asked.

He nodded. "Well, I try to. It's more ceremonial every year, but it keeps people aware."

"It's a mystery, that's for sure."

"What do you think happened?" Parker asked.

Doc Hollis gazed across the street where the police had discovered the Camry all those years ago. He looked down the road and then back to the spot across the street. "I guess I'm like most everyone else. The girl was drinking and driving, and the car broke down. She stumbled into the woods, and one day we'll find her on the hill somewhere. I hope I'm wrong, of course." The doctor said goodbye and headed to his grid.

Parker watched him disappear into the woods. She missed walking.

"Did Sophie tell you about what happened?"

"To Sammy?" Parker asked. "Yeah. He was a friend of mine."

Danny didn't say anything.

"Do you think he suffered?"

The kid answered without hesitation. "Yeah."

"You don't sugarcoat anything, do you?"

"What do you mean?"

Her face felt flush. "I mean, he was my friend, and you just told me he suffered, like it was no big thing."

He put his hand on hers. It was red and cold. "I'm sorry. I don't always think right when I talk."

Parker nodded, her anger fading. "Sit in this chair beside me, and put your hands under my blanket. But don't get any ideas."

He did as he was told, his hands trembling.

She grabbed them and rubbed them.

"She didn't go into the woods."

Parker snorted. "Why do you say that?"

Danny looked serious. "I see almost everything. She's not up there."

Parker looked across the road into the snow-covered bushes and trees. She saw a few people mulling about, but most of the searchers were deep into the woods now. They were alone except for a few crows standing in the center of the street. They stared at her as if trying to decide if she was alive or some carcass to be picked at. They must have made a quick decision, because they all flew away together.

"What happened to her then?" she asked.

Danny looked down Route 29, which eventually led to Augusta, and then back the other way, which would have brought Rachel Randall into Abbot Pond. "Someone must have pulled over and taken her."

"A lot of people have theories. It's all over the internet. What makes you so sure someone took her?"

"Because she didn't go into the woods."

They remained quiet for a moment as searchers exited their grids. A yellow school truck parked beside them. The bus kept running, but the door opened, and the driver popped out. He asked for coffee, and Danny poured him some—the first drink he'd gotten right all day. The guy thanked them and headed back to the warmth of his bus.

She took his hands again, even though they had warmed up. She didn't exactly know why she did it, but he sure didn't mind. She looked at his face and realized it had filled in a little during the week he had been in town. Mrs. Morgan was feeding him well.

They sat for a while, wordless, watching people saunter to and fro, most of them rushing to get on the bus. The snow was slowing down, but it was still steady. She saw Sophie and Freddie exiting the woodlands and reflexively jerked her hand from his. She looked at Danny, and he gave her a goofy grin.

She whispered, "I've been thinking about the other day."

"At bowling?

"Yeah. When you did that thing to my back."

He didn't say anything; he just looked at her.

"Do you think you could do it again?"

CHAPTER EIGHT

ANOTHER MYSTERY

Maureen watched the white Chevy pull up the driveway and into Freddie's spot in the carport almost to the railing, and the driver fluidly exited the car. He stopped to look across the pond, as everyone did, before walking up the path to the steps. She waited for him to knock before she stepped away from the window to open the front door. Maureen thought it best to make him wait.

He was tall and lean, like most of the young cops in Camden, and he had a nice face. His hair was light and thin, and she decided he wasn't bad to look at. He looked familiar to her.

"Mrs. Morgan? I'm Detective Nault. We talked a bit on the phone this morning."

"Of course, Detective. Why don't you come in? I'll hang up your jacket, and you can put your shoes over there."

He didn't argue. He handed her his L.L. Bean jacket, removed his shoes and placed them neatly beside the others on the rubber shoe pad. She gestured him toward the couch, approached the closet and looked for a spot. It wasn't as empty as usual, because Jackie had started to bring back his stuff. It made her warm just to look at all his beat-up things.

She sat in one of the chairs. "Jack will be right down. He's fixing a leg on a dresser in Freddie's room."

They regarded each other for a moment. He wore nice pants and a light sweater over his shirt and tie. He looked like one of her young salesmen. "You seem a little young to be a detective already."

"They hired me in that capacity. I was an MP in the service and moved up quick in CID, short for criminal investigation division. My mom got sick, so I decided to move back home and find a job in the real world."

She nodded. "Jackie was in the army. He served in the first Gulf War."

As if he was waiting at the top of the steps for his introduction, Jackie came stomping down the wooden steps. His damn work boots were probably scuffing the wood with each step. He entered the room wearing ripped worked pants and a white t-shirt, looked at the detective and then at her. He looked annoyed. "Who's this?"

"Jackie, this is Detective Nault. I told you he was coming over this morning."

Jack didn't say anything. His work boots clomped loudly as he approached her. "What does he want?"

"You know what he wants, Jackie. He needs to know about what happened the other night."

He faced the young detective. "I already told the other cops everything I know."

Nault smiled. "It's procedure that I come and talk with you."

Jackie grunted and walked into the kitchen. He returned with an apple and took a bite. "Well, ask away."

"Okay." Nault wrote on a pad of paper. "You were at the house on Chamberlain Street."

"Right." Jackie sounded annoyed.

"You were with a young man. A teenager?"

"Danny. Daniel Cole. He's staying with us."

"All right. What is his relation to you folks? Is he family?"

Jackie looked at Maureen as he searched for the right words. "I guess not. Not exactly."

Nault scratched his chin with the side of his pen. "What does that mean, Mr. Morgan?"

"He means Danny is like family to us," Maureen said. "His parents are not currently capable of taking care of him, so we are temporarily providing a home for the boy."

"Where is Mr. Cole right now?"

"He and Freddie are volunteering over at the Lakeside. They have some, er, friends who volunteer to spend time with the patients, and they needed a little extra help."

Jackie said, "That's what our boys do. They're good kids."

"I understand. Didn't Mr. Burns work at that facility?"

Jackie looked ready to say something that might come out wrong, so she grabbed his hand. "That is true, Detective. It's a small town."

He smiled. "Call me Paul."

"Okay, Paul. We didn't know he worked there until Sophie, Freddie's friend, told him that she'd seen him there last week."

"Did your son know Mr. Burns?"

Jackie wiped some sweat from his forehead. His voice got a little louder. "They played basketball together, but they weren't pals or anything. Why do you want to know about Freddie? He wasn't even there."

Maureen smoothed the sides of her dark dress and straightened her back. She loved that he was protective of the family, but he tended to say the wrong thing when someone pushed him. "Jackie, he's asking reasonable questions. Don't you want to find out what happened to poor Sammy?"

Her husband was losing his cool. He didn't like anyone other than Maureen telling him what to do. Plus, she knew he thought the cops weren't looking out for his interests. He'd had a few brushes with the law.

"Your son isn't a suspect, Mr. Morgan." Nault maintained an even tone and seemed to not notice her husband's minor meltdown. He was obviously well trained.

"No?"

"The house at Three Chamberlain is occupied. They saw some people in the area last week, and one of them matched Mr. Burns' description."

"And the others?" Maureen asked.

Nault shook his head. "I can't get into any of that except to say that all of the people of interest are Caucasian. I believe your son is Hispanic?"

"Well, don't that beat all," Jackie said, grinning. "It's gotta be the first time a kid being Spanish kept him out of trouble."

Nault's face sharpened. "Are you implying I would investigate your son simply because of his ethnicity?"

Jackie didn't answer.

"I'm sure that's not what my husband means, Paul. What other questions might you have?"

Detective Nault took a piece of paper from the pad and unfolded it. It was a picture of a pretty blonde girl, maybe fifteen or sixteen years old. "Does this girl look at all familiar to you?"

Maureen took the photo and looked into the young girl's eyes. She looked very innocent.

Jackie took the photo from her and shook his head. "Who is she?"

"Ciara. Ciara Clark. She lives at Three Chamberlain Drive. She's been missing for about a week."

CHAPTER NINE

LAUNDRY AT THE LAKESIDE

There weren't many visitors at the Lakeside Residence. Sophie knew a few patients were home visiting families for Thanksgiving. This was always a problem when they returned. She had seen big men cry when their children dropped them off. In her opinion, the patients should stay here for good after they move in. Sure, there were field trips for the less afflicted into Camden for ice cream or hot dogs at Wasses, but going home just distressed the poor folks. Anyway, Lakeside always hosted a Thanksgiving dinner, and the food was pretty good.

The Sentry was nowhere to be seen when they walked in. She hoped Lucy was sleeping or with family, but it was a bad sign that she wasn't at her post. The Sentry never shirked her duties, meaning Lucy was probably taking a turn for the worse. Parker looked for her too, and the girls shared an expression.

Sophie shrugged.

"What will we be doing today?" Freddie asked. "We're ready to work."

Freddie and Danny both wore jeans and tees. Freddie had been here a few times and knew he would be wearing some stains on his clothes before he left. She wasn't usually a big t-shirt person, but Freddie looked so fit whenever he wore one. The shirts were always too tight on his chest, and his biceps popped right when the sleeve ended and his skin began. Danny didn't look quite as skinny as he had just a few days ago. Still, they looked like a very odd couple.

"Betty says they could use some help with the dishes. There shouldn't be too many."

Freddie nodded and pulled Danny toward the kitchen.

Parker scrutinized Danny, like she couldn't figure something out. Sophie guessed lots of people regarded him that way, especially at school. This look was different though, like they shared a secret. Why was she so interested in the kid?

"What's going on between you two anyway?" she asked.

Parker shook her head. "I don't know. There's something about him though."

"You know he's kind of weird, right?" Sophie asked. "I'm not judging, but he's a little different."

Parker fiddled with the charms on her bracelet. Most of them were random, and a few were from her parents. The one that said *Sisters* on one side and had a wavy design on the other was from Sophie. Parker had cried when she gave it to her last summer. Sophie couldn't imagine her life without Parker.

"Let's just get to work. What are we doing first?"

Sophie braced herself. "Laundry. We're doing laundry."

Parker wheeled for the door. "Hell, no. I'm not touching those clothes, and I hate that room."

Sophie ran to her friend and grabbed the hand grips on the back of her chair. She popped Parker backward slightly and spun her around. Sophie pushed hard and fast and led them to the little laundry room near Doc Hollis' office.

His door was open, and he waved at them. Sophie held fast to the wheelchair, but Parker waved back. They were giggling by the time they arrived at Sophie's destination.

"You know this room is haunted, don't you?" Parker asked. "The ghosts are always banging on the walls."

Sophie had heard the knocking before, when the laundry wasn't running, and the door was closed. "It's just the pipes. This building is wicked old."

Four washers and three dryers rested near the wall, and a sturdy folding table sat in the center of the room. She eyed the heavy metal door in the corner of the room. It was always locked, and Sophie had no idea where it went. Probably nowhere. The building had been rebuilt so many times, it might just lead into a brick wall.

A full-size trash can, lined with an industrial trash bag, stood beside the big table. Several cloth laundry bags were strewn about the room. Sophie picked them up, because Parker couldn't, and put them on the table. Sophie had seen some disgusting things come out of these bags, things much scarier than clanking pipes. She was not looking forward to this. Not at all.

⁕

Parker was alone, grabbing clothes from the table and folding them on her lap. Most of the stuff had a patient's name on it somewhere, which was helpful. The other clothes, ones with no name or the name of a long-dead patient, she put in a miscellaneous pile on the floor. The orderlies and assistants were good at returning the clothes to the right people. She wondered which of the old ladies wore the sexy G-string but decided she didn't really need to know. Maybe old habits just die hard, even if you're living with dementia.

Danny walked in and locked eyes with her.

She wanted to look away, but that didn't happen; his eyes were brown and deep and ever so innocent.

"Sophie said you might need some help. We're finished with the dishes."

"What's she doing now?"

"I don't know. Talking with Freddie, I guess."

Parker looked away. "How are you at folding? Better than you are at pouring hot chocolate?"

"I'm getting better."

"Good. We just have to wait for the final load to finish drying."

"Okay."

The room was quiet except for the hum of the dryer. Danny fidgeted then walked around. He surveyed the table then the washer and dryer. Finally, he put his hands on the big iron door. "Where does this go?"

"I don't know. Probably somewhere spooky."

He grinned. "I could open it, if you want."

"It's probably locked for a reason, Danny."

"Still …"

The dryer clanked to a stop.

"Grab the clothes, and bring them over here," she said.

"Do you do this a lot? I mean, help these people?"

She wheeled closer to him. Part of her, the smartest part, wanted to tell him to shut up and get to work. Instead, they played their little eye-contact game again. "Not as long as Sophie, but for a while."

He nodded. "You guys do most everything together, right?"

"We weren't always friends, you know."

He looked a little surprised, but he kept quiet, waiting for her to finish her thought.

"We weren't exactly enemies, but we always competed. We were both into sports, and even if we were on the same team, we'd compete. Then we got to high school, and her mother wouldn't let her do sports, so she started being all girlie girl. I mean, she has the greatest taste in clothes. I think it's another kind of competition to her, dressing better than everyone else."

Danny understood. "Freddie really likes how she dresses. I see him staring at her, and I know he's looking at all of her—her clothes, her hair, her smile."

"I see that too. Anyway, one day, my mother's driving me to school, and she swerves to get around a squirrel. A *squirrel*. And bang—she slams into a pickup truck. I'm awake for the whole thing, and I can just *feel* my legs shutting down. It didn't even hurt much. I wish it had."

He reached to take her hand, but she wouldn't let him. Not yet.

"So, I get out of the hospital, and I'm not in school for a couple weeks. One morning, Sophie shows up, and says she'll drive me. And I did. I went to school with her."

"And you've been best friends ever since?"

"Yeah. Why do you think she did it?"

Danny put his hand to his chin and stroked an imaginary bear. "I think she was always your friend, in her own way. When things changed for you, they changed for her."

Parker ran her fingers through her dark hair and thought about his words. First, *How could he know things like this*? And, second, *Why hadn't I thought about it more*? Originally, she had thought Sophie just felt sorry for her, but that sure wasn't the case. Maybe one day, she would sit down with her best friend and ask her about it. She was pretty sure Sophie might not really have an answer either. It didn't really matter now, did it?

They folded some clothes until he stopped and took a step toward her. "I can do it again, if you want."

She wanted to pretend she didn't know what he was talking about, that she wasn't craving the feeling he'd given her that day—like she supposed a drug addict craved heroin. Instead, she said, "Okay."

He kneeled beside her and placed his hand on her shoulder. His fingers followed the same path they had taken just a few days ago. Again, he turned his hand, and again, she felt the spark. This time, it burned hotter, and she was sure she saw a flash of light where his hand and her back met. Something electric surged through her legs, all the way to the very tips of her toes. It sort of burned, but it felt like her legs were alive. She felt almost whole again.

Parker realized she had closed her eyes while she experienced the new/old sensations. When she opened them, his face was just a few inches away—creased with lines—and he looked pale. He rubbed his cheeks and eyes, and life came back to them. The goofy grin had returned.

Parker grabbed his head and pulled him close. She kissed him as hard and as long as she had ever kissed a boy.

Finally, she pulled away. "I don't know why I did that."

He grabbed her hand. "I don't mind."

Freddie finished vacuuming the dining room floor. It had taken quite a while to get all the food bits and whatever, but he looked almost balletic—if that was a word—in his effort. His mom had trained him well in all things domestic. He was a pretty well-rounded guy.

He saw Sophie looking at him, and he walked over. "How's the laundry going?"

She wrinkled her nose. "We don't even bother to separate the lights and the darks. And we always wash everything twice, including the laundry bags. In hot water."

He smiled that smile.

"What?" she asked.

"It's just that you don't want to do it, but you volunteer anyway. Because no one else will do it, right?"

Sophie nodded. "Somebody has to do it, especially since they're one employee short."

"An orderly told me they already hired someone else for Sammy's job, one of the kids on the football team."

"Not Mike Gillette?"

He shook his head. "No, Bobby Stevens. They call him *Bobby Boots*."

"Why?"

"Because he always wears boots. Except when he's playing football. He's all right, but he's rough. And big."

"Bigger than you?"

"Easily."

She went to hug him, but he stepped backward. "I'm not sure if I should do that after you handled all that laundry."

She pretended to smack him on the chest.

He laughed and gave her the hug. "I'll just shower as soon as I get home."

"I know I will. Sometimes weird things come out of pockets when you fold them, like forks or ice-cream cones. Or worse."

She followed him as he returned to the vacuum and wound up the power cord.

"I had the dream last night," he said. "But it was a little different."

Sophie was intrigued. She had been following his dream since the old lady was just a figure in the shadows. "What's she doing now?"

He lowered his head and spoke quietly. "She's not really bouncing on me anymore. She's pointing at me, but then I realize she's pointing behind me. And she says something new."

Sophie was caught in Freddie's dreamworld. "What? What did she say?"

"Either *peligro* or *el peligro*. Either way, it means danger. There's danger behind me."

"Have you talked to Richard about it?"

"I called him this morning, that's how I knew what it meant. He thinks the lady might be on my side, like a guardian angel or something. I could practically feel him doing the Catholic cross thing when he said it to me."

"Who do you think she's warning you about?"

"I don't know. It's just a dream, I guess. I don't have any enemies putting me in danger right now."

Parker and Danny strolled—as much as Parker could stroll in that chair—from the laundry room. They were both smiling. Parker looked sort of shiny, like she'd exfoliated or something.

Sophie felt something had happened, but neither of them would tell her what. Like, when she'd seen them handing out coffee the other day, trying to look innocent. But she knew something was up.

"What's going on?" Sophie asked.

Parker said, "Nothing. We folded all the laundry and kept all the ones with names on them together. There's a pile of clothes on the table we couldn't decide who belonged to what. Danny figured out a bunch of them though."

"The staff is pretty good at straightening that all out. Good job, guys."

Freddie said, "Maybe we could get going? My mom texted me a while ago."

"She wants you home?"

He nodded. "She said we all could come and maybe have dinner."

Sophie couldn't remember a time when the Morgans had invited her to dinner. "My mom's expecting me."

"I told her. Then she asked if you wanted to come over for Thanksgiving. Parker too."

Sophie's head spun. "I don't think she's said three words to me since I met her. What's gotten into her?"

"She's been pretty happy lately. Happy *for her*, I mean. Maybe it's because my dad moved back in."

"Where's Danny going?" Parker asked.

He was heading into the main room. Most of the residents were napping in the chairs and sofas. One lady was making baby noises and pretending to talk to her mother. A sad-looking nurse sat at a table, staring straight ahead, probably reconsidering her career choices. The television was tuned to an old cowboy show. It all looked so depressing to Sophie.

Danny sat by Lucy Diamond, who was relaxing on the main sofa, and they talked. She moved her hands a lot and leaned in when she spoke to him.

He didn't recoil as so many—Sophie included—sometimes did when crazy, old ladies with food on their faces babbled at them. He didn't seem to care about any of that. He was listening.

They followed and stood beside him, the girls careful not to touch the sofa.

The Sentry said, "You know what you have to do, right?"

Danny nodded slowly. "Don't worry."

Lucy eyed them suspiciously. "Can we trust them?"

"They won't let us down."

"Good," she said. Her eyes narrowed, and she counted to ten without the five and the seven over and over again. Finally, she remembered the seven but forgot the nine. This continued for a while. Numbers reappeared in her brain, expelling other ones. Her addled mind only had so much room for memories.

Danny stood and started to leave.

"What was that about?" Freddie asked.

"She just wanted my help, that's all."

"Help with what?" Sophie asked.

He ran his fingers through his crazy black hair. "She thinks trouble is coming. She wasn't clear."

"Okay," Freddie said. "Time to go."

CHAPTER TEN

The Water Calls

Freddie sat at his desk, reading an old book his father had recommended about a boy joining a star fleet and becoming a man while in outer space. Jack liked the old science fiction writers and was always rereading his dusty paperbacks. Heinlein was his favorite, but he liked Blish and Niven and just about anyone else that wrote sci-fi in the 60s and 70s. His dad didn't look like a big reader, but everything about him was contradictory.

Freddie didn't need to move to outer space to become a man. He enjoyed his house on the big pond. His parents were great, and he knew what he wanted to do with his life. He was happy here. Occasionally, he got a look from someone when he was out with Sophie—the look of disapproval—but otherwise, Abbot Pond was great.

His phone buzzed, and he saw a text from Sophie. *How was dinner? Sorry I couldn't come.*

He wrote quickly, *That's all right. Hoping you get the okay for Thanksgiving.*

She answered, *I'll find a way. I want your mom to like me.*

He wrote back, *Weird news here. Parents talked to cops. A girl is missing in Camden.*

It was a minute before she responded. *That's horrible. Why did they tell your parents?*

The top corner of his phone told him it was almost midnight. The house was quiet now. He heard a faraway rumble that could only be his father snoring on the couch. *At least he's back in the house*, he thought. And they weren't fighting.

He wrote, *Near the property in Camden. The one with the dead body.*

Another pause. *Do they think it's related?*

He answered, *I think so. Not sure. Why else would they tell my parents? It wasn't on the news.*

She stopped replying, so he returned to the space book. He was almost finished with his chapter when the phone buzzed again. *Keep me in the loop on that. We have another possible problem.*

He wrote, *What?*

She fired back, *You have to talk to Danny. Something weird is going on between him and Parker. I'm really uncomfortable with it.*

Freddie felt a flash of anger at his girlfriend. It passed, and he wondered why he felt so upset about her words. He answered, *What's wrong with her liking Danny?*

Her response came quickly. *I don't know. But something odd is happening. Can you talk to him?*

He wanted to tell her that it wasn't his business. Instead, he said he would talk to Danny first thing in the morning.

She sent a smiley face and said, *TY. Sleep well. Don't take any crap from the dream lady.*

He tried to revisit the book, but her words reverberated. Was something weird happening between Danny and Parker? They did seem a little too friendly at the hot chocolate stand, and they had been laughing a bit too much when they exited the laundry room. Why did it matter? Danny didn't seem so bad lately, and Parker could use a new friend. Maybe Sophie was a little jealous of their friendship? He made a mental note to never mention that thought to his girlfriend. She wouldn't take it well.

Freddie stood and stretched. He looked out the window onto the ice. It always glowed in the moonlight, and the moon was almost full. Something moved across the pond. It wasn't a stray dog, it was too big, and it stood on two feet. Some nitwit was trying to walk across the ice. He thought of Ryan, who had not been a nitwit. Whoever it was seemed tall and unsteady; however, that could be because the ice was slippery. Another thought struck him.

He opened his door, entered the hallway and tapped quietly on Danny's door. With no response, Freddie opened it. He turned on the light and saw the room was empty. His heart beat like a jungle drum. This couldn't happen again; Freddie's parents would never recover.

Freddie took the steps two at a time. He found the downstairs closet and threw on his parka. He didn't bother looking for socks and just popped his bare feet into his boots. The back door was creaky, but he opened it slow enough that it didn't sound too bad. He closed the door behind him and rushed to the dock.

"Danny," he called out, hoping his folks didn't hear. "Danny, what are you doing?"

The pond wind blustered in all directions, and he doubted his words could even reach the kid. It felt like it might be snowing, but he decided it was just the wind blowing snow from the ground, into the air and onto the ground again—freaky Maine weather.

Danny's lanky frame scurried from him.

Freddie's eyes hurt from the bright light reflecting from the ice. He blinked a couple times, and the feeling subsided a bit. He stepped onto the thick ice, hoping it wasn't a soft spot. Ryan had stepped on a soft spot years ago, and they didn't find him for three days.

He took three more steps before he slipped and landed on his butt, spinning in an almost complete circle. His tailbone hurt, but he got up and continued. "Danny! Get back here!"

Danny stopped maybe fifty yards away. He got on his knees and seemed to be caressing the ice.

Freddie was sure the kid hadn't noticed him. He hollered again, louder, hoping he'd snap out of it. Was he sleepwalking? That had been one of the theories that floated around about Ryan's death. *Maybe he had sleepwalked down the stairs, unlocked the door and walked onto the ice.* Except the door was locked on the inside. Danny seemed out of it though, and his face seemed blank.

Freddie panicked and quickened his pace. He took a few more steps before his foot broke through thin ice, cold water splashing his pants as his leg sank. His pant leg was soaked to his knee, and his boot filled with frigid water.

He wriggled backward and stood up, glad he hadn't gone under. His wet leg burned at first but then numbed. He knew the soaked leg wouldn't respond well to the cold temperature, but he couldn't turn back. He had to get to Danny.

His hands were red and trembling, so he shoved them into his pockets. He limped closer to Danny. "Danny, what are you doing? Snap out of it."

The wind seemed to increase with each step across the ice. His eyes watered, and he reached to wipe the tears. The moisture was frozen to his face before he could brush it away. He was getting close, so he called out again.

Danny looked at him and seemed to shake himself from his fog. He jogged across the ice, almost slipping with each step, and stopped in front of Freddie. "What are you doing here? The ice is dangerous."

"No shit, the ice is dangerous. What are you doing?"

"What happened to your leg?"

"Thin ice is everywhere here. You have to get off the ice."

"I see the ice better than you do. You shouldn't be out here."

Freddie's leg was completely numb, and the rest of him shivered. He felt a sudden urge to smack the kid. "We have to get off of here alive and without my parents finding out. They'll have a double heart attack."

"This is where your brother drowned? Back, long ago?"

"Yeah, my— Ryan drowned, and we will too. You should never go on the ice until at least January."

Danny grabbed his arm. "He was your brother, Freddie. You have the same parents. Believe that."

Freddie shook his head, which he realized was bare. He pulled up his hood and put his hands back in his pockets, feeling a little stupid. Why did he rush onto the ice? He should have gotten his parents. Last year, he would not have chased after the kid. Why was it so different now?

"I'm fine, Freddie. I can see the ice better than you. Follow my lead back to the dock."

For some reason, he complied. It made no sense that Danny could see any better than Freddie. As a matter of fact, Danny used to wear glasses. Why hadn't he noticed that before? He wasn't wearing glasses anymore. Still, Freddie followed his friend's lead.

Danny walked his normal pace, as though he were strolling on a sidewalk or along a familiar footpath. Occasionally, he yanked Freddie's arm, and they detoured this way or that way. But they made it to the dock in only a few minutes.

"What were you thinking?" Freddie asked.

"I don't know, exactly. I guess the water was calling for me."

"Calling for you?"

"I guess."

Freddie shook his head. "How did you even get out? I didn't hear you."

Danny grinned. "The window in my room is loose on one side. I just popped it out and I crawled onto the ledge. It popped back in easy, then I shinnied down the birch tree."

Freddie just looked at him. "I have to get in. I have no feeling in my leg."

Danny took a knee, grabbed Freddie's leg and rubbed.

"Hey, watch it now. That's not cool."

"How's it feel now?"

Freddie shook his leg and it felt fine, kind of warm. "It feels okay."

"Good. Now, how are we getting back in the house without your parents noticing?"

"I don't know. Maybe you can pop out another window."

CHAPTER ELEVEN

SNOW PRINTS

The young detective pulled up next to his truck.

Jack turned off the wipers, hoping the misty weather didn't turn into more snow. More snow meant more snow blowing, and he was getting a little bit on in years. His snowblower mileage was a little high. Maybe he could talk Maureen into investing in a snowplow attachment for his truck. Damn, that would be fun.

Jack took a long sip from his coffee. There was just a hint of sugar and cream, just enough to take the bite from the black stuff. The girl at Dunkin' made it perfect for him. He would hand her a five and tell her to keep the change. She always had it ready for him before he entered. It was a nice arrangement.

Nault climbed from his little Chevy and waited for him.

Jack sighed and got out too. He wasn't looking forward to a pow-wow with this kid when he had work to do. He had to change the locks on this property, replace the lights at another spot and he had painting and plumbing everywhere. Painting and plumbing. He should start a business.

"Thanks for meeting me here, Mr. Morgan."

Jack nodded, taking another sip from his cup.

"I've seen the inside of the property. Looks like you have some work to do."

"If I can ever get to it."

"Could you hold off on any work here for a while longer? We processed the scene before we knew about the girl."

Jack looked down the road at the Clark house. He didn't even know a kid had lived there until he learned she was missing. "Right. Now you think she may have been in our house?"

Nault shrugged. "Maybe. Probably. It seems unlikely the two crimes happened on the same street at probably the same time and were unconnected. We want to have a team analyze the scene again. Is that all right?"

Jack doubted he had a choice. "Sure. Freddie wasn't pals with that kid, but he liked him, and we'd like to know what happened. And it's not right about the girl."

The detective leaned against his car. "We don't think the kids came here in a vehicle."

"This place is kind of hard to reach on foot, Detective. "Unless …"

"Yes?"

Jack didn't like working with the cops. They'd given him enough grief throughout the years. Police were great for traffic duty, but otherwise, he'd rather handle things himself. Still, Maureen's voice rang in his ear. She'd want him to help.

Nault looked annoyed. Cold and annoyed. "You have something to share?"

"There's nothing but woods behind us. I've gone hunting around here before."

"They weren't dressed like hunters, Mr. Morgan."

"Jeez, I know that. What I'm telling you is there are trails that hook up with other streets, some of them with no houses."

The detective started toward the trees. "Show me."

Jack grabbed a heavy parka from his truck. It used to be Freddie's, but he'd outgrown it when he hit high school. He locked the truck and put on the jacket without zipping it. "All right. Wait up."

The back yard was big and rectangular. Jack headed to the corner, the snow already up to his calves, and stepped between two birch trees.

Nault followed him apprehensively, like he was entering a swamp or something.

Jack didn't mind making the kid feel uncomfortable. It amused him a little.

"You for sure know where we're headed?" Nault asked.

Jack trudged along as snow collected in his boots. It didn't bother him. "You'd see the path if the snow weren't here. And *lookee* beside us. Footprints."

Jack had hunted in snow enough to recognize human footprints. Paw prints always seemed to expand, making the animal appear bigger than it really was. Human prints just sort of folded down and withered into oval holes. He stopped and said, "A few different prints."

The detective stopped and examined the different-sized holes in front of him. He didn't look too sure about them. "Try not to get too close. I'll have the team take a look."

"I bet these prints bring us right to Churchill Street. There are some houses but not at the end where this path would let out. There's a couple more streets after that too. But those streets have a lot of families."

They continued along the path, avoiding the old prints.

Nault stopped, pulled out a pencil and dug into a footprint. He retrieved a small white sneaker with pink laces—definitely a girl's sneaker. The kid had a keen eye to spot that in the snow.

"I think we're done, Mr. Morgan. We can't take the chance of ruining any more evidence."

"Her sneaker?"

"I think so. It matches the description."

"You think the rest of her is out here?"

Nault shrugged.

Jack was shivering. He wondered if it was from the cold or from the thought of what they might be standing on. "Her poor parents."

"We don't know anything yet. She may have just lost her shoe, and they were in a rush to get to the car."

Jack suddenly wished he still smoked. "Took a few days to find my boy."

"Ryan?"

"Right. Ryan. Is that in my file?"

"I went to school with your son, back in the day."

"Oh. Were you friends?"

"I went over for his birthday party once. We all went swimming, and you belly flopped off the pier with a beer in your hand."

Jack chortled. "That was a good day."

"We were still friends when it happened. I remember thinking that maybe it was another of his Houdini stunts, and he would appear down the street, laughing at everybody, like Tom Sawyer."

"Not that time. There's no escape from the ice."

"I'm sorry for mentioning him. I can see it's a sore spot."

"I'm not ashamed to cry over my son, Detective."

"Of course not."

Jack rubbed his hands together then blew into them. "I remember you now. You were the long-haired kid with the life jacket. You were scared of the water, but you jumped in anyway."

"I couldn't swim. I took lessons that fall. I'm racing in the Abbot Pond Swim this year, hoping for a strong finish."

"Freddie won that last year. Biggest guy in the race."

"Jack, can you backtrack to the house and lead my guys here. I'll stay here. I don't want to leave this spot until we've looked around."

"Sure. Sure, Paulie. I can do that."

CHAPTER TWELVE

THE MONSTER SQUAD

Sophie's dad looked handsome in his medium-expensive Joseph Abboud charcoal-colored sport coat. He shopped a lot at Men's Wearhouse, and sometimes that wasn't a great look for a guy. But he really sold it, with his lean build and thick brown hair. She knew some of her friends thought he was hot, which was a gross thought, but she just felt he looked distinguished, like a fine lawyer should.

He looked at her and smiled.

She was holding his hand but wanted to pull it away. After all, she was a senior in high school now, so why did she need to hold hands with her dad at a funeral? He read her mind and let go, but she caught herself grabbing it again when the priest spoke about Sammy's immortal soul. She didn't know if she had an immortal soul, but she hoped she did. She watched the priest talk for a long time, but his words weren't staying with her. It was like trying to pay attention in trigonometry. Impossible.

The big church brightened, and everyone lined up to pay their respect to Sammy's mom. It was a school day, and not too many kids from Abbott Academy were there. Mrs. Burns hugged one of Sophie's second grade teachers. They were crying but laughing a little too. Some doctors from the Lakeside Residence stood in line in front of them. Doc Hollis was one of them, and he caught her eye and winked. Some kids behind her were being loud, but she didn't turn around. They were from the football team—Mike Gillette among them—and they weren't even dressed up, just jeans and football jackets. How did they even know Sammy? He played basketball.

Her dad nudged her, and she realized the line was moving.

"I'm sorry Freddie couldn't make it, honey," he said. "I hope I'm a worthy substitute."

Sophie straightened her Lauren Conrad printed bell sleeve top. She'd bought the shirt at Kohl's, of all places, but loved it. It went well with her Ann Taylor petite straight leg pants. She shivered, but she had decided against wearing her coat during the service. Outer wear is for outside; inner wear is for inside. Basic.

She smiled at her dad. "You're nobody's substitute."

He beamed but didn't say anything. She knew he was having trouble with the whole daughter-growing-up thing. He was much cooler about it than her mom though. Sophie hoped she would come around soon. Sometimes it felt like her mother didn't even live with them anymore, like she was a living reminder of a woman who had once been full of life.

It was their turn, and Mrs. Burns remembered her. She was a little overweight but not too bad for an older lady. Her face was pretty but lined with wrinkles and runny mascara. She held a tissue in one hand and Sophie's hand with the other. "I know Samuel was quite fond of you, especially when you were kids. I'm sure he'd be glad you came."

Sophie wanted to introduce her father, but Mrs. Burns was already hugging him. "Warren, it's been so long. How are you?"

"Fine, fine. I'm so sorry, Marie. Sophie tells me that he was a wonderful boy."

She nodded. "So full of promise."

Sophie thought about saying goodbye to Sammy. A nice-looking guy in an inexpensive but not cheaply made suit stood by the coffin. She saw him earlier standing in the far corner of the church studying the mourners like he was trying to solve a Where's Waldo? puzzle. Now he looked into the coffin with an odd expression on his face. He looked sad enough, but it was more empathic, like he didn't know Sammy, but he sure felt for the family. He locked eyes with Sophie and smiled. He whispered something to Sammy and left.

They approached the casket and Sophie looked at her friend. Sophie had never seen a dead person before, and it was terrible. Sammy wore a ton of makeup, and his face looked fake, like he was a weird wax figure at that museum in France or wherever. He wore a dark suit and held a chain with a cross in one hand. She touched his arm, which was cold, but didn't say anything. She just walked away.

People filled the back room, and the heat from the crowd warmed her. Her dad was talking, and she was only getting bits and pieces, but she didn't say anything—lawyers just liked to talk. He even talked in his sleep.

He chewed a sugar cookie while he explained to someone about his hiking trip along part of the Appalachian trail. She knew the story, and it ended with a bear cub in his camp. The momma bear didn't show up, so they took off as fast as they could. The story never changed. He was a just-the-facts kind of lawyer.

She wandered into the hallway and could breathe easier. Crucifixes, pictures of Jesus, and photos of church outings hung on the wall. One photo was of the older priest who'd just officiated the service. His silver hair was darker in the picture, and he looked happy. He had a nice smile.

Sophie removed her cell and read her messages. Most of them seemed oddly unimportant, except for the one from Freddie. *Thinking of you. Sorry I couldn't be there.*

Freddie and his mother were at some meeting in Portland. She didn't understand it all, but it was something about trading cars with another dealership. Freddie tried to get out of it, but Mrs. Morgan was clear that this was an important part of the job. Sophie wondered how important it was for her seventeen-year-old son to know this part of the job before he was even out of high school, but she wasn't the business genius Freddie's mom was. She just knew she missed him.

She wrote, *I miss you. I understand.*

She heard voices and turned to see Derek Matthews, Mike Gillette, and another kid. This boy was taller than Freddie, and wider—all of them were wide though, way bigger than last year.

"Derek," she said. "How are you?"

He smiled that phony smile, and she worried he might try to hug her or something. He didn't. "We're okay. We're just sad, of course."

"I didn't know you knew Sammy. Did you have classes together?"

Derek shook his head. "We knew him more from when we were kids. We played all the parks-and-rec stuff together. He was always a great basketball player, and he'd have been good at football too, if he'd wanted."

Mike stared at her as though he wanted to say something, but he kept whatever it was to himself. He looked sad though. He was teary-eyed, and his face was drawn. Maybe that was just a remnant of the beatdown from Freddie at the bowling alley—maybe it was permanent damage.

Derek said, "Do you know Bobby Boots?"

The big kid smiled at her, which was terrifying. His yellowed teeth were all over the place. Pock marks covered his face, and his nose had veins popping from it. His hair was dark and crazy curly. She knew the clerks would never card him at the Shop and Save. He grunted, which she hoped meant he wouldn't kill her today.

She knew she should acknowledge him. "Freddie says you're taking over for Sammy at the Lakeside Residence?"

His voice was low and croaky. "I hear you work there too."

She was surprised Frankenstein even knew who she was. This was the first time she remembered seeing him. Hopefully, it would be the last. "I … I just volunteer every now and then."

"Are you going to introduce me to your friends?" It was her father.

Thank God. Did she just think that in church?

He stepped in front of her, looked Derek straight in the eye and shook his hand. If he noticed that he was surrounded by *roided-up* jocks, he didn't show it. It was just another business meeting to him. He never looked scared.

"We're friends of Freddie," Derek said. "We were just leaving."

She watched them walk away. A few people were in the corridor, and they pressed themselves as far away from the big men as possible.

Derek looked back and waved.

Sophie realized she'd wrapped her arm around her father's. She smiled as best she could and waved with her other hand, not wanting to release her grip on her dad's arm.

"What the hell kind of monster squad was that?" Warren asked.

"I'm glad Freddie doesn't hang with those kids anymore. He's not like them."

Her father nodded. "And he helps me with my taxes."

"He's nothing like them. Nothing at all."

CHAPTER THIRTEEN

THE WHEELCHAIR WORKOUT

"I don't understand why that man was so upset."

Parker said, "Jessica, you stopped right in front of him and waved people into the circle. He was probably afraid someone would slam into him."

Jessica Bradley shrugged. "I was just being nice. He didn't have to beep."

You were nice to the squirrel too, Parker thought. *It's probably very grateful.*

Parker's mother turned up their driveway and stopped by the ramp. Their beat-up white SUV wasn't specially equipped for Parker's wheelchair. She didn't want it, and her mother couldn't afford it. She waited for Jessica to grab the chair from the back. She opened the door, and Parker dropped into the seat. Her mother guided her, but she mainly relied on good aim and gravity.

She rolled to the unlocked door and entered. One of the cats, Copper, jumped in her lap and acted like she would lay down in it before she jumped up and ran off. The cats still liked her, even though she occasionally ran over their tails. She heard Copper thundering up the stairs, probably chasing a shadow. Parker wanted to thunder up the stairs.

Jessica carried the mail inside and stomped her feet on the mat. She handed it to Parker and returned outside.

Parker tore through the envelopes—nothing from Drexel or the University of Arizona, only a few bills and a card from an aunt.

Her mother stomped back inside. She had three Shop and Save bags in each arm and panted. Jessica's dark hair was wet from the snow.

"Jessica, I could have helped," Parker said.

"It wasn't that much, honey. Remember, I'm not getting a turkey this year."

Her mother wore way-too-tight jeans and a pink sweater. Her hair was dyed a little too dark, but it looked okay. She wore just enough makeup to cover the worry lines. The woman always tried to look younger than she was, which was silly. Jessica wasn't even forty yet, and Parker thought she was beautiful. A lot of old guys in their thirties and forties agreed, but Jessica didn't really go out much since the accident.

"I can stay home if you want. I don't have to go," Parker said.

"No. You're a young woman now, and it stands to reason that you'll start making other plans."

Parker grabbed the bag with frozen stuff and rolled to the refrigerator. "I asked you first, remember?" She opened the freezer side and put away some frozen vegetables, three Weight Watcher meals, and a Ben and Jerry's. "How often do I get invited out?"

Her mother nodded. "If you can get in good with Maureen Morgan, maybe she'll give me a deal on a car. The Cherokee's about to die."

Parker laughed. "I wouldn't count on that. Freddie bought his car there used, and he's making payments. No special treatment for him."

After they had unpacked the groceries, they headed toward the living room. It was still carpeted, but Parker didn't struggle any more. The wheels had worn a path. Plus, her arms were stronger now. She had done thirty pull-ups in gym class a few weeks ago. *I could do my own workout video*, she thought. *Bigger arms in just two years with* The Wheelchair Workout.

"I'm surprised Sophie's mom is letting her go," Jessica said.

"Everybody's a lawyer there, Jessica. They made a deal. Sophie's doing Thanksgiving early there, and then she's picking me up, and we're going over to Freddie's."

Parker was sure her mother didn't like Mrs. Lindstrom, but she wasn't sure why. Sure, Sophie's mom was a little high strung, but she let Parker sleep over a lot, and she was always nice. She was just a little cold, like she'd given up on something.

"Let's make some cookies later, and you can bring them over with you."

An image of Danny two-fisting chocolate cookies popped into her head, and she laughed. "That sounds good. I just want to rest for a while first."

Her mother eyed her. "You need to rest?"

"I'm a little tired, yes."

Parker wheeled to the stairs and climbed onto the stairlift. They'd held a fundraiser when the doctors discharged her from the hospital that had paid for the lift. The company that installed it had done the work for free. Her mom cried the first time Parker used it. Parker felt like crying every time she got on it. Sometimes, she butt-bumped down the stairs instead. It probably wasn't good for her damaged spine, but it made her feel like she had some control over her body.

Her old chair sat at the top of the stairs, and she plopped into it then rolled to her bedroom and closed the door. The room looked about the same as it did when she had the accident. A Belieber poster hung by her desk. She should get some new stuff for the walls, maybe Drake or Ed Sheeran. But she would need help to do that, and she promised herself she would do it one day alone—not even Sophie would be there.

Parker wheeled to the bed and pulled herself onto it. She looked at her door, making sure the knob wasn't turning. She didn't need her mother to see what she was doing. She wouldn't understand.

She rubbed her memory charms for luck and thought, *I hope this works.*

Parker sat at the edge of the bed and dropped her feet toward the floor. She could feel the frayed bottoms of her long, baggy jeans brush against her heels. It wasn't her imagination; she *felt* it.

Whatever Danny was doing was awakening her legs. She didn't know how he was doing it, and she didn't really care. Short of a deal with the Devil, she'd do anything to walk again. And Danny wasn't the Devil. He was too cute.

Parker eased her body downward, her feet catching the floor, and she stood. She gasped. Her legs felt locked, and they weren't moving. Parker looked at her feet and wiggled her toes. She used a hand to move her knee, and she shuffled a step. Her body trembled from the strain. She tried to take another step but instead tumbled face first onto the floor. Her head ached, but she didn't care.

"Parker, are you okay?" Jessica yelled. "I thought I heard something."

Still laying on the floor, she yelled back, "I'm fine, Jessica."

CHAPTER FOURTEEN

Danny Makes a Friend

"Hi, Freddie," the cashier said. "That'll be twenty-eight dollars and sixty-eight cents."

Freddie remembered her from algebra. The girl wasn't afraid to ask questions and had a grasp of the equations some other kids didn't. She was tall and pretty, and he remembered dancing with her couple years ago, before he knew Sophie. "Hi, Cassidy."

Danny stood behind him in line. He pulled some cash from his pocket and handed it to her. "I think that's enough."

She smiled and took his money. "How are you, Danny?"

Danny didn't seem to recognize her. "I'm good. Happy Thanksgiving."

The Shop and Save was open till one o'clock for last-minute shoppers. Freddie noticed that many of the store's carriages were filled with beer and wine. Thanksgiving was going to be festive this year.

"Danny, Mom gave me money for the stuff," Freddie said.

Danny took his change. "I'm leaving soon enough. I can't take all the money your father's given me for helping him. When I'm gone, you should have it."

Freddie smiled at the girl as they walked away. "Of course you can take it with you. Buy a wallet."

Thick slush filled the parking lot, and the plows hadn't arrived yet. They approached Freddie's black Mustang in silence, each of them carrying two bags. Their feet made splat noises as they trudged along. Freddie was warm in his parka and boots. Danny seemed fine in his sweatshirt and sneakers. At least he was wearing a hat. *Baby steps.*

"Freddie," Danny said. "That's Rachel's father."

He followed Danny's gaze and saw a Volvo parked diagonally across from their spot. Its motor idled roughly, and too much smoke came from the tailpipe. The plates were green.

"Maybe."

Danny dropped his bags on top of the trunk and scampered toward the Volvo.

Freddie yelled after him to stop, but he paid no mind. Freddie opened the trunk and put the bags inside. He slammed it shut then hoofed after Danny. The kid had problems with impulse control.

Danny knocked on the driver side window, and it slid down. "Are you Mr. Randall?"

Freddie caught up. "I'm sorry, sir. My friend gets carried away sometimes."

It was Mr. Randall, and he looked old. His hair had always been grey, but now it was shock white. The lines on his face were deeper, and his eyes were sadder. Freddie hadn't gotten close enough to notice during the memorial, but the change was stark.

"That's okay, boys. How can I help you?"

Danny regarded the man longer than he should have. "Are you here to look for your daughter?"

No filter, Freddie thought.

Mr. Randall appeared almost amused, like he was used to people watching what they say around him—and then here comes Danny. Danny didn't worry too much about what came from his mouth. He said whatever he was thinking. Funny that he also seemed to be keeping the biggest secrets too.

"I'm Danny Cole, and this is Freddie Morgan."

"I recognize you from the service. Thanks for helping out."

"Are you searching for her now? In the snow?"

Mr. Randall looked at Danny and then at Freddie. He probably thought they were a pair of nuts. "Yes, I am. I woke up this morning and thought she deserved another effort today. Why should I stop because of a holiday, right? We don't really celebrate it much anyway. So, I jumped in the car and drove here."

Freddie grabbed Danny's shoulder. "We'll let you go, sir."

Danny wriggled from his grip. "Can we help you? We don't really have to be home for another couple of hours. That's when our friends are coming over."

"Danny, he probably wants to be left alone. I'm sorry, sir."

Mr. Randall tried to smile, but he couldn't quite do it. He shook his head. "Honestly, I wouldn't mind the company."

Route 29 was dark and unplowed. The Mustang skidded when Freddie parked behind the Volvo, and Freddie was glad he didn't bang into the back of it.

Danny got out before him and jogged to poor Mr. Randall. Danny's balance was better now, but he seemed slower.

Freddie struggled for a word. *Lethargic*, he thought. A little *lethargic*.

They were parked across from the Townsend's field, and Mr. Randall crossed the street to look it over. His gloved hands stroked the back of his head. "She might have gone up there. There wasn't as much snow then, and it does seem like somebody might live up there, especially in the dark."

Danny shook his head. "She didn't go up there."

Mr. Randall stopped walking. "Oh, and why not?"

Don't tell him you see everything better, Freddie thought. *Please don't do it.*

"I see things better than most people. She didn't go up there."

Mr. Randall eyed Danny then Freddie. "He sees things better than other people?"

Freddie smiled.

Mr. Randall sounded angry. "Is it true, Mr. Morgan? Does your friend have special eyesight?"

"I hate to say it, but he seems to have … I don't know, um, a weird knack. Ask him something."

"How many fingers do I have up behind my back."

"Two."

Mr. Randall brought his hand from behind his back. Three fingers were showing.

Danny frowned. "You had two fingers up. You changed it when you moved your hand."

"Maybe. What else can you see?"

"That's not the right question," Danny said. "It's what I don't see. I don't see Rachel anywhere near the field or in any of these woods."

"Danny, why don't we just help Mr. Randall look and not give our opinions."

Mr. Randall surveyed the field again. "She's not there, you say? Where else isn't she?"

Danny didn't answer.

Mr. Randall pulled a flask from his pocket and took a quick gulp. "I know it's not right, but the whiskey helps."

They walked toward the spot where the police had found Rachel's car all those years ago. Freddie wanted to say something encouraging, but the guy was lost in his thoughts. Danny had an expression on his face like he knew something, but he wasn't talking. They walked a little farther, staring into the hills. Where did she go? They might never know.

"Have you always had great vision, Mr. Cole?"

"You can call me Danny, sir."

"Okay, Danny. Call me Vince."

"Danny had an accident a few months ago," Freddie said. "He's been a little different since."

"What kind of accident was it, Danny?"

"Honestly, Vince, I guess it was an overdose. I don't remember much from before."

"An overdose? You're a damned addict?"

Freddie wished his friend had kept that to himself. "Danny's not the same since then. He was dead for three minutes."

Mr. Randall stopped. "You were dead. Light-in-a-tunnel dead?"

"I guess so."

Mr. Randall leaned down and grabbed a handful of snow. He rolled it into a ball and tossed it deep into the trees. He glanced down the road toward the parked cars then back the other way. "That's where she came from. She stormed out of the house and jumped in my car and just took off. We thought she was going to a friend's, but I guess she remembered a vacation we took in Camden one year. Have you ever skied the Snow Bowl?"

Freddie nodded.

"And then she was gone. Probably forever."

"You don't know that," Freddie said. "If she's not in the field or in the hills, she must be somewhere."

Mr. Randall grabbed Danny's bare hand. "What do you remember of those three minutes."

"I can't explain."

The man pulled Danny closer. "When you were … in those three minutes, when it happened, could you see anything—anything that could help me? I don't really believe that nonsense, but tell me what you saw."

Danny shook his head.

The snow turned to heavy rain and splattered Mr. Randall's glasses. He tried to clear them with his jacket sleeve, but that only smeared them more. He looked desperate. He started to cry and made a muted noise, sort of a whimper. "Please tell me what you know, Danny."

"She's not on the other side. I would have seen her."

Chapter Fifteen

Danny's Room

The door swung open, and the boys entered, carrying bags from Shop and Save. They banged their shoes and removed them. Freddie's mom rose from her chair and took Freddie's jacket. Danny's sweatshirt was soaked. He took it off, and Mrs. Morgan took that too.

Sophie sat on the couch, her feet tapping nervously. "Where have you been? I texted you."

Parker was locked in place beside her. They'd arrived early, only to discover the boys weren't back from the store yet. This led to almost half an hour of conversation with Mrs. Morgan. Freddie knew Mrs. Morgan made her nervous. What took so long? She was sweating through her crepe V-neck top from Forever 21. She didn't want to smell around her boyfriend's family.

"We went out to Route 29 with Rachel Randall's father and helped him look around."

Sophie wanted to say something clever. Instead, she said, "Oh."

"That was very thoughtful of you boys," Mrs. Morgan said. "How did this come to pass?"

Freddie told her that they had met him in the parking lot and offered to help. "He's very sad. He was drinking from a flask."

"You should have invited him here to let him sober up a bit."

Freddie shook his head. "We did invite him, but he had to head home. I don't think he was drunk. He said whiskey helped a little with the pain."

Mr. Morgan came from the bedroom. He must have heard some of the conversation. "Sometimes it helps a little too much."

Freddie's mom said, "The pain is in the not knowing. When we lost Ryan, we … we knew what happened pretty quickly. The footprints led to a hole in the ice. We searched for a few days and found him. I can't imagine how I would feel if I didn't know what happened."

Mr. Morgan took her hand. "Well, that's enough of that talk. Who wants some snacks?"

Parker said, "I brought some cookies."

"Cookies?" Danny said. "What kind?"

"Chocolate chip."

The boy shook with excitement. "Maybe we can eat them in my room. Can I show Parker my room?"

Freddie said, "I don't think my mother wants us bringing people up there, Danny."

Mrs. Morgan said, "No, I trust you kids. I just ask that you keep your doors open, and keep in mind one of us will be by if we need your help."

Freddie looked shocked. Sophie was aware of the house rules, and no girls in your room was number one on the list. Maybe she was just being nice because it was Thanksgiving. Whatever, she was just happy to be with Freddie.

Parker said, "How should I …"

Mr. Morgan grinned. "Freddie, I'll take the handles, and you take the wheels. We'll just carry you up, like you're Cleopatra on the Nile."

Sophie went up the stairs first. She had been there before, but Freddie's parents didn't know about it. Or maybe they did. Freddie's dad led the way; he gripped the handles hard, and his muscles swelled under his long-sleeve shirt. Freddie did the bulk of the lifting, grasping the wheels, but didn't look tired at all. Parker sat in her chair looking embarrassed but sort of happy too. Danny was last. He carried the Tupperware bowl with cookies. He was eating one of them already.

Freddie led the crew into Ryan's room. "This is it."

Sophie looked around. The room was obviously decorated for someone a few years younger than Danny, but he seemed to fit. A small pile of comic books sat on a desk, and games and puzzles littered the room. One of the shelves had some baseball stuff and some trophies. Danny was a bit of a slob, and he had some clothes piled in a corner. The bed was small but not too small for a skinny guy like him. A George Strait poster hung on the wall across from the bed. It looked just like the one Freddie had.

Danny stopped eating and looked at Parker. "Do you like it? I really like it."

She smiled. "It's a great room, Danny."

Sophie felt that uneasy feeling again and wished Freddie felt it too. But he was getting to like Danny, and he didn't see the problem. She knew something wrong was going on between Parker and the kid, and it worried her. "Looks like you're making it your own."

"Well, I know I'm not here for long, but I sure like it here."

Parker said, "You don't know how long you're here for. It could be longer than you think."

"Maybe."

Danny showed everyone Ryan's *Star Wars* collection and then moved on to his baseball cards. Some were recent and Sophie realized Danny must be adding to the collection. How would Mrs. Morgan feel about that?

Freddie said, "Do you want to see my room, Sophie?"

"Yes," she said. "I've always wondered what your room looks like." She followed him across the hallway into his room. The room was bright from the shiny pond outside his window and clean for a boy's room. A poster of a country girl and the George Strait poster hung on the wall. "I do like your room."

Freddie walked to the doorway, peered down the hallway and whispered, "All clear."

She wanted to say something about him not answering her texts, but there would be time for that. He kissed her lightly, and then again. When he pulled away, he looked nervous, like a little boy who'd broken a toy and didn't want anyone to know. "I just know she'll check on us."

Sophie took his hand and sat beside him on the bed. "Maybe you could just play me some music, and we can talk about school."

He looked relieved.

"The toughest boy I know is scared of his mother."

He nodded. "You got that right."

"I guess I can't really blame you. She scares me a little."

Freddie stepped closer. "She has a secret."

"What secret?"

"She had a tattoo. On the top of her arm, near her shoulder."

Sophie giggled. "A tattoo of what?"

"She won't say. But she has one of those removal scars that look so weird. I hope it was a pirate skull or something tough like that."

Sophie wondered if she'd ever figure out Mrs. Morgan.

"When did you decide to be a doctor?" Danny asked Parker. "I think it's really cool."

"I guess always, but ever since I've been talking to Dr. Hollis about it. He's only part time at the home; though he practically lives there lately. He's mainly a general doctor. I've been seeing him since I was little. He thinks I can do it."

Danny nodded. "So do I. I wish I was going to be around to see it."

"You might be here longer than you think. Maybe you'll stay here permanently. Your parents are in jail. You're seventeen years old. You could stay."

Danny sat on his desk chair. He rolled it close to her. "I'm pretty sure I'm going to have to go home soon. I'm only here for a visit."

Parker's tears welled up. "I don't want you to go, Danny. I think you *are* home."

He brushed his hands through her hair. His face was fuller, but he looked tired. "I promise I'll find a way to visit again. I promise."

His brown eyes looked hungry for something. He kissed her, and she tasted chocolate chips.

She pulled away. "Can't you just try to stay?"

He shook his head. "I don't think I can stop what's going to happen."

Parker grabbed a magic toy from his desk. It was three big rings, all of them connected. "Can you work this?"

He grinned and took the rings. He turned around, and when he turned back, they were separated. "Ta-dah."

"How do you do that?"

"I can't tell you. It's the code of the magicians."

She smiled. "Like the trick with my legs."

"That's not a trick."

She told him about standing the other day and about falling, too. "It took me a few minutes to get back into my chair."

"I bet you only need my help once more. Then it's probably just a matter of time."

She wanted to say no. "Okay. One more time."

He rolled his chair beside her and did the thing with her back again. The spark felt stronger this time, like his phaser was no longer set on Stun.

Parker's body rocked in her chair, her arms spasming, and her legs trembled. Her skin felt like she was blushing all over. All her thoughts were cloudy and happy. She panted, like she'd just finished a 10k.

It took a moment, but her head cleared. Danny sat next to her, his head down. He must have fallen from the chair. He looked at her and smiled, but he looked sickly.

"Are you all right?" she whispered.

He blinked a few times and stood slowly. "I probably just need another cookie." His legs buckled, and he dropped to his knees.

"Danny, can you move? Are you okay?"

He struggled to his feet again. This time, his face was clearer, his eyes more alert.

Parker felt panic set in. "This is because of me, isn't it? It was too much."

He shook his head. Sweat matted his hair.

"Take it back, Danny. I don't want you to get hurt. Take it back."

"It doesn't work like that, Parker. It's a gift."

Mr. Morgan knocked on the open door. "The bird's ready. Let's get you downstairs so I can say Grace. Afterward, Maureen wants to take some pictures."

Danny looked about normal again. He grabbed Parker's arm and held it. "Can I say Grace this year, Mr. Morgan? I have a lot that I'm thankful for."

Mr. Morgan nodded. "I think we all do, Danny."

CHAPTER SIXTEEN

Playing Catch

The Mountain View Road property was the only one the Morgans owned in Abbot Pond. It wasn't anywhere near the pond and didn't overlook any mountain that he was aware of. It was a well-developed neighborhood close to Camden and wasn't rented out as an apartment. It was a medium-sized, one-story traditional white ranch with enough back yard to cook out and play horseshoes. His mother had rented the place three times, and all three times the renters had trashed the house. Every tenant passed a credit check and seemed normal, but not a single occupant left the house without breaking at least one window.

They had the lights on, but they didn't need to. The sun was bright, and its reflection on the snow and ice around the house brightened every inch of the open concept home, just like the pond brightened his room at the house—just another reason to love living in Maine. He never wanted to move.

Freddie and Danny were on cleanup duty. Freddie's mom wanted the floors cleared of debris and mopped to perfection. The floors, under all the dust and glass, were real hardwood, and she used them as a key selling point whenever she listed the house. They were supposed to clean up and take some nice pictures, minus the broken window, and email the photos to her office.

Danny wore the sweats Jack had bought him and dirty work boots. He went right to work with the push broom.

Freddie said, "You look like you know what you're doing."

Danny grinned. "Your dad doesn't let me just sit around when he's paying me to work."

"Well, you've come a long way since when you got here." Freddie grabbed the other broom and headed to the opposite side of the room—the one with all the broken glass. He swept the junk toward the middle of the main room.

Danny pushed the debris from his side to the same spot. After a while, a sizeable pile took up space in the center of the floor.

It dawned on Freddie that he didn't mind working with Danny. He enjoyed his company. His phone buzzed. It was a short one from Sophie. *OMW*

He wrote back, *K*, then said, "Sophie's meeting us here in a while. Her mom's dropping her off."

"Great. I like her.

"She likes you too. She thinks your interesting."

Danny stopped sweeping and smiled at him. "It's okay, Freddie. I know she doesn't like me very much."

"She likes you, but you make her nervous."

"I understand. I'm different."

"I know what it's like to be different, Danny. People stare at me when I'm out with Sophie. The other Hispanic kids at school barely talk to me, because I only speak English, and I never know what the white kids think about me."

"You don't look so different, Freddie. Most people see you another way—anybody who knows you, I mean."

Danny returned to sweeping. He moved the broom in odd patterns, creating large piles of dirt. He looked good now, almost not underweight. His hair was better since they visited Supercuts, and his color was coming back. He'd been pale since Thanksgiving, and Freddie had been worried. But now, a few meals later, he looked good. He was still walking a little slow though. Hopefully, that would get better as well.

"She's just concerned for Parker, is all," Freddie said, getting back on subject. "She worries about her. Worrying is good."

Danny nodded and kept sweeping.

"And now you're planning this big date with her, just the two of you. That'll drive Sophie crazy."

"We just want to spend some time together. I wish I could drive."

"You have a license. You could borrow my car."

Danny shook his head. "I don't remember how. It wouldn't be safe."

"I don't mind dropping you guys off at Applebee's, but the movie theater will be a pain. You'll have to cut through the Hampton Inn parking lot and then go down the long driveway to the cinema. And it'll be dark."

"We can manage, Freddie. I really appreciate you driving us and picking us up. I kinda feel like a little kid though. Maybe you and I could go driving when the weather's better, and I can practice. I'm sure it'll come back to me."

Freddie didn't mind. In fact, it made him feel like they were part of a normal family. He loved his parents, but there was nothing normal about them. Work consumed his mother most of the time, and his father was more than a little quirky. Taking Danny to practice driving just felt right. He liked it, even if Sophie couldn't understand. She'd come around.

Freddie spotted a pink rubber ball on the floor. It was smaller than a baseball. He picked it up, bounced it and grinned at Danny. "Heads up!" He whipped the ball near the pile of trash, and it bounced off the ground.

Danny casually snatched it and smiled. "I used to play baseball." He bounced the ball back with more force than Freddie expected.

He caught it and threw it back. "When did you play baseball? I don't remember that."

"A while back."

Freddie bounced it again, and Danny caught it without looking. They went through the process, and the kid did it again. His hands moved to where he knew the ball would be, but he almost looked like he wasn't paying attention. Freddie moved around the room, and Danny shuffled slowly away from him, still sweeping. He put more spin on the ball and bounced it at odd angles. Every time, his friend snatched the ball, like some blind ninja in an old kung fu movie. If the ball bounced to his broom side, he just flipped the stick to the other hand and grabbed the ball with his weak hand. All in one move.

This would make a great YouTube video, he thought. *But everyone would think it was fake.*

"You should try out for the baseball team this spring," Freddie said. "You've got wicked good reflexes."

"I will, if you will. If I'm still here."

Freddie thought about it. "You know what? I just might."

Someone knocked on the door, and Freddie turned to look. The ball bounced past him and smashed through the already broken back window. "Oh, shit."

The boys looked at each other and laughed.

The door opened, and Sophie entered, looking perfect. Freddie could practically hear his heart beating.

"Did you guys just break something?" she asked.

Freddie said, "Our official story is that the window was already broken."

She wore what passed for her work clothes—white jeans and a retro-80s t-shirt that had bright pictures of a band he'd never heard of. She wasn't wearing her jacket. Her blond hair was wet from the snow. He knew she'd rather look good than be warm. She was like a famous painter who suffered for her art. Except, she would put on the jacket if it got too cold. She wasn't crazy.

"Hi, Sophie," Danny said. "I like your shirt."

"Thanks. I see you got a haircut. It's good."

Danny blushed. "Thanks, Sophie."

"What were you guys up to?"

Freddie found another ball, a smaller one, and bounced it to his friend.

Danny nonchalantly caught it while sweeping. He looked like a marionette with invisible strings, his arms floating in awkward directions.

"He's a natural," Freddie said.

Danny bounced it back, but she grabbed it.

Her reflexes impressed Freddie, but she looked serious.

She whispered, "Don't you think it's a little odd that he didn't even look, and he caught the ball?"

Freddie took the ball and tossed it back to Danny. "He sees things better than we do."

Sophie sighed. "I've heard that about him."

CHAPTER SEVENTEEN

OFF THE RECORD

Freddie had to park in his mother's spot.

"Whose car is that?" Sophie asked, unfastening her seatbelt.

"I don't know," Freddie said. "But I guess that's why my dad called us back to the house."

Danny was in the back of the Mustang, his gangly legs knocking against the back of Sophie's seat. "It's the policeman's car. The one who was here before."

Sophie turned. "Now, how would you know that?"

"Mr. Morgan said the detective drives a Chevrolet. A small one."

Freddie said, "If it's him, he's got the wrong car for this area. Malibus are no good in the snow."

Freddie turned off the lights, and they exited the car. It wasn't even supper time and it was already dusk. The front light was on to help them travel the familiar path through the snow, up the stairs and through the front door.

Sophie wanted to stay in the car, but she knew how that would look. Mrs. Morgan already viewed her like some criminal whenever they talked. Maybe they'd be out of here before she got home.

Mr. Morgan sat in one of the chairs, drinking from a coffee cup. A familiar tall guy stood next to him. He looked casual in his dockers and sweater.

"I know you. You were at the funeral," Sophie said.

He smiled. "Yes, that was me. You were behind me in line."

Mrs. Morgan said, "Freddie, why don't you grab everybody's coats and have a seat?"

Freddie did what she had instructed while Sophie sat on the couch.

Danny disappeared for a moment and returned with a bowl of barbecue chips. He offered her a chip, and she shook her head. She was wearing light pants, and she knew the kid would get some on her. He was like one of those sharks rolling their eyes back into their head when they were eating seals on the Discovery Channel. He lost all control. She remembered the chocolate chip cookies on Thanksgiving. They'd had no chance against the kid.

Freddie returned and sat beside her. He reached across her and grabbed some chips, like they were all watching a football game or something. She saw that he'd managed to get a few crumbs on her pants and resisted the urge to brush them off. Mrs. Morgan didn't want crumbs on her floor.

"My name's Paul Nault. I'm a detective in Camden, and I'm investigating Samuel Burns' death."

Danny said, "You're a detective? That's great."

"Uh, thanks. My mother is very proud."

"I bet she is."

Nault studied the kid like he was trying to figure him out. *Good luck with that.* The detective shook his head. "Anyway, I'll be honest. I got nothing. None of you are in trouble or implicated in any way, but I was just trying to look at the case from any angle I can find. Jack—Mr. Morgan—said it would be okay if I talked to you boys off the record."

Freddie said, "I don't know that we can help you much. I wasn't close with Sammy."

"I was with Mr. Morgan when he found the body," Danny said. "That was the first time I remember seeing him, but my memory's a little shaky."

Nault scanned his notepad. "That's right. You had an episode. You're better now?"

"Yes, thanks. My memory gives me a few problems, but I'm getting better. How are you?"

Sophie restrained herself from shaking her head. "I knew Sammy. I volunteer at the Lakeside, and he worked there too. He said college was more expensive than he had expected."

The detective asked her what her name was and then wrote it down. "You're under no obligation to talk to me. I haven't asked for your parents' consent."

"My parents are lawyers."

He smirked, and she suddenly realized he was kind of cute. "Now I'm *sure* they don't want you talking to me."

"I think it's okay. I liked Sammy."

Nault scratched his head. "It seems as though everyone liked him. That's the problem. Somebody must have had it in for him. He didn't just fall on his head."

Danny said, "I think it has something to do with the missing girl down the street."

Nault said, "I do too. Why do you think so?"

Danny tilted his head. "Somebody broke into Mr. and Mrs. Morgan's property down the road from where she lived. I doubt it's a coincidence."

"Why's that, Mr. Cole?"

"Well, I've seen *Law and Order*. A dead body up the street from a kidnapping? It seems suspicious."

"You like mysteries, Mr. Cole?"

Mr. Morgan chuckled. "He's got a new way of looking at things, that's for sure."

Danny said, "I've always been good at puzzles. I like to look at things from a lot of directions."

The detective looked at Danny funny again. "Have we met before, Mr. Cole?"

Danny said, "I don't think, so but my memory's weird. You can call me Danny."

"Is that what you think, Detective?" Sophie asked. "The missing girl had something to do with Sammy getting killed?"

"I can't say officially, but I'm not a big believer in coincidences." He nodded at Danny. "I used to watch that show too."

Freddie said, "None of us knew him real well. I played basketball with him when I was a kid."

The detective stood and looked around. He stared at a picture of Ryan on the wall, looking like he was trying to decide, then nodded. "Okay, I'm going to ask you something in confidence, okay?"

The detective flipped through his notebook and stopped after a few pages. "How would Sammy get ahold of drugs in a nice town like Abbot Pond?"

Sophie felt like he had punched her in the gut. She'd smoked pot once, and it wasn't fun, and Freddie was squeaky clean.

Danny said, "What kind of drugs?"

Finally, a subject this kid has experience with, Sophie thought.

"Look, it doesn't leave this room, but he had a dangerous combination of narcotics in his system—traces of methamphetamine, cocaine, and anabolic steroids and a couple other things, opioids. Not enough to kill him, but enough to wire him up."

Sophie said, "I heard he overslept for work a couple of times. He said he was always trying to keep up with his schoolwork."

"A weird mix like that will make you crash, that's for sure," Nault said. "He was playing a dangerous game."

Mr. Morgan half raised his hand. "If he was buying that stuff, he must have had a dealer. You know the streets are crawling with them on the coast."

Nault nodded. "It was a problem back when I was in school, Jack. But this particular mix is an unfamiliar blend to our department."

Danny said, "Why did he need steroids? Was he still playing basketball?"

"Good question. We checked the community college, and they don't even have a team. He was so overwhelmed with classes, he didn't seem to have any new friends. It was work and school for him. Steroids are drugs though, and people can become addicted."

Freddie's dad said, "Well, he was with *somebody* when he died."

Sophie thought of Parker. She was pretty sure her and Sammy had gone out on a few dates before the accident. No way she would tell that to the cute cop, but she would mention it to her later. Maybe she'd remember something.

Nault said, "The missing girl was seen with three youths shortly before she went missing. They were described as Caucasian and large."

Freddie dramatically wiped his brow. "Rules me out."

"Me, too," Danny said, patting his stomach. "I'm skinny."

Sophie said, "Did any of her friends match that description?"

"She has a lot of friends," the detective said. "Not a one looks anything like that. I've spoken to all the basketball and football players in her school. That was a nightmare."

"Sammy was big," Danny said.

"Right, but he seemed pretty friendless at the time of his death."

Sophie felt a sense of guilt ride across her conscience. She had talked to Sammy every few weeks and had never asked him how things were going or how his grades were. He had been a nice kid and must have been having a tough time.

Freddie grabbed her hand and squeezed; he knew what she was thinking.

"So, you kids have no idea what he might have been up to? Nothing at all?"

Sophie fidgeted in her seat.

"You have something, Miss Lindstrom?" Nault asked.

"Well, it's the funeral. Some kids were there I wouldn't have expected to be there."

Freddie said, "Sometimes kids will go funerals just to get out of school."

"Yeah, that's what I was thinking."

Nault said, "I remember seeing some kids behind you in line. At the time, I thought they might be friends of yours. One of them looked like Herman Munster. He was certainly big."

She nodded.

"Can you give me their names? I'll talk to them."

"I don't know. I'm sure they had nothing to do with any of this."

Detective Nault said, "Your name won't come up. I'll tell them I saw them at the funeral and have a few questions."

Sophie looked at Freddie. "One of them was Freddie's old, um, teammate. Derek Matthews. He was with Mike Gillette and a really big kid. Bobby Boots. He was your Munster guy."

Freddie looked a little shocked that she'd brought his friends into the conversation. "Stevens. Bobby Boots is just his nickname."

The detective raised an eyebrow. "Why Boots?"

"Because he wears boots all the time."

Nault looked disappointed. "Oh."

Freddie said, "Derek used to be one of my best friends. He wouldn't do anything like what you're thinking."

The detective closed his notepad. "I'm sure you're right, but, like I said before, I got nothing. It can't hurt to see if these kids know anything."

CHAPTER EIGHTEEN

THE COAT RACK

Parker knew Sophie wasn't used to shopping at Target, but she just wanted a nice shirt that didn't cost much. She didn't care about the name on the tag or the origin of the threads that weaved the material into a blouse. She just wanted a shirt that Danny might like on her.

"Oh, this is a cute store. Very red."

"You've never been to Target?"

Sophie laughed. "My parents aren't rich enough for me to be that snobby, Parker. I like it here."

Parker smiled. "I'm sorry, Soph, but your clothes are usually kind of fancy, and we've never been here together."

"You've never worn those boots before either."

Parker smiled. The brown boots had been in her closet since sophomore year. They were tallish with buckles on the side. "My dad bought them for me, right before he left."

"Well, say what you will about the guy, he had pretty good taste in lady's footwear."

"He's helping with my college. That's something."

"Have you heard from any more schools?"

Parker shook her head. "Not the ones I'm most interested in. The ones I've heard from are offering me partial scholarships though."

"I like Drexel. It's not as far away as Arizona."

"Me too, and Dr. Hollis went there. He loved it."

Sophie nodded. Parker knew she didn't like the idea of her moving so far away, but Sophie had applications out too. They'll be apart a lot in the years to come. That's just the way life works.

"I like Arizona too. No snow to wheel through, and the ground is really flat. It could work."

It was hot in the store. Whenever a cold snap hit, the big stores always overcompensated with a heat blast of their own. Christmas music was blaring already, even though it was just the beginning of December. Target wasn't that busy yet, but it was still early in the afternoon. Foot traffic would pick up soon. Friday nights were always crazy in December.

They moved down the main aisle toward the rear of the store. A few people looked at her weirdly, but she pretended not to notice. Before the accident, she would have been like that. People don't usually mean anything when they looked at her or said something to a friend. Sometimes they were mean though. Like Mike Gillette was mean.

"We should go to Ruby Tuesday's after," Sophie said. "Maybe just get appetizers."

Parker wasn't sure if she'd have enough money after shopping. "We'll see. Let's get a shirt first."

Parker liked Target for a lot of reasons, but a big one was how much room she had to maneuver her wheelchair. Most mall stores were a little tight for her chair. Even Walmart was hard for her to traverse, which she found surprising. Half the people she saw in those funny Walmart YouTube videos were crashing around in those motorized chairs before they demolished the store. Target was the best.

She wanted to go to the women's section, but Sophie guided her to the young adult clothes. The walls had pictures of kids in hip, bright clothes, and she thought that might work. All she saw from the aisle were Fortnite t-shirts and sweatpants.

Sophie knew where to go though, and she brought her to a quiet corner with youthful shirts and sweaters on the wall. "You should get a nice sweater. It'll go well with those faded jeans you're always wearing."

She was right, of course, but Parker said she wanted to look around first. She knew she'd end up back in the corner with the sweaters. Sophie Lindstrom was never wrong about fashion.

Sophie messed with her charcoal grey scrunchie. She pulled at her hair and tugged at the tie until she looked perfect. A lot of blond girls went to their school, but most of the others had dark roots coming out of their skulls. Sophie was the real deal—so pretty, so perfect. Parker hated that she was a little jealous of her friend.

"I bet they'd serve you a drink at Ruby Tuesday's," Sophie said.

"What?" Parker asked.

"Because of the chair. You look almost old enough, and you're in that wheelchair. I bet the server would be too afraid to card you."

"Why would I do that?"

Sophie shrugged. "I don't like to drink, as you know. Beer is gross, and wine is sour."

Parker nodded.

"I'd like to be on a beach somewhere and drink the fancy drinks, like piña coladas and strawberry margaritas. Freddie would have one too instead of water. We'd sit at the beach bar and stare across the ocean. Maybe we'd see some frolicking dolphins."

"Freddie's at your beach too?"

"Of course. He's the best."

Parker looked at a pair of oversized sweatshirts. They were light and kind of cute, but the sweaters they had looked at before were better. She sighed and moved back toward the corner.

Sophie didn't say anything, but she was probably gloating on the inside.

"Would you take Danny to this hypothetical beach?" Sophie asked. "I mean, if you think about the beach, do you see yourself with him?"

She thought for a minute. "Danny's just here for a visit. I wish that wasn't the case, but it is."

Sophie pulled a striped fuzzy pullover from a rack and placed it against her friend's chest. "Why don't you try this one on?"

The pullover was comprised of a variety of light colors and looked perfect. "I think I like it."

"Speaking of Danny," Sophie started. "I was there when a detective questioned him and Freddie about Sammy and about the missing girl in Camden. It doesn't sound like they have many clues."

"It's not right about Sammy. Or the girl."

Sophie moved closer and whispered, "He had drugs in his system. A lot of them."

Parker nodded.

"You're not surprised?"

Parker started toward the changing room. "I wish I was."

The girl at the counter handed them a plastic card with a big number one on it, and they entered one of the rooms. Parker removed her jacket and tried on the sweater. She had to be careful not to run over Sophie's foot when she turned toward the big wall mirror. The sweater was just right. She thought she looked pretty cute, if you forgot about the wheelchair.

"Is that why you stopped seeing him?"

Parker didn't want to dredge up old memories. "It's the main reason."

"You didn't do them too?"

"Not everybody's perfect, Sophie."

Sophie shook her head. "I didn't mean anything. I just asked."

"We only went out for a while, and he was kind of up and down. Anyway, he talked me into trying it one morning when we were supposed to be at school. He had a line of the stuff on his mother's glass table in their living room, and he showed me what to do. I remember we were watching *The Price is Right*."

Sophie was wide-eyed. "And …?"

"And it burned my nose, and it made my head feel weird. I hated it."

Sophie looked relieved. "I've never tried it. I'm glad you didn't get hooked or anything."

Parker snorted. "Hooked?"

Sophie smiled. "You know what I mean. And that was why you stopped seeing him?"

"Mainly. He had issues. He was a sweet guy, but he didn't like himself all that much. I just couldn't deal with it. Anyway, we were kids."

"Hmm."

They left the dressing room and handed the card to the girl.

"What's the *hmm* for?"

"Nothing, it's just …"

"Just what?"

Sophie's face tightened. "You broke up with one guy who liked drugs, and now you're going on a date with a boy who actually died from drugs."

Parker felt the blood rush to her face. "That's not fair, Sophie. That was *Old Danny*."

"*Old Danny?* For all you know, he's still rummaging through bathroom vanities and stealing pills. That's what he used to do."

"I like him, Sophie. So does your boyfriend and so do a bunch of people at school lately. You don't know what he's done for me."

"You've known him off and on for years, and you act like you just met him. He has a history."

"He's not that guy anymore, Sophie. I thought you saw that."

Sophie rolled her eyes. "Maybe he's not, or maybe he's the same guy he always was and he's just trying out a new act."

Sophie was still walking, so Parker spun and rolled as quickly as she could toward the back of the store. She turned into the men's department and looked to see if Sophie was following her. A flash of blonde came in her direction, so she plowed into a round stand filled with men's parkas. The rack wasn't too full, so she had room to squeeze in. The floor was dusty, and she fought the urge to sneeze as she pushed in as close to the center as she could. She heard movement outside the coats and held her breath.

"Parker, I can see your wheels."

Damn, she thought. "Just go away, Sophie. I can't do this."

Sophie's voice sounded tearful, but she couldn't tell for sure through the thick jackets. "I'm sorry, Parker. I shouldn't have said anything."

"Sophie, I'm embarrassed enough to be hiding in this rack. Can't you just leave, and I'll have Jessica pick me up?"

"I'll take you home, Parker. I'll shut up about Danny. Your mother doesn't want to drive all the way out to Topsham. She's not good in the snow."

Tears streaked her cheeks now. "Sophie, I don't want to go with you. You know Jessica will come."

"I'm sorry, Parker. I thought we could tell each other anything. Remember the memory charm …"

"I don't have too many guys knocking down my door these days, and the one guy who doesn't even notice my wheelchair is the guy you won't stop bitching about. Just leave me alone." She felt warm from the jackets, like she'd gone to bed with too many comforters. "Sophie?"

"I'll leave."

Parker waited and then tried to roll from the rack, but one of her wheels was caught on the metal stand. She took a breath and stood enough to work the chair over the obstruction. She sat down and rolled out. An old woman eyed her funny, but she didn't care. Sophie was nowhere to be seen.

She brushed the dust and tears from her cheek and pulled her phone from her purse. Her mother answered on the first ring. "I need you to come pick me up."

"Where are you?"

Parker told her.

"It'll take a little while. Give me forty minutes."

Parker hung up and looked around. No sign of Sophie. Did she really leave?

She thought about returning the sweater to the dressing room and having them put it back, but she really liked it. Instead, she wheeled around the big store, browsing the new Blu-rays, looking at videogames for Danny and grabbing Fritos for her mother. That killed ten minutes. She thought she saw Sophie in the music section, but it was another girl not as pretty as Sophie.

Parker rolled to the front and grabbed a candy bar to eat on the way home. What else could she do now? For sure, she wouldn't wait outside in the subzero. She got in line and paid for her stuff then wheeled to the little café that sold pizza. She parked near the window and saw Sophie's car wasn't where they had parked. Did she really leave?

She welled up again but fought it off. Nobody wants to see a handicapped girl crying in the corner of a Target. She focused on her candy bar and watched for her mother. "Silent Night" played over the intercom. It looked to be snowing, but it was the kind that was sort of rain too. It wouldn't pile up like the thick stuff. It was turning into an awful day.

Her mother's white SUV pulled in front of the store.

Parker threw away her candy wrapper and headed for the front door. The cold blast from the outside knocked her from her melancholy, and she scrambled for the car. Jessica was parked in a fire lane, and somebody beeped a long and exaggerated beep at them as Parker climbed into the Chevy. She hoped her mother didn't notice how easily she did it. Parker wasn't ready for the world to know about her legs.

Jessica wasn't wearing a jacket, and she shivered as she exited the car. She gave the finger to the beeper without looking at them and grabbed the wheelchair. She tossed it in the back and hopped into the car. She looked at her daughter and affectionally rubbed her arm.

Parker scanned the parking lot for the brown Audi, but it was nowhere. She sighed.

"She's parked behind that van over there. She's kinda ducked down," her mother said.

"She didn't leave."

"Of course, she didn't. She's your best friend, your sister from another mister."

Parker smiled. "Don't ever say that again."

Jessica pulled away from the fire lane, and someone beeped at her again. She ignored them and turned toward the main road.

Parker looked in the mirror and saw the Audi pull into traffic a few cars back. She knew Sophie didn't trust Jessica's driving.

"I guess you have a guardian angel," her mother said. "You want me to lose her?"

The idea of Jessica trying to lose someone in traffic terrified her. "Let's just go home, okay?"

CHAPTER NINETEEN

Good News

"What do you think they're talking about in there?" Freddie asked.

He and his father sat outside the counselor's office. They brought Danny to Bangor every other Saturday for his appointment. The Ground Round was still open in town, and they usually went to lunch afterward. It was sort of a thing.

Jack wore dockers and a heavy plaid shirt, with no coat. "I don't know. She probably wants to know about the overdose. You know, was it accidental or on purpose? Or maybe she wants to know if he's happy with us. He didn't used to be."

"He likes Dr. Williams. He says she's fun."

"She's nice. There weren't too many Oriental doctors around Bangor when I was coming up."

Freddie shook his head. "I think you mean *Asian* doctors."

"She's from the Orient, isn't she?"

"I don't think so. Her last name is Williams, and she sounds like she's from around here."

Freddie's phone buzzed with another message from Sophie. *She's still not answering me.*

He typed back, *Just give her time.*

His dad smiled. "Women troubles?"

"No, not exactly."

"When I was in high school, I had my pick of the ladies."

"Really?"

"Sure. I had so many that I had to hand out applications. I interviewed the top three applicants, and the winner got to go out with me."

Freddie laughed. "That's not true."

Jack winked at him. "Sure, it is."

His phone buzzed again. *How are you? Any new dreams?*

He tapped back, *Sort of. Just a minor change. I'll tell you later.*

The old lady didn't say anything different last night, but she did grab him while she pointed behind him. She looked sad and a little afraid. He remembered turning around, but then he woke up. Freddie felt he was close to figuring out what upset the old lady so much. He just had to stay asleep next time.

The door opened, and Danny exited.

Dr. Williams followed him, smiling broadly. "You're very funny, Danny."

Dr. Williams was tall and had dark hair. She sometimes wore glasses, but she wasn't wearing them now. She didn't wear a lab coat or anything formal like that, just jeans and a dark blouse. Freddie thought she was kind of cute but too old for him. He only liked girls his own age.

Danny was holding something. "Dr. Williams gave me a jigsaw puzzle for Christmas. It's a *Star Wars* one."

"In case I don't see you before then, Danny."

Danny gave her a hug. "Goodbye."

"Jack, could I talk to you for a few minutes?" she asked.

He stood up. "Sure, Linda. Sure. Boys, I'll be right back."

Danny took Jack's spot and stared at his present. "It's got five-hundred pieces."

"That should take you about twenty minutes," Freddie said.

"Do you want to help me?"

"If you want. It won't be until tomorrow though. I have to go see Sophie later."

"Okay."

"How'd it go in there?"

"It was all right. She kept trying to talk about before my accident, and I kept telling her I didn't really remember much of that."

"What did she say?"

Danny scrunched his face. "She thinks I've, um, *repressed* my memories."

"What do you think?"

He shook his head. "You know that's not it."

His phone buzzed again. *Do you think I should just go over there? I could just knock until she answers.*

Freddie most definitely did not think that was a good idea. He wrote, *It's up to you.*

Freddie said, "Did she say anything else, besides, 'You have repressed memories, and here's a neat Christmas present'?"

Danny nodded. "She wants me to see a doctor. She's worried because I'm moving kind of slow."

"You went to Doc Hollis before. We can probably make an appointment there."

Danny didn't seem to care. "Is everything okay with Sophie? She's texting you a lot."

The phone went off again. *You're right. I should give her some space. I'll go over tomorrow.*

Freddie smiled.

"Is she okay?"

"She and Parker had a fight. I didn't want to tell you about it until after your appointment."

"A fight? Was it about me?"

Freddie didn't reply.

"It's about the date, isn't it?"

"I think that's part of it, but there's other stuff too."

Danny frowned. "It's mainly me. She's worried that I'm a weirdo."

"That's not exactly it, Danny. And you're not a weirdo. A goofball, maybe …"

"Don't be mad at her, Freddie. She's right. I overdosed and died. Then I come back and act like I'm a different person. Sophie's just looking out for Parker."

The door opened, and Jack exited, smiling.

"Everything okay, Dad?"

He closed the door and put his hand on Danny's shoulder. "She seems to think you can probably stay with us indefinitely."

Freddie felt a rush of joy. "What?"

Jack led them to the door. "Your mom's still in … still in jail. You're seventeen now and a senior, and you've told her how much you like it with us. It's pretty much up to you where you stay. Maureen and I have temporary custody anyway, so not much stands in the way."

Danny remained quiet.

Jack opened the door and stepped into the cold. The walkway and driveway were both neatly shoveled, and no ice was on the ground. The big green house resembled any other house on the street, except it had a side entrance which led to a doctor's office.

Jack asked, "Do you want to stay with us, Danny?"

Danny was only wearing sweatshirt, and he was shivering. As usual, he didn't notice. "I want to stay with you for as long as I can."

Jack let out a *whoop*. "Well, let's go celebrate."

Danny said, "Does Mrs. Morgan want me to stay?"

Freddie grabbed his shoulder. "You know she does, Danny. She loves you."

The kid looked all misty-eyed. "Can we go look at Stephen King's house, like you said?"

"Absolutely. We're close to his street. I'll take a picture of you two in front of his fence."

"The one with the bats on it?" Danny asked. "That seems cool."

"Yeah. You'll like it."

They climbed into Jack's truck. Danny got in the back. Jack was grinning, and Freddie realized he was too. He couldn't read Danny's face, but he had the feeling Danny knew something they didn't. Freddie could feel the air being let out the bag.

Danny said, "Do you think Mr. King is home now?"

Jack said, "Not if he's got any sense. With his money, he should be in Saint-Tropez or Hawaii or someplace like that. This weather's for poor people."

CHAPTER TWENTY

A Friendly Little Conversation

"Thanks for going along with this, Mick," Detective Nault said. "I know it's a little sketchy, but these kids won't answer anything at the station, not if their parents lawyer them up."

They stood in the hallway of their old high school, leaning against the concrete wall. A row of lockers lined the opposite wall, stopping at the next classroom. The row continued down the other side of the doorway and out of the detective's line of sight. Nault felt like a teenager again for just a moment then remembered why he was here.

"You just gonna talk to them out here? Nothing private?" his friend asked. He was still lean, probably only a few pounds heavier than his high-school weight. His nose was bent from Golden Gloves, and his hair was short from military habit. He was a solid guy, inside and out. Nault trusted him.

"Yep. I want them to think we're just talking and they're in no trouble. A friendly little conversation. But I want them a little nervous too."

Mick Roberts had been his friend since before he could remember. They played baseball together, went on dates together and even enlisted together. "But you think they know something?"

"Can't hurt to ask."

The door to room 217, Mrs. Lander's old room, opened, and a couple kids exited, followed by Vice Principal Meyer. He was aging, and he was small, and they were big, but he had all the power over them. They kept their heads down when he spoke to them and stood where he told them. He introduced them to Detective Nault and stood to the side. He wasn't going anywhere.

Mr. Meyer wore a powder-blue suit. It probably looked great back in the 80s. "Just a few minutes, gentlemen. Okay?"

Mick said, "Absolutely. We just have a couple of questions."

Nault said, "Hi, guys. I'm Detective Paul Nault from the Camden Police Department, and you may know Detective Roberts from the Abbot Pond Police Department. We're looking into a couple of things, and we're hoping you could help."

Derek Matthews, a tall, blonde kid wearing slacks and a polo shirt with the collar flipped up—who still does that?—looked a little cocky and seemed like a talker. "Are we in some sort of trouble?"

He was taller than the other kid, but the one with the buzzed hair was much wider. They were both way too big to be high-school kids, almost comically too big. He hadn't noticed from the distance during the funeral, but they were jacked. Unnaturally so.

Mick chuckled. "Hardly. Detective Nault just has a few questions, which you do not have to answer. You can call your parents, if you like."

"Well, what's this about?" Matthews asked.

Nault smiled. "Sammy Burns. We're trying to talk to any of his friends who might have an idea of what he was up to."

"We barely knew the guy," Matthews said. "Right, Mike?"

The Gillette kid grunted agreement. He wore jean shorts and a sweatshirt. His bare legs rippled with muscles. The kid knew how to do squats.

Nault said, "You two were at his funeral, right? I saw you there with another kid who looked like he was part Wookie."

Mike laughed. "Wookie. That was Bobby Boots."

"How'd you track us down from the funeral?" Matthews asked.

Nault smiled. "I'm a detective."

Matthews glanced at Mr. Meyer. "I'm not proud of this, Officer, but we mainly just wanted to get out of school that day. I mean, we *did* know him growing up, but he was a year older, and he wasn't a football kid in high school. He only played basketball."

Nault scribbled in his notepad. "But you knew him when you were younger?"

Buzz Cut said, "He played in pee wee and up. He was pretty good on offense, but he didn't like playing D."

"Officer Roberts here played corner and wide receiver back in the day. He could cover anyone."

Mick said, "Stop it. I'm gonna blush."

Nault leaned against the wall, looking all comfortable, and the kids stood at ease in front of him. "Sammy didn't seem to have an enemy in the world. Can you think of anyone who might want to hurt him?"

Both boys shook their heads.

"It doesn't make any sense," Matthews said.

Mick could be such a smartass. "What about you, Haircut? Can you think of anyone at all that didn't like him?"

The Gillette kid looked at his friend then shook his head.

Nault wrote a little more then scratched his temple with the safe end of his pen. He glanced up, contemplating his next question. He wanted to keep everything all friendly, but he felt the Matthews kid was a little suspicious. Gillette acted nervous, but kids were usually nervous around the police.

"You guys ever see him with a girl. A blonde girl?"

"No, sir. Like I said though, we weren't close or anything."

"You've never been to the house in Camden where we found Mr. Burns?"

Mr. Meyer interrupted. "The bell will be ringing soon, detectives."

Matthews looked confused. "Why would I have been to that house? I don't know where it is now."

Nault said, "Well, the Morgan family owns that property, and their kid used to play on your team. He was the captain before you, right?"

Matthews replied, "I did not know that. Freddie's parents own a lot of properties."

"Any idea why he stopped playing with you guys?"

Mike said, "I heard he started working for his mother at their car place."

"That's right," Matthews said. "Too bad for us. He was an animal."

Nault remembered Freddie sitting beside his girlfriend, laughing at the weird foster kid's jokes. He didn't seem like an animal, but people are different on the field, he knew. "How so?"

The kid looked all innocent. "Well, he's a great kid, but …"

Nault waited.

"He's got a bit of a temper, you know. He punched Mike in the head a few weeks back at the bowling alley for talking to his girlfriend or something like that. That's not really cool to do to your old teammates, your friends."

Nault looked at Gillette. He was a monster. "What position do you play?"

"I'm mainly a linebacker, but I'm on the offensive line a lot."

"And Freddie just up and hit you? You punch him back?"

The big kid shrugged. "Freddie's pretty tough."

The vice principal interrupted again. "Are you finished with your conversation?"

"Yes, thank you, Mr. Meyer. Thanks, kids."

He handed each a card and told them to call if they remembered anything.

The Matthews kid put the card in his pocket without looking at it. He started to enter the classroom, but the bell rang, and a stream of kids pushed him farther back into the hallway.

The other kid read it and put it safely into his pocket. He looked at the detectives then turned away. The mob of kids went around him, everyone apparently knowing better than to bump into him.

Except, a kid like Freddie would just walk up and punch him? He needed to ask for Freddie's version of the story.

Outside, the detectives stood as their cars heated up.

Mick bundled himself in a police jacket, his gloved hands buried deep into his armpits. "Supposed to be warm the next few days."

"I heard that," Nault replied. "It'll be a nice break."

"Yeah. What'd you think about the interview?"

Nault tightened his overcoat. His teeth chattered as they talked—bring on the heat wave. "Something's a little funny about those boys, especially the talker."

His friend nodded. "He sure was fast to throw that Morgan kid under the bus, being as they're such good friends."

"Yeah. He definitely wanted me to take a hard look at Freddie. I bet he's got a different story about the punch at the bowling alley."

"Well, if he's anything like Ryan, I'm taking the side of the Morgan kid."

"He's not a lot like him when you meet him, but you get a sense he'd get along great with Ryan, like they'd play off each other pretty good."

"A day doesn't go by that I pass that pond and I don't think of Houdini. I'll never understand why he went on the ice like that. Never."

"Yeah. I've been thinking about him a lot lately."

"Because of the case?"

Nault shrugged. "Maybe. I've met with his dad a bit, and I kind of get a kick out of him."

"I've met him too. He scares me a little, and I'm a cop. He doesn't seem to like us."

"You just have to get to know him."

Mick outstretched his hand. "I've got some other work to get to. It was cool working together, Paulie."

Nault reached. "Thanks for extending me this courtesy, Detective Roberts."

Mick patted him on the shoulder. "Let me know if we have any overlap."

"Will do."

"And don't forget about dinner Saturday. Alice is going to try to set you up with a friend of hers."

"What's she like?"

"She's a nice girl who is more fun to hang out with than your mom. No offense to your mother."

Nault got in the car and drove off.

The young detective leaned against his and stared into the complex of buildings that made up Abbot Pond Academy. Some kids were getting out early and strolling to their cars, maybe heading to a part-time job at Shop N Save. One kid seemed to be having trouble turning his car over. Somewhere, a gym teacher blew a whistle, and sneakers squeaked on a gym floor. He smiled because he kind of missed this place.

But he knew something was wrong here.

CHAPTER TWENTY-ONE

BABYSITTING BELLE

Belle was sitting up in her bed, her legs under the covers. She wore white pajamas with funny little pictures of Goofy and Mickey.

Sophie sat across from her, a wrinkled paperback in her hand. *The Boxcar Children* was one of Belle's favorites, and they were working their way through the final chapters. Sophie had never read any of the sequels, because she didn't think the book needed anything like that. It ended happily, and the story was over.

"I don't think I'd want to live in a railroad car," Belle said. "There's no electricity, and wherever was the bathroom anyway?"

"I think you're giving the book a little too much thought, sweetie. It's just a story."

The light was still on, and Sophie scanned the walls. A poster of a different Disney princess hung on each wall and one on the door. Oddly, none of the posters were from *Beauty and the Beast*. The walls were off-white, and a Barbie dreamhouse sat on the floor. Sophie's Barbie was wearing a tiara.

"I hope you're happier next time you babysit," Belle said. "I hate when you're sad."

Sophie smiled. "I'm sure I will be."

Belle handed her a brush, and Sophie got to work on the little girl's long hair, which was still a little wet from her shower. It smelled of lilacs, and all the hairs were soon in place.

"Beautiful," Sophie said as her phone vibrated, but she ignored it. "All right, under the covers. I was supposed to have you in dreamland by eight-thirty, and it's almost nine now. You want me to get fired?"

The girl's eyes were already droopy. She squirmed more of her body under the covers and rolled onto her side. She whispered, "I love you, Sophie."

"Me too. A lot."

"What are you getting me for Christmas?"

Sophie laughed. "Something nice, I promise."

She sat on the bed until she heard her little friend snore. It was a low whistle, almost like a flute. For just a second, she forgot about the fight with Parker, and she enjoyed the moment. She turned off the light and half-closed the door as she left. Belle liked the hall light on when she first went to sleep, so Sophie left it alone and went downstairs to watch the television.

She took a few bites from the half-eaten bowl of popcorn on the couch. Belle liked lots of butter, but sometimes that made Sophie's stomach burn. She chewed a few more pieces and decided that was enough. Freddie and Danny really liked popcorn and would have emptied the bowl. She wished Freddie was with her. She felt so alone.

The phone vibrated again, and she pulled it from her pocket. It was Parker's mom. She hit the green button and said, "Hello?"

"Sophie, hi. This is Jessica."

"I know. Your picture comes up when you call me."

"Right. Technology. Is Parker with you?"

Sophie felt something like a shiver, only deeper and almost painful. "What do you mean? You know she's all mad at me."

The phone went silent for a moment. "I know, but I got home a few hours ago, and she wasn't here. It's getting a little late, and I still haven't heard from her. You know she'd text me if she was going somewhere. She never—*almost* never goes out without you."

"Look, Mrs. Bradley, I'm sure she's okay. I'm watching Belle now, but I can come over right after her parents get home. I'll text her now."

Jessica sounded a little relieved. "Okay, I'll see you in a little while."

Sophie hung up and thought about the situation. Who would Parker be with? The answer came fast, and she quickly typed a message to Freddie. *Is Danny with you? Important.*

She didn't wait for an answer from her boyfriend. She sent a quick message to Parker. *Parker, are you okay? Your mom is really worried.*

She brought the popcorn bowl into the kitchen. She didn't dump it, because she knew Mr. St. Cyr would probably eat what was left over. Sophie put the bowl on top of the kitchen table and glared at their fat, orange cat. "Stay away from the human food, Queenie. I've already fed you."

The cat stared back at her.

She sat and checked her phone. Nothing. She must have gotten a ride to the Morgan's house or met up with Danny somewhere for a burger and a deep conversation about Obi Skywalker's light sword. Her chest still felt tight, but she knew she was probably right. Sophie wasn't ready to panic yet.

Her phone vibrated. It was Freddie. *We hooked up the Xbox. Playing Gears of War.*

Lights flashed through the big window, and she knew Belle's parents were home. She heard two doors slam and looked for her coat.

The phone vibrated again. *Why?*

Her twill field jacket was neatly folded and hanging over a kitchen chair. It was a nice shade of green that the people at Old Navy called *Hunter Pines.* It was really cute, and she wore it because the temperatures had risen to almost fifty degrees near the coast. The warm weather was supposed to last almost a week, which was nice. Freddie didn't like it though. High temperatures meant the pond ice would crack, and some idiot would lose his truck ice fishing. She put on the jacket and searched for her boots.

Belle's parents entered. Her mother, Amanda, had two pints of Ben and Jerry's, and Sophie knew one of them was for her. Sophie got along with Amanda, and she knew about the fight with Parker.

"I think I've got a partial cure for your situation, Sophie. Maybe you could stay, and we could watch *Music and Lyrics* again? I know you love that movie."

Sophie shook her head. "Something's kind of come up. I have to get going."

"Is everything all right?"

Her body trembled. "I don't know. Parker's mom doesn't know where she is."

Amanda frowned. Premature grey streaked her dark hair, and thick strands fell across her eyes. She pushed them back. "She's probably with that boy."

Sophie typed another message for Freddie. *Is Parker with you? Tell the truth, because Jessica is worried.*

His response was quick. *No. We've been here all day. Sort of a marathon.*

Sophie didn't want to think about Freddie and Danny playing videogames all day. Their friendship, or whatever it was, sort of pissed her off. She wondered if she was kind of jealous of Danny. She pushed away the thought and tapped, *Can you meet me at Parker's house? I'm leaving Belle's now.*

"Anything new?" Amanda asked.

Mr. St. Cyr said, "I'm sure everything's fine with your friend. Are you going to eat the ice cream?"

Amanda said, "Larry, we got it for Sophie."

Sophie smiled. "No, you can have it."

Larry snatched the pint from his wife and headed toward the living room. He stopped and grabbed the half-empty bowl of popcorn with his free hand and disappeared from the kitchen. She didn't know a single father who didn't like ice cream, popcorn, and watching TV in the living room. It must be in their DNA.

"She's not with Danny," Sophie said. "I'm going over to Parker's house now."

"Let me pay you first," Amanda said. "Be mindful of the road, okay? Big puddles are everywhere, and a weird fog rolled in."

She slipped her boots on. "Okay."

Amanda held the door for her, and Sophie stepped onto the farmer's porch. She heard Belle's dad calling for a spoon. She sort of wished she'd taken the ice cream with her.

The Audi roared to life. She shifted it into gear then put it back into Park. Her phone was vibrating. It was Parker. *It's all ok. Tell Mom I'm with a friend. I will be home soon. Love you.*

Sophie wrote, *What's going on, Parker?*

She waited for almost a minute. Finally, the response, *I'm just chillin. Will talk soon.*

Sophie turned down the loud music and reread the message. Then again. She dialed Jessica's number.

Jessica answered with a question. "Have you heard anything?"

"I just got a message."

"Oh, thank God. Is she okay? She's with that boy, isn't she?"

"Jessica, I think you need to call the police. Something's not right."

"What do you mean?"

Sophie sighed. "I've gotten a million texts from Parker before, and this just doesn't sound like her. I don't think it's her using the phone."

CHAPTER TWENTY-TWO

Where's Parker?

The door opened and Paul walked in. He was wearing jeans and a thin jacket and looked tired, like he'd probably done a double shift today. Detective Mick Roberts was talking to the uniformed officer, but he waved over his friend. Paul glanced at the table and nodded at Freddie Morgan and the weird kid. The kid's name was Danny Cole, and his face looked grim. Did he know something?

"All right. What's going on?"

"Girl hasn't come home," Roberts said. "Apparently, she's been texting her friend, but her friend thinks it's somebody else. I thought I had it handled, but in comes the Morgan kid and his buddy. Seemed like an odd coincidence, him showing up right after we were talking about him. So, I called you."

"Who's missing?"

The uniformed cop said, "Parker Bradley, seventeen. She was home alone all day, and she's limited with her mobility. She's a paraplegic."

Mick said, "Technically, she's not yet a missing person, but we're treating it that way. Hard for her to just run away, stuck in her wheelchair."

"Where's the mother?"

"Upstairs with the friend. They're with another officer."

Roberts steered his friend toward the door. "This is just weird, and I thought you could help. You have some familiarity with these kids."

Paul nodded. "How thoroughly have you searched the house?"

"She's not here. There's no blood, thank God. We checked for signs of a break in. The front door was unlocked, the mother says. But kids never lock doors."

His friend scribbled in his notepad. Roberts wondered how many pads his friend went through every month.

"Let's talk to the kids," Paul said.

Roberts stood, and Paul sat across from the Morgan kid. "You know Detective Nault?"

The boys nodded. The Cole kid said, "Hi."

"Freddie, how are you involved?" Paul asked.

The boy leaned forward. "Sophie texted me that Parker was missing. So I came over. The cops were already here and had us sit here. I still haven't seen Sophie."

"How does Sophie know this girl?"

"They're best friends," Freddie said.

Roberts looked at Danny Cole. "How do you know Miss Bradley?"

"We're friends. We're supposed to go on a date."

Roberts thought it was odd that a kid would want to date a disabled girl. He knew that was a pretty shallow thought. "When was that supposed to happen?"

"Tomorrow. We're going to a movie."

Officer Davies entered with two blondes—a teenager and one in her late thirties. Mick liked Davies. The officer was smart and tough and didn't make mistakes. She'll climb the ladder fast.

Officer Davies still wore gloves. "Nothing appears to be missing."

"Who was the last to see her?" Paul asked.

Davies nodded at Jessica Bradley. "Mother went out shopping this afternoon. Around one-thirty, she says."

"Anyone else? UPS or something?"

"The mailman comes to the door if there's something for Parker," Jessica said. "I don't think he's supposed to do that, but he knows about her injury. She's waiting on a few colleges."

Roberts looked at Davies. "Find out about the mailman."

She nodded and stepped outside.

"Miss Lindstrom," Paul said. "This girl is your friend?"

Sophie's eyes were puffy. "She's my best friend."

"Does she have any other friends she might be with?"

The girl eyed Danny. "He's the only one I could think of, but he's been with Freddie all day."

"You haven't spoken to her, Danny?"

The kid stood. He was taller than he looked somehow. "I haven't heard from her all day, Mickey."

"She didn't text you?"

He shook his head. "I don't have a cellphone."

That was odd. "Any idea where she might have gone?"

"She wouldn't just take off. Anyway, I think she was getting ready to call Sophie tonight. I talked to her on the phone yesterday, and she said she was going to do it."

Sophie brightened. "Really?"

"Yeah, I told her I thought you were right to worry about her, and she agreed. She was still a little mad though."

Mick glanced at Paul. "Hold on. Why was she calling you?"

The girl was tired, and her face was a little swollen, but she was a looker. "We had a dumb fight the other day, and we haven't been talking."

"What about?" Mick asked.

Sophie didn't answer.

"Me," Danny said. "They were arguing about me."

Mick regarded Danny. "How do I know you?"

The kid half-smiled. "I don't know. I had an accident, and I don't remember too much."

"You have amnesia?"

He nodded. "Sort of."

"What kind of accident did you have?"

Danny didn't say anything.

"He had an overdose." Freddie answered.

Roberts had a flash of memory. "You're Danny Cole. I busted you once. You shoplifted some videogames from GameStop."

Danny shook his head. "I don't remember."

"You look a lot better now. Healthier."

Parker's mother had been standing in silence. "Nobody told me anything about an overdose or shoplifting. Why would my daughter date a junkie?"

"He's a nice kid," Sophie said, "but he's weird. I mean, he says weird stuff, and he can do things."

"Like what?"

Freddie held Sophie's hand. He was only wearing a t-shirt, and his arms stretched the short sleeves beyond capacity. He seemed annoyed. "This doesn't have anything to do with anything. Danny's not that guy anymore. That was old Danny."

"We need anything that's relevant," Paul said.

"You seem upset, Mr. Morgan," Roberts said. "Do you have a temper?"

"What?"

Roberts wanted to see the kid's reaction. Maybe he really could lose his shit too fast, like the Matthews boy had claimed. "I heard you popped some kid in the mouth at the bowling alley."

Freddie shook his head. "That's not what happened."

"He was just protecting us," Sophie said. "Mike Gillette was making fun of Parker. When Freddie told him to stop, he wouldn't."

The Gillette kid was a little bigger than Freddie, but Freddie looked like he could take care of himself. Roberts asked, "Does he have a history of any sort with Miss Bradley?"

Sophie looked horrified. "No. Yuck. She didn't even recognize him."

"What was his problem then?" Paul asked.

"The other one wanted him to do it," the Cole kid said. "To test him."

"What other one?"

"Derek," Sophie said.

"We don't know that for sure," Freddie said. "Derek's my friend."

"Derek Matthews?" Roberts asked.

Sophie nodded.

"Okay, we're getting way off topic," Mick said. "You received a text from the missing girl?"

"From her phone, yes."

"When?"

She checked her phone. "Nine forty-seven."

"But you don't believe it was her on the other end?"

Sophie shook her head.

"Why not?"

Sophie's face tightened. "It just didn't sound like her. She always calls her mom *Jessica* in her texts. And she never tells me she loves me. Not even in real life. Plus, what seventeen-year-old girl uses the word *chillin'* in a sentence?"

"She's right," Jessica said. "Parker hasn't called me *Mom* since the accident. She blames me for it. She doesn't say so, but she does."

"I'm going to need to borrow your phone, okay?" the detective said.

She looked embarrassed. "I have another one. In case I misplace this one."

Roberts nudged his friend. "Let's go outside."

They stepped onto the porch and walked to the bottom of the wheelchair ramp. There was too much traffic at the house. Cars were parked on the street. At least none of the cruisers had on their emergency lights.

"What do you think?" Detective Roberts asked.

Paul rubbed the back of his head. "Well, Freddie had access to the house with the stiff. He knows Parker, and he's recently gotten into a fistfight with one of my suspects in the Ciara Clark case."

"Right. The Cole kid is weird, has a thing for the girl and is a known drug abuser."

"And we both know drugs are involved somehow."

"For sure."

"Or it could be the Gillette kid and his friend. Maybe they hold a grudge."

"Or she could be out with some new friend."

Davies approached from across the street. "You should see this."

They followed her to the edge of the neighbor's yard. The street was all slush and puddles from the warm up, and neither man wore boots. They didn't really care. It was all about the case now. The house was medium sized with a garage. They could see someone peering through the blinds.

"What are we looking for?"

"In the ditch," she said. "Something's sticking out of the snow."

A light fog covered the top few inches of the snow. It had made driving here a bitch and made snooping in the dark nearly impossible.

Roberts couldn't see whatever he was supposed to see. "What is it?"

He was rattled to hear the Cole kid's voice behind him. "It's her wheelchair. It's Parker's wheelchair."

Jesus, Mick thought. *He's right.*

"You have to back away, son," Davies said.

"We have to search immediately," Paul said. "Maybe it's a hit and run."

Detective Roberts' stomach felt queasy. He didn't want to find a dead kid buried in the snow. He remembered Ryan Morgan lying in that fancy coffin, makeup caked all over his face. His mind flashed to a time he had found the leftover pieces of a nice, old widow who a snowplow had run over. He'd held it together till he got home. Then, he threw up all night.

The other kids were there, and Parker's mother stood behind them.

"What happened?" Sophie asked.

Freddie grabbed her and held her. He was a tough kid, but he looked scared. "Danny?"

What could Danny do?

The kid walked like a slow, awkward robot. His face was hard, like a soldier who had returned from war. He surveyed the ditch and front lawn covered with snow and fog. He turned and scanned the Bradley's front yard. "She's not here."

"What makes you say that?" Officer Davies asked. "We haven't had a chance to search."

The kid shrugged. "She's not here."

CHAPTER TWENTY-THREE

Public Announcement

The temps were in the mid-forties, and most of the kids were dressed like it was spring. Many of the boys wore shorts, usually matched with comfortable sweatshirts and sneakers. The girls mainly wore jeans and light jackets. Sophie sported a pair of upper-end Dockers and her green field jacket. She wore sensible boots, knowing much of the snow had turned to slush and water. Last minute, she remembered she hadn't showered, so she wore Parker's softball cap to conceal her dirty hair.

Jessica stood with the police in front of the television reporters. She was crying a little, but she was doing all right; she was putting one foot in front of the other. Freddie was parking the car down at the Shop and Save. There weren't any spots in the school parking lot, so he just dropped her and Danny off and drove away. He said he'd be right back.

Danny was a wreck. His hair was messier than hers, and he wasn't hiding it. He looked as though he hadn't eaten in the week since Parker disappeared, his body only fueled by a slow-boiling rage. The goofy grin was gone now, replaced by a pained grimace. Still, he remained kind to her in their brief conversations. Once, he briefly took her hand and gripped it. He'd said nothing, but she knew what he was saying.

"I won't go with you," he said. "I don't want to be a distraction."

"I understand. I'm sorry."

The story was big. Two girls missing in the town where Rachel Randall had disappeared in all those years ago. Who was the obvious suspect? The local press centered on the oddball loner spending time with Parker. The fact he'd died once from a drug overdose meant he was troubled, and it stoked the flames of suspicion. Even Sophie's mother asked her about him, like she was worried about Sophie or something. Please.

Danny got it pretty bad at school, and a carload of reporters tried to camp out in front of his house. Mr. Morgan had fired off his shotgun, and they scurried off. Probably illegal, she guessed, but it worked. At least for now.

Sophie passed the policewoman from the other night and nodded at her as she approached Parker's mom, who was talking to a middle-aged couple. She wore jeans and a long sleeve with a brown winter vest.

Jessica stopped to hug her. "Sophie, this is Mr. and Mrs. Clark. Their daughter … Their daughter is Ciara Clark, the girl from Camden."

"I'm sorry to meet you guys like this. I have friends in Camden, and they say Ciara's a great girl."

Mrs. Clark was brown-haired and a little chunky. "We're glad to meet you, Sophie. Jessica has told us how much help you've been."

Some tech guy was assembling a desk with microphones, so the two detectives could give an update. Nault gave her a wave, and she smiled back. The other one sort of nodded, but he was all business. Each was in uniform—the first time she'd seen either of them dressed like that. They looked different, more serious. It was a good look.

"Where's Freddie and his friend?" Jessica asked.

"Freddie's parking, and Danny's trying to keep out of the way."

"I wish I'd known more about him before," Jessica said. "I would have said something to her, not that she'd listen to me."

Sophie didn't want to have this conversation again. "Just stay strong here, and we'll get through it, okay? Together."

Jessica pressed her hand tightly. "You're family to us, Sophie."

Sophie didn't mind crying a little, because she wasn't wearing makeup. "That's how I feel too."

Davies tapped her on the shoulder. "Why don't you guys take a seat, and we'll get this thing started."

The speakers came to life. "Good afternoon, folks. I'm Detective Michael Roberts of the Abbot Pond Police Department, and I'm here to update you on the Parker Bradley case. Detective Paul Nault of the Camden Police Department will update you on the Ciara Clark case. With us are some representatives from the state police and from the governor's office. I can assure you in advance that we don't have much new to report, and we're still not even certain that the cases are related."

Freddie pushed through the crowd of mainly kids from the school and some of their parents. He saw Arnie from the bowling alley with his brother and their wives listening intently. He knew Arnie had lost a daughter in a car accident, and things like this really resonated with him. That was probably why he never gave Parker any grief about her wheelchair scuffing the floor.

He heard Detective Roberts answering questions, but the crowd's murmuring muffled the questions. The detective sounded annoyed and mainly answered with *yes* or *no*. Occasionally, he used *I just don't know*. Both detectives seemed honest and straightforward. He liked them.

He moved near the front of the crowd. Most people there were talking into their phones or taking pictures. Some of them shouted questions. A lot of those were about Danny. Was it true Danny discovered the dead boy in Camden? Did he know Ciara? What was the extent of his relationship with Parker? Are the rumors of her pregnancy true? Freddie's brain burned when he heard that crap.

Detective Roberts said, "As I have clearly stated several times, Mr. Cole is not a suspect. We have corroborated his alibi. You folks should leave the boy alone."

He caught a glimpse of Danny to his right, leaning against the fence that separated the school parking lot from the 7-Eleven. Over time, students from the past had somehow made a hole in the fence, and kids liked to duck into the store during their free periods. Sometimes, there was a fight behind the store, and kids watched from the school side of the fence. Freddie usually went around the fence, because the hole was tight, and the metal wires scratched his arms when he climbed through.

A couple kids spoke to Danny. He didn't know them, but they were bigger than him, and they were doing most of the talking. Danny wasn't paying much attention to them, and that seemed to be frustrating them. Freddie picked up his pace.

A girl said *hi* to him, but he kept walking. The crowd was living and breathing, so it was hard for him to keep an eye on his friend. Everyone just kept moving a little here and a little there. His sneakers squeaked from the puddles in the parking lot, and his toes felt damp. He didn't care about that. He had to get to Danny.

When he saw them again, Mike Gillette was talking to the boys. He towered over the kids. Freddie burned inside. He wouldn't hold back this time if Mike was starting more crap. Danny was already on the edge. He didn't need this.

Mike had one of the kids by the arm and threw him into the fence, which rattled with the impact. He said something to the other kid, and they both took off. The one Mike had thrown was holding his back. They didn't look back.

"What's going on?" Freddie asked.

Mike turned and nodded at him. "Just taking out the trash, Freddie. I know you could have done it, but I didn't know you were here."

Freddie eyed Danny. "What happened?"

Danny looked terrible. His hair was all over, and huge bags hung under his eyes. "They were asking me where I buried Parker."

"Oh, God," Freddie said. "I'm sorry. Let's just stay together from now on."

Danny almost flashed his crazy grin. "Okay."

"Thanks for the help, Mike," Freddie said.

Mike patted Danny on the shoulder. "I could tell how you felt about her that night, Danny. I know you couldn't do anything like that to her. People can be such assholes."

"Yeah. Thanks for your help, Mike."

"I'm surprised you're here," Freddie said. "And without the team."

Mike smiled. "The season's over, Freddie. I'm taking a break from those guys."

Freddie could see Mike wanted to say something else. Instead, he just waved and moved into the crowd. He wore pants for a change and a dark red sweat jacket. Most of the kids got out of his way as he maneuvered through them. Freddie thought he was even bigger than he had been that night at the bowling alley.

"Why'd you even come, Danny? You knew this might happen."

"I could have stopped them if I wanted to."

I don't want to know how, Freddie thought. *But I believe you.*

"Anyway, I needed to know who's here today."

"You can see everybody in the crowd?"

Danny shrugged. He wore those baggy jeans he liked and a t-shirt. Big, raised goosebumps dotted his arms, and he shivered.

"You have to start taking better care of yourself, Danny."

"We have to find Parker."

"She needs you healthy, if we're doing that."

He shrugged again.

Freddie looked up at the grey sky. The sun wasn't even bothering to try to burn through the clouds. Crappy weather was on its way, and it wouldn't leave any time soon.

"Let's get Sophie and get out of here. I'll blast the heat for you in the Mustang."

The crowd was mainly gone. The Clarks spoke tearfully about Ciara and then left without taking any questions. Jessica answered a few, mainly about Danny's and Parker's relationship. She made a big point about Parker not being pregnant. Sophie thought she looked shocked, like it had been even worse than she had expected, and she grabbed her hand when she sat back down.

After a while, Sophie blocked out the questions and answers. She knew what they would say. *The investigation is ongoing, and please contact us if you have any information.* The same stuff they always said when one of these things was on CNN or FOX. Only this time, it was about Parker.

The policewoman was saying something to her. "Sophie, are you listening?"

"I'm sorry. What?"

"I'm taking Miss Bradley home. Do you need a lift?"

The wind had started, and the winter warm up was beginning to chill. She turned up her jacket's collar and shook her head. "Freddie's here somewhere. He's taking me back."

She hugged Jessica and stood. Workers were already disassembling the desk and microphone, and someone grabbed her chair almost as she stood. She searched for Freddie and Danny, but they weren't in sight. They knew where she was, so she would just wait.

A soft hand touched her arm. "Sophie?"

She turned. "Mom? What are you doing here?"

Sophie talked to her mother a little during the week, mostly about Parker and a little about Freddie and Danny. She wanted to be as honest as possible about what was happening. Valerie had been uncharacteristically restrained and even a little understanding. Sophie hoped that would last.

Valerie was a little taller than her daughter and a little less blonde. She was still hot, Sophie knew. She worked out a lot, and Sophie knew guys checked her out. It was funny she didn't want Sophie to play sports anymore, but she was always taking some new workout class or buying that expensive stationary bike. All that didn't much matter now. Only Parker mattered.

"Your father's at work, and I thought you could use a little moral support."

Boy, was she right. "I'm so glad you're here."

Her mother squeezed her hand. "I know I'm not the most sentimental person, Sophie, but I do love you. I'm so sorry about this. I brought some clothes from your closet. They're in the trunk. I brought a few things, because I don't know how long you'll be staying at Parker's. Until she comes home, I imagine."

She hugged her mother, trying to remember the last time that had happened. "Hopefully, it'll be soon." She saw Freddie and Danny behind her mother. "My mom brought me some clothes."

Freddie looked surprised. "That's great. That's very thoughtful."

"Yeah, Sophie likes clothes," Danny said.

Sophie's mom laughed. "Don't let those people get to you, young man. If my Sophie says you're a good guy, then you're a good guy."

Danny grinned. "You said that, Sophie?"

"Maybe. I don't remember."

CHAPTER TWENTY-FOUR

A Reward

Maureen watched through the front door window as her husband shoveled the snow. It was only a few inches, but he wanted Freddie to be able to park without fishtailing. Jackie wore jeans and his boots, of course. No jacket. No hat. For some crazy reason, he'd cut the sleeves off his heavy plaid shirt, so he was shoveling in a *Maine* muscle shirt. She'd married and divorced a crazy one, that was for sure.

He hustled up the path and inside, shaking snow from his head and torso, like a mangy dog. He flexed for her. "I saw you checking me out, Maureen. You still appreciate the gun show?"

"You have lost your mind."

He smirked. "You were watching, and probably half the lonely housewives on the pond were watching too."

"I was watching a damn fool shoveling snow in a sleeveless shirt. It's a wonder you don't catch cold."

"Name a time you saw me sick, Maureen. Just one time."

It was true. Crazy as he was, he'd never been sick a day in his life. "That doesn't mean you should *try* to catch pneumonia."

"I'm fine."

He kicked off his boots and scooted into the kitchen, and she followed. The house felt so much more alive since he'd moved back in, like the world was just a little sunnier since the reconciliation. Freddie was happier, at least he had been until this terrible Parker thing. And along comes Danny to fill out the family. She felt guilty about her run of good luck, especially considering what was happening.

Jackie rummaged through the refrigerator for something specific. He transferred the milk onto the table and rearranged and Tupperware bowls like chess pieces. "Damn it. This refrigerator couldn't get more full. Danny's gotta start eating again."

The poor boy barely picked at his food now.

"I've been trying everything. I even baked cookies," Maureen said.

"Have you heard from the boys?"

She nodded. "They're dropping Sophie off at Parker's, then they're driving around. Danny needs to search more."

"He's damn near obsessed, that boy."

Maureen whispered, "I think this whole thing is killing Danny. It's too much for him."

Her husband stopped digging and put his arms around her. They *were* still quite impressive arms, and their strength calmed her a bit.

"You know he's stronger than that. He's just focused on Parker right now. They both are."

Jackie resumed his refrigerator hunt while she sat at the table. Finally, he gave up and put the milk back in. He opened the freezer and grabbed his favorite Ben & Jerry's—the chocolate one with lots of nuts. He fished around the silverware drawer for a spoon.

"You're having ice cream right after shoveling?"

"Well, I couldn't find the leftover Chinese."

She rolled her eyes. "That was over a month ago, Jackie. I threw it out."

"You shouldn't have. The microwave makes all leftovers good again."

Maureen didn't want to argue with his logic. She watched him eat his ice cream and thought of Ryan. That boy had loved his ice cream too. It didn't matter if it was chocolate or strawberry, just so long as he could pour some jimmies on top. And he was never a picky eater, like so many kids today. She cooked it, and he ate it—such a good kid.

"Thinking about Ryan?"

"How'd you know?"

Jackie smiled. "You had your look. You know he's closer than you think."

Maureen understood. "Maybe."

"You get that picture from Thanksgiving framed yet? Those kids looked so happy."

She nodded. "I haven't put it up yet. Poor Parker's in it, and I don't want to hang it until she's back. I know that sound Pollyannaish."

He finished the pint, but he didn't get up. "What the hell is wrong with people, Maureen? Who would steal little girls from their parents? Or kill young men and just dump them in somebody's basement? I've done things I'm not proud of but never anything like that. Just a little hellraising."

She thought of her Bible. "Evil is a real thing, Jackie."

The big clock chimed ten o'clock.

Maureen said, "So, we're making the announcement tomorrow."

"About the reward?"

"Yes, first thing in the morning. It's going to be brief. 'Morgan Nissan announces ten-thousand-dollar reward for any information leading to the safe return of Parker Bradley and/or Ciara Clark.' My guys will write it better than I said it."

"You said it just fine. The boys will be so proud."

Maureen rose to get some water. "I hope it helps."

"What if there are two kidnappers, and we get information about both cases?"

She sipped from her glass. "I guess we pay out double. I doubt it'll turn out like that. I think it's the same guy. There can't be that many kidnappers walking the streets of Camden and Abbot Pond. We're not New Hope, for God's sake."

"What about the other thing?"

She couldn't restrain a smile. "I spoke to the lawyer, and he didn't think we'll have a problem. He thinks we can convince Danny's mother to sign some papers. We'll probably just have to give her a little, um, gift."

"Shame on her. But good for us. Now, we just have to talk to Danny about it."

"After this Parker thing sorts itself out. We need to help him through this before he makes any big decisions."

Jackie was right, she knew. It could wait. With the Lord's help, Parker would soon be back where she belonged, and her family could be whole again.

Jackie said, "The kids are out. You know what we should do?"

"What?"

He took her hand. "Let's watch TV together. When was the last time we did that?"

Maureen giggled. "I don't even know if the damn thing works."

"You look so beautiful, Maureen. I mean that. With all that's happening, you still make me feel like when we were in high school."

Maureen felt a flutter. "Oh, shut up. Turn on the damn television."

CHAPTER TWENTY-FIVE

The Charm

A new woman was at the sign-in desk.

"Where's Betty?" Freddie asked.

She was a younger woman, probably twenty-two or twenty-three. Green streaks highlighted her dark hair, and she wore a black dress. "I don't know, sir. I just work for an agency."

Freddie nodded. "We're here to see Dr. Hollis. His other office is closed, but he said he could see us here."

"I'll let him know you're here. You can sit down at one of these tables."

"We thought we might visit some of the patients while we're waiting," Danny said. "We're volunteers sometimes."

The new girl frowned. "I'll have to buzz you through."

Freddie realized the keypad was gone. "I guess they've tightened security. How do we get out?"

She smiled. "There's a buzzer on the other side. I'll see you on my camera and buzz you back. Or, in your case, the doctor will find you and escort you out through his office."

The technology may have upgraded, but the patients remained the same. An old detective show played on the TV, but no one was watching. A smattering of older ladies paced aimlessly about the room. The Whizzer was asleep in a chair. Lucy Diamond was nowhere to be seen. Freddie hoped that didn't mean anything. Hopefully, she was just taking a nap or something in her room.

Danny's hair and clothes were all clean. He still looked tired and weak, and his mood hadn't improved. "How long do we have to wait?"

"I'm sure not too long, Danny. He was nice to even see you today."

Danny examined some photos outside of a patient's room locked in a glass cabinet. Freddie knew the staff called the cabinets *memory cages*. He didn't recognize the patient by his old pictures. The young man in the photos was strong looking, with a large forehead and dark curly hair. He was smiling in all the pictures, and kids surrounded him. Freddie thought the guy looked like he was always the life of a party. Now, the poor guy was stuck here.

"Hello, boys. Thanks for meeting me here. I never seem to have enough time in a day." Doc Hollis wore a white smock over a blue shirt. He seemed a little broken down, and Freddie wondered how old he really was. He'd been around town all Freddie's life, which wasn't that long. Late 40s or early 50s? Probably more. His hair was greying, and a few wrinkles lined his face. Maybe he was worried about Parker. Freddie knew they were close.

"Thanks for letting Danny come in," Freddie said. "We know you're busy."

The doctor smiled. "Your mother called me personally. I always seem to have trouble denying her requests."

Freddie chuckled. "Me too."

"How long will this take?" Danny asked. "I have to … I have things to do."

"I don't think this'll take long, Danny. Why don't you come in, and I'll examine you, and then your friend can come in. We'll all talk then."

Danny followed the doctor into his office.

Freddie wandered around outside, peering through the edges of Dr. Hollis' shaded windows. The doctor was poking and prodding Danny on a table. Danny jumped down and stood on one leg then the other. He nearly fell both times. Freddie had to look away. His friend had come so far the last few weeks, and now he couldn't even stand on one leg. It wasn't fair.

He walked past the office and checked out the other rooms. The off-duty doctors' offices were dark. The light was on in the laundry room, and Freddie stepped inside. The machines were all running, and he was glad he didn't have to fold anything—certainly one of his least-favorite activities here. That and cleaning the bathrooms. No, thanks.

Bobby Bones walked in with a big laundry basket. "Hey, Freddie. What are you doing here?"

He extended his giant hand, and Freddie shook it. He had always felt sorry for Bobby when the kids picked on him for being fat. Now, he was this massive football player who scared just about everybody in school. Freddie still sort of felt bad for him though. He wasn't completely sure why. Maybe because he was still an outsider, more than Freddie ever was.

"Just waiting for Danny. Doc Hollis is examining him."

"That was nice of him. To see your friend, I mean."

Freddie nodded. "How do you like it here?"

"It's not so bad. The patients are all in their own little worlds, you know? We just kinda have to herd them around a little. One old lady never says a word, but she sings along with the piano, and she sounds perfect—like she could be a professional."

"That's Shirley. I've heard her."

Bobby smiled—or maybe grimaced. "I hope I'm never like that, Freddie. It's not a good way to end up."

"No, it's not."

"But not a single patient has ever mentioned my size or my looks. You have no idea what kind of relief that is. It's kind of, what's the word? Liberating."

Freddie understood. "You're free to be you for a change."

"Right."

Freddie heard the doctor calling for him. "I know what you mean, Bobby. I'll see you later."

He hurried into the office and stood by Danny seated on a chair opposite the doctor's desk.

"How'd it go?" Freddie asked.

The doctor sat back in his comfortable chair. "Well, he's very tired. He admits he's not eating well. His reflexes are surprisingly good though."

Freddie remembered the game of catch at the property in Camden.

"Frankly," the doctor continued. "I'm not sure what's going on."

"I'm fine," Danny said. "I've just been preoccupied."

"Maybe," Dr. Hollis said. "Or maybe there's more. I'm worried there may have been more nerve damage than we thought when you had your little adventure last spring. The doctors may have missed something with your brain. Loss of blood to the brain might explain the lethargy."

Danny shook his head.

Doc Hollis smiled. "Or you may just need some sleep and a better eating regimen."

Danny looked at framed certificates on the wall. "You went to Drexel?"

"What? Yes."

"One of your diplomas says Drexel. William R. Hollis. Nineteen seventy-nine."

The doctor stood, removed the diploma from the wall and handed it to Danny. "Those were probably my best years. I don't want you boys to be in a hurry to grow up. Enjoy every minute."

Danny traced the words on the diploma with his finger. "Parker wants to go there. She said you went."

Freddie didn't think talking about Parker was a good idea. "Um, so what should we tell my mother? About Danny, I mean."

The doctor walked around his desk. He moved some papers from the edge and sat down, his eyes locking with Danny's. "I'm recommending a battery of tests. We'll start easy with some blood testing, but I'll want to schedule an MRI and see if everything's working right inside your brain."

Danny didn't seem like he was listening. "Parker really wants to be a doctor."

"I know," Dr. Hollis said. "She's been picking my brain for years."

"Danny can't think of much else since she's been gone."

The doctor stood and put a hand on Danny's shoulder. "She needs you strong, son. You need to get your diet in order and sleep a bit more. Maybe start taking a multivitamin. Doctor's orders."

"Do you miss her?" Danny asked.

Doc Hollis frowned. "I can't believe she's gone. I can't believe any of this. We just have to hold out hope that our police can find her."

Danny stared at the doctor and then handed him his diploma. "One day, Parker will have one of these too."

It sounded more like a threat than a casual comment.

"Of course."

Freddie tapped Danny's arm and told him it was time to go.

"You can take the shortcut out my side door," the doctor said.

Danny shook his head. "I think we want to visit the patients a little longer, if you don't mind."

"Sure, you just have to buzz out."

"Thanks for everything, Doc," Freddie said. "We know you're busy here."

"You can go into the lab on Main Street for the bloodwork. Don't go before school though. And eat something after."

"Freddie will take me," Danny said.

"Good. I'm glad you have each other."

Danny studied the room and spotted the Sentry standing face first in the far corner. She looked like a teacher was punishing her or something. Freddie was relieved to see her, even if she was suck in a corner. Like a turtle turned over on its shell, she couldn't figure out how to turn around. Bobby Bones was right about not wanting to end up like that. Freddie's heart ached for her.

Danny took one arm and gently turned her around.

She stared at her feet the whole time but seemed to recognize his touch. She turned her head just a little. "Do you know what you have to do now?"

He nodded. "I think so."

A light snow dusted the parking lot, and Freddie wanted to get into his Mustang. "Come on, buddy. Let's get going."

"Which car is the doctor's?"

Freddie almost didn't want to tell him. "The red BMW, why?"

"That's an expensive car, right?"

"He's a doctor."

Danny moved toward the BMW.

"What are you doing?"

Danny circled the car and stopped at the driver's side. He tilted his head back and forth, resting one arm on the side window. He rubbed his chin with his free hand.

"I don't know what you're thinking, but don't do it. He's probably got an alarm on that thing."

Danny's hands rested on the door handle, but Freddie couldn't quite see what he was doing. After a minute, he pulled the handle, and the door swung open. "I guess he didn't lock it."

Adrenaline raced through Freddie's veins. "We can't just break into cars, Danny. We could get arrested."

"Okay." He climbed inside and reached under the front seats. "It's leather. It smells better than your car."

"Danny, get out."

Instead, his friend climbed into the narrow back seat and began feeling around. "This car is much nicer than your Mustang, Freddie. Which one is faster?"

"I don't know. I think it's close."

Danny stuck his hand under the seat in front of him and searched for what seemed like hours. Freddie checked to see if anyone was watching from a window or something. His mother would kill them both if she knew what they were doing.

Finally, Danny pulled his hand from underneath the seat. "I found it."

"What is that?"

Danny's voice lowered. "A charm. You know, from a bracelet."

He handed it to Freddie as he climbed out of the car. He closed the door, and they headed to the Mustang.

"Do you recognize it?" Danny asked.

It was shiny and had a cool design on one side. The word *Sisters* was engraved on the other side. Freddie felt a shock. "Yeah. I went with Sophie when she bought it."

Danny nodded. "When I asked him if he missed Parker, I knew he was lying. I know when people are lying."

Freddie's hands trembled. "We have to tell somebody."

"She's in there, Freddie. I'm sure of it. He took her."

They sat the Mustang with the engine running. Freddie didn't know where to go. "What do we do?"

"I think she left it there for me to find. She knows I'm coming for her."

Freddie looked at his frail friend. "I don't know if you're strong enough, Danny."

Danny slammed his fist against the glovebox and something sparked. "I'm not leaving until Parker is back. Do you understand? I'll do it without you, if I have to."

Freddie put the car in Drive. "We do it together, Danny. You know that."

CHAPTER TWENTY-SIX

The Patient

"You have to take the pills, Ciara," Parker whispered. "You have to fight." She brushed the girl's sweaty hair from her brow. Her face was puffy, not like the colorful picture Parker had seen a few weeks ago. She couldn't recognize this girl from that photograph. This girl would probably never look that way again. Too much damage.

Ciara's head was raised a little from the extra pillow, but her breathing was still labored. Her eyes were open, though she seemed lost, sort of like the patients upstairs—like she was halfway out the door already and didn't care what happened next.

Parker popped the pills into the girl's mouth and helped her drink from her cup.

"Parker … Parker?"

Parker tried to smile. "Yes, Ciara?"

Ciara shook her head and closed her eyes.

Parker washed her face with a clean towel then wheeled to the laundry basket by the door. It was hard for her to move around in the cumbersome chair. The wheels were heavy, and she couldn't grip them easily. These hospital wheelchairs were designed to push patients, not for them to move themselves around. Her fingers were already blistered from her frustrating attempts at mobility. No matter though. She knew something they didn't.

The room was bright from the overhead fluorescent lights. They hummed loudly, and their flickering gave her a headache. The walls smelled of fresh paint, the odor growing stronger when the radiator kicked in with a sizzle. Ciara's bed looked like any of the beds Parker had helped change upstairs. It probably was one of them. She only had a cot to sleep on.

Somebody banged on the metal door. "Stand back."

She didn't stand, but she did roll back.

The metal door creaked open, and Derek swaggered in. He looked at Ciara. "How is she?"

"She's getting worse. She needs real treatment at a real hospital."

He shook his head. "Parker, it's very important for you to do your job. He brought you in and gave you a simple task. Don't disappoint him."

"What is wrong with you, Derek? Doesn't it even bother you that he did this to her, and she could die? Why are you helping him?"

He didn't look like he cared. In fact, he smiled.

She wheeled back a bit more and stared at him. He wore light pants, a blue jacket, and white retro Converse sneakers that looked like basketball shoes. His blond hair was wet from snow or rain. Parker guessed he had somewhere to be. Maybe he had a date with one of the cheerleaders. They all liked him.

"He's coming to check on her later. You might want the place to look nice and clean. He likes everything just so."

"You tell him that she needs something stronger for her swelling. I think her infections are spreading."

"Okay. How's her pain?"

She frowned. "You guys definitely have that covered."

Derek snorted. "At least she has that."

She pointed at the laundry basket. "We need more towels and probably another gown. She's … She's bled into the one she has. And new sheets too."

The smirk on his face burned at her. "No problem. One of us will be down with all that in a while. Just remember to pick up."

After he left, she checked the lock. She knew it wasn't likely that he'd forget it, but Derek and Bobby were tweaked out on something. That makes people sloppy to begin with, and neither of her *guards* were great thinkers. Especially Bobby. He would make a mistake soon enough, and she would be ready.

The bathroom was all right. The toilet seat was low enough to slide onto, and the shower was handicap friendly. A door was to the side, which she figured probably led to an identical room. Patients had to share bathrooms back in the day, she guessed. It was locked now, but Danny had told her a few times that any lock can be picked. She just had to find the right tool to open it with.

This room smelled of fresh paint too—blue paint. They must have been planning this for a while. They'd repainted the rooms, hung some paintings and even placed flowers on the table. The cot looked last minute, and it was. Probably nobody expected a little teenage girl to put up such a fight when the doctor arrived. Good for her, but what a price to pay. Now, they needed a nurse.

"Parker, don't let him …" Ciara squirmed on the bed again.

Parker wheeled over and grabbed her arm.

"Parker, don't let him do it again."

"*Shh*. We need to get you strong before we can figure a way out of here."

"And don't trust Derek. He's bad."

The girl wiggled a little, and soon her grip loosened, and she faded off again.

Another pounding shook the door. "Step back."

The door opened, and Derek entered with fresh linen and a new laundry basket.

Doctor Hollis followed him in dressed in his doctor's robe, looking like he was just doing his rounds. "How's the patient?"

Parker wanted to tell him Ciara Clark wasn't his patient but his victim. "Her infection's getting worse."

He smiled at her like they were still friends. "Have you been cleaning the wounds?"

"Yes. And she's been taking your pills. They're not enough."

Hollis eyed her calmly. "You're not a doctor yet, Parker. Let me take a look at her."

"But she just went back to sleep."

He kneeled beside the girl to move the white sheets and lift the dressing. Ciara howled in pain and surprise and began to cry.

Parker heard Derek snickering. "Does he have to be here while you do this, *Doctor*? Shouldn't Ciara have a little privacy?"

Hollis turned his head. "Step outside, Matthews. I'll be right along."

She looked at Derek, and he stuck out his tongue at her.

After he left, Dr. Hollis said, "Come take a look at her wounds, Parker. The bruising has subsided, which could be good or bad. The swelling isn't worse, it's just not better. You're doing a fine job."

She wanted to call him an asshole. "Thanks, Doctor. I'm doing my best."

He patted her hand. "You're doing fine. And you're right—she does need a stronger prescription. I'll get right on that."

"Dr. Hollis, what'll you do when she gets better? I mean, with me?" Parker needed to know how much time she had. She wasn't stupid. They needed her to nurse Ciara, but, after that, what other use could they have for her? They'd have to get rid of the evidence. And she was the evidence.

"Don't you worry about that, Parker. I'm sorry you got yourself involved in this whole affair. I'm very fond of you."

"I just wanted to know why Drexel thought you were dead. You could have just told me it was a mistake."

The doctor finished redressing Ciara. He sat on the edge of the bed, as if a suffering girl wasn't fighting for her life beside him, and sighed. "Because I know you, Parker. You would have investigated it and asked me questions or called them and told them that they were wrong and that I was your mentor here in Abbot Pond or something else that might have brought my world crashing down. No, I couldn't take the risk."

"I just want to go home," Parker said.

He stood up. "We'll worry about that when the time comes, Parker. You're doing an extraordinary job. I'm very pleased. Now, change the dressing when she wakes up. Then take care of the gown and her sheets. Derek will take care of the linen."

"Thank you," she mumbled. "Uh, thank you."

He nodded. "But, Parker, you really need to keep this room tidy. We have rules here."

"Okay."

After he left, Parker wheeled to the small couch imprinted with a vague floral design and a strong odor of disinfectant and plopped onto it. Rule number one was to not touch the furniture upstairs, but she needed to get out of the chair. Her back hurt in it, and her legs ached. Yes, ached. She needed to stretch out when no one was looking. Her legs needed to be strong for when Danny came.

When she could block out the steam from the radiator and the humming from the lights, the room was deathly quiet. That wouldn't last, she knew. After a while, she heard the giggling. Parker wasn't sure where it came from—probably the pipes above her—but somebody was happy. Some of the patients talked baby talk, so, initially, she guessed the pipes just echoed their weird babbles. But it sounded more real to her, like a nearby child was playing with her doll or chasing her puppy.

But that seemed unlikely.

CHAPTER TWENTY-SEVEN

A New Lead

It was the middle of the week, so the bowling alley was nearly dead. The detectives were dressed in jeans and jackets and didn't stick out too much. The kid didn't want anyone to know he was talking to the cops, and who could blame him? Young people were disappearing and dying across two towns.

"Place hasn't changed much, has it?" Paul asked. "I'm not sure Arnie's as much as repainted this place since we hung out here back in the day."

Detective Roberts nodded. "Kids still love it though. Especially on Friday nights with the glow lights and the prizes."

"I had a birthday party here once," Paul said, "just before all the kids started joining their little cliques and pretending not to know each other."

"I was there," Mick said. "And I still know you."

Arnie at the desk waved to them as they headed toward the pool tables. The place was empty except for Arnie and the big kid in shorts playing pool by himself. He cracked the stick, and balls jumped into the holes.

"Not bad," Mick marveled. "You know what you're doing."

Mike Gillette shrugged. "We have a table at the house. My old man used to be a bit of a hustler before he started selling insurance."

The two detectives stood on opposite sides of the table and watched Mike as he cleared the table. Mick thought the kid could be a hustler too, if he wanted. The boy put down his stick and grabbed a Coke bottle he had placed on another table. He gulped most of it down.

"So, we're here," Roberts said.

Mike nodded. "I appreciate you meeting me here. No one's ever here this early in the day."

"Shouldn't you be at school now?" Paul asked.

Mike didn't answer.

"What did you want to talk to us about?" Detective Roberts asked.

The kid looked nervous. "I just want you to know that I'm not involved in any of this, but … I don't know. I think my friends might be. I guess, I'm sure of it."

"Which friends?" Paul asked.

"You know. Derek and Bobby. Derek, for sure."

"Why do you say that?" Roberts asked.

The kid beckoned them into the corner by the basketball machine. Mick was suddenly aware of the kid's size as he towered over the two detectives. Mike looked around before he said, "Derek's really *happy* lately. I don't know if I can explain it, but he's cockier than usual."

"Maybe he got laid," Mick said. "This doesn't help us."

Paul smiled. "Detective Roberts is right, son. Cocky and happy aren't admissible in court."

"I know. Things have gotten weird on the team since Freddie left. Derek became team captain, and everything turned sideways."

"Define *sideways*."

"Well, everyone liked Freddie, and he kind of led by example. He's great on offense and defense. Colleges were scouting him. Then he decides to focus on the family business, and he says he's not playing senior year."

"He didn't want a scholarship?"

Mike shook his head. "He's still getting offers. He's a better student than he is an athlete."

"Why'd you all vote Derek as captain if you didn't exactly like him?" Paul asked.

"The coaches liked him, and it seemed to make sense. He was Freddie's best friend, sort of, so we all kind of thought he'd be like Freddie."

Neither detective spoke.

"Derek really looked up to Freddie, but he talked bad about him behind his back. You know, racial stuff about Freddie dating white girls. I think Freddie's nature kind of kept Derek from going *full-on Derek*, you know? But now, Freddie's not around to rein him in."

"Okay," Roberts said. "So, Derek takes over. Then what?"

Mike looked embarrassed. "Then came the drugs."

"Wait. You're saying Derek Matthews is a dealer?"

Mike nodded. "At first, he gave us stuff for free. You know, steroids. And we all were getting jacked. Crazy jacked. And fast too."

Mick looked at his friend and wanted to say *ah-hah*. These things always come down to drugs. Always.

"Then we had to pay. And I've heard he sells other stuff—meth and oxy, that kind of stuff."

Paul stood at attention, like everything had suddenly become serious. "Let me ask you a question, Mike. Was he selling to Sammy Burns?"

The kid lowered his head. "I think so, but I never saw any of it. I think that's how Sammy got his job at the mental hospital place."

"What mental hospital?" Mick asked.

Mike waved his hands. "You know, for old people."

"You mean the Lakeside Residence? By the pond?"

"Right."

Roberts scratched his head. "How could the captain of your football team be getting jobs for schoolmates at a medical facility?"

Mike looked tired. He had bags under his eyes, and he was sweating. His sweatshirt was wrinkled and dirty. Roberts knew the kid was wrestling with his priorities. Loyalty to friends versus doing the right thing were tough choices at any age. Maybe his parents had raised him right, because here he was, unloading all his suspicions about his friends.

"I've seen him hanging with Dr. Hollis—like, driving around together. Everybody knows Dr. Hollis spends a lot of time at the hospital. He won some award."

The sound of candlepins hitting the floor made the kid jump.

Mick eyed the lanes and saw a pair of older men laughing. "I don't think you have to worry about them."

Mike looked doubtful. He didn't know who to trust.

Mick asked, "Did any of your other friends get work at the facility?"

"Bobby Boots works there. All sorts of weird hours too."

Paul put his hand on the kid's shoulder. "Why are you telling us all this, Mike?"

The kid straightened. "My dad always tells me to do the right thing. This year, I haven't exactly done that. I took the steroids to get bigger, and I got away with it. Nobody said anything—nobody that counted. Derek tells me to start a fight with Freddie, I do it. I get my head handed to me, but I do it. I'm tired of being the bad guy. I am *not* the bad guy."

"No, you're not," Paul said. "Not at all."

Detective Roberts nodded. "If anything comes of this, you may have to testify. At least about the drug dealing. Can you do that?"

"I didn't call you down here to not help. I'll do it."

They all shook hands, and the kid walked away. Mick thought he looked like he was walking a little straighter now that he'd unburdened himself. Hopefully, his friends wouldn't find out about this conversation any time soon. Sammy Burns had probably wanted to unburden himself too.

Paul put some quarters in the basketball machine and began sinking shots. The hoop moved back and forth then side to side, but Paul didn't miss. When the game ended, he put his initials in as the high scorer. He was sweating.

"Are you through?" Mick asked.

Paul shook his head. "Not by a long shot."

"I guess we start looking real hard at the good doctor."

CHAPTER TWENTY-EIGHT

LATE NIGHT DINNER

Somebody pounded on the door. "Step back."

Parker was in her chair, holding poor Ciara's hand. Ciara mumbled something about cheerleader tryouts. Parker told her not to worry. She'd make the team.

The door opened, and Bobby Boots' enormous frame filled the doorway. He wore his white work pants and shirt. "Doc wants to know, how is she?"

"She's healing. The infection seems to be getting better. She's still pretty loopy though."

He stepped inside and looked at Ciara. "You think she'll be okay?"

Parker shook her head. "She'll never be okay after this, after what he did to her."

"You know what I mean, Parker."

She knew what he meant, and the truth was Ciara *was* getting better. The swelling and the redness was slowly fading, and she could move a little without screaming. Parker figured she had a couple of days before it became obvious they wouldn't need her anymore. Dr. Hollis could protest all he wanted, but she knew what would happen to her. He wasn't leaving any witnesses.

He inched closer and examined Ciara's pale, sleeping form. "You've done a great job, Parker. Dr. Hollis is very happy."

She shook her head. "You know he's going to kill me, Bobby. Or have one of you two do it. Either way, I'm dead."

He looked horrified. "I would never do that, Parker."

Parker remembered the red BMW pulling into her driveway just a few weeks back. Dr. Hollis had beeped and waved, and she had come out to see him. She had rolled onto the porch to talk to him, to listen to his explanation. Drexel was a huge school, with lots of alumni, and she knew there could have been a clerical error or something. William Hollis was probably a common name, and the school was just confused. The next thing she had known, Bobby's gorilla arms had wrapped around her. His grip had been so strong she couldn't breathe or scream. Dr. Hollis had swung open the side door, and Bobby had stuffed her into the back of the BMW.

"Get rid of the chair," she'd heard. She'd seen it fly across the road.

Bobby had jumped into the car, shaking it like an earthquake, and they had driven off. It all happened in a matter of seconds.

"I remember you hurting me before, Bobby," she said. "My ribs still hurt."

He looked sheepish.

Bobby was a little too close, so she rolled back until her wheels tapped Ciara's bed. "Is that all?"

"You don't have to be so sore at me, Parker. I didn't want to hurt you."

Parker shook her head.

He stared at her like she was his favorite burger at Five Guys.

He can do anything he wants to me right now. And I can't stop him.

"Do you want to go for a walk with me?" he asked.

"What?"

"Just down the hall."

"I don't think your boss wants you taking me for a walk."

Bobby shrugged. "He won't know. Come on."

Her heart pounded. "Is this it? You'll march me out of here and throw me into the furnace or something. At least be honest with me, Bobby."

Bobby was offended. "The doc's not here and neither is Derek. I just thought you might want to get out for a few minutes. Anyway, you wouldn't fit in the furnace."

He could kill her any time he wanted, that was for sure. It didn't matter if it was in this room or in the hallway. She might as well play along. "I can't leave Ciara for too long. She doesn't like to be alone."

His weird monster voice sounded giddy. "I won't keep you out too late. Come on."

She followed him into the hallway and waited while he locked the door. The cement floor was choppy, and she had trouble moving the hospital chair over the debris. He grabbed the handles and pushed her down the hallway. Some of the overhead lights flickered, and it was tough to see. She looked back at the smiling giant and shuddered. Where was he taking her?

They passed more rooms like hers, but they weren't fixed up or painted. Most didn't even have doors and were filled with rubble. Dust clouds erupted as her wheels rolled down the craggy walkway. She heard a dull hum that she thought may have come from a generator. At last, they came upon a room with lighting, and he turned into it. The lights were so bright she had to squint until her eyes adjusted.

"It's a cafeteria," she said. "You have your own little cafeteria."

The room was about twice the size of her cell and cooler. Three tables were on one side of the room and a refrigerator and a stove on the other. A small counter that was home to a microwave and an open bag of potato chips separated the appliances. Parker couldn't help eyeballing the chips. She missed junk food.

He wheeled her to one of the tables. "We've got everything. You want a burrito?"

She wanted to say *no*. "Yes, please."

He took two from the fridge and put them in the microwave. He collected some paper plates from a cabinet on the wall and put them on the counter. Bobby stared eagerly at the microwave until it beeped. He placed one on each plate and brought them to her table. He looked so satisfied, as if he'd just given her a winning lottery ticket.

"You want soda? We've got Pepsi."

She liked Coke. "Okay."

Bobby returned to the refrigerator and grabbed two cans from one of several six-packs. Beer was in there too. He closed the door and delivered the drinks to the table. He sat across from her and smiled.

Parker suddenly realized they were on a date, at least in his mind. Out of habit, she said, "Thank you."

When he smiled, his crooked teeth didn't look as menacing. "No problem."

There were no utensils, so she picked up the burrito and ate, the tortilla bread lightly burning her fingertips. It tasted so much better than the slop Derek usually brought her—cold, crusty leftovers from the patients, soup for Ciara. They would leave a plastic pitcher and some cups in her room. She would fill it with water from the sink. Meanwhile, Derek and Bobby had opened their own little restaurant right down the hallway.

Bobby ate with his mouth open, naturally, and burped a bit. Danny would lose control when he ate too, but it was cuter when he did it. She remembered him double fisting cookies on Thanksgiving. He had been so happy she'd made them. He'd been so grateful.

"Won't they miss you upstairs?" she asked.

"No. It's the middle of the night, and the nurses are all gossiping."

"It's night? I guess I thought it was afternoon." Parker finished her burrito and licked her fingers. She hated Pepsi but couldn't stop herself from gulping the can dry.

He watched her as she did it. "Do you want some more?"

"No, thanks. I should probably be heading back to Ciara."

"How about some chips."

She spied the bag and licked her lips. "Maybe just a few."

He put some on a paper towel and brought them to her. They were a little stale, but she didn't care. The taste of salt made her eyes roll with satisfaction. How could she have missed salt this much? She hardly ever ate junk like this.

"We can do this more if you want to."

"Do what?"

He blushed. "You know. Walk around a little, eat snacks. We have pizzas in the freezer."

She shook her head. "Bobby, *I'll* be in a freezer in a few days. You know that."

"No, Parker. Don't talk like that."

Maybe she was feeling strong from the junk food. "I'm only alive because I've had a little medical training and you happened to have kidnapped me at the right time. Ciara's getting better. Dr. Hollis won't need me after that."

"I don't want that, Parker."

She laughed at him. "It's not up to you, Bobby. You're Igor, he's Dr. Frankenstein."

Bobby stood and walked into the hallway. Judging from his footsteps, she guessed he was pacing. He made some noise that sounded like a seal barking. Was he crying?

Parker wheeled to the counter and grabbed the chips. Might as well have a few more before he strangles her. She didn't want to die hungry, after all. She smiled at her dark humor. Then, she ate more chips.

He stomped back in. "I have an idea."

I doubt that.

"I'll talk to Dr. Hollis."

"Okay, good for you. Can I go back to my room?"

He pounded his fist onto the wooden table, and a long crack formed at the point of impact. "Listen to me."

Now, she was scared. "Okay, calm down. I'm sorry."

"What if I ask him if I can keep you?"

Her stomach turned. "Keep me? Like a pet?"

He put his hand on her arm. "I think you're nice, Parker. And you're pretty."

Parker rolled slowly away from him.

"Stop, Parker. I'm serious."

Her voice quivered. "Bobby, I'm not a girl you're asking to the prom. I'm a prisoner. Can't you understand that?"

"Don't you like me? I'm nice to you."

"If you wanted to, you could sneak me out of this place right now. You could carry me up the stairs, wherever they are, and out the door. Who could stop you? You could be a hero."

Bobby glared at her.

"Will you do that, Bobby? Could you save me?"

He shook his head slowly, tears forming. "I can't."

"Why don't you bring me back to my room now, okay? I need to check on Ciara."

CHAPTER TWENTY-NINE

BIG CHANGES AT LAKESIDE

The girl with green streaks in her hair wasn't at the desk. This time, it was a guy in a red and white polo sweater. "Who are you visiting today?"

Sophie wore baggy jeans and an old blouse. Most of her clothes were loose lately. "We're volunteers. We were just planning to kind of say *hi* to everyone. Is Lucy doing all right? She wasn't talking much last time we were here."

"I don't know any of the residents personally."

Danny was chewing on a no-bake cookie he'd bought at the gas station. He was still skinny, but his hair was better, and his mood had improved. "Well, I'd like to see her. She likes me."

The guy sniffed. "I'll have to check with someone. I believe they're reorganizing the volunteer program. Generally, it's family only."

Danny took another bite. "Why don't you check with Doc Hollis. I saw his car in the parking lot."

The guy picked up the phone and turned away.

Freddie came in, his hair wet from the snow. He stomped his feet on the carpet. "What's going on?"

"The volunteer program is being reorganized," Sophie said.

"*Hmm* ... Lots of changes around here."

Sophie noticed a camera mounted at the front entrance and another one near Dr. Hollis's office. More cars were in the parking lot than normal, and a smiling security guard was posted by the front entrance. Security was getting a major upgrade.

Dr. Hollis came from his office wearing his white smock. His eyes were puffy, and purple bags hung under them, as though he had been missing sleep. "I see your appetite's back, Danny."

Danny smiled. "A little bit, yeah. And I went to that lab yesterday."

"Good, good. And now you're looking to help out around the hospital today?"

"It was important to Parker," Sophie said. "*Is* important to Parker."

"Sure, sure. We don't need much help these days. The kitchen staff has been upgraded, and the orderlies have been taking care of the laundry and the janitorial services. You folks are certainly welcome to visit with the patients though. That's where you can be the most helpful. Danny, the kitchen has a surplus of cookies this week." He nodded at the guy with the sweater. "Jerry will buzz you in as soon as you're by the door."

"Thanks, Dr. Hollis. For everything," Danny said.

Hollis looked compassionate. "Just doing my job, son."

Sophie smiled to herself.

The intercom was playing only Christmas music, and a big tree stood in the corner of the room. Sophie thought Bing Crosby was singing, but it could have been Dean Martin. A John Wayne movie played on the television. He punched someone, and a few patients laughed. Sophie knew her dad liked John Wayne almost as much as he liked Clint Eastwood. She wished her generation had real movie stars like that—mysterious people who didn't go on talk shows or tweet about their butts.

Freddie was talking to a stocky new patient. She seemed to think he was one of her students. Sophie heard her say, "I can't keep giving you do-overs, Mr. Brown. It's not fair to the other students."

"Yes, ma'am," Freddie said. "I'll do this one on time. I promise."

The *teacher* nodded firmly then stood and walked to the couch to scold some invisible students. After a minute, she put her head back and fell asleep, snoring loudly.

"Where'd Danny go?"

"I think he's investigating the kitchen," Freddie said.

Sophie smiled. "It's good to see him eating again. Let me, rephrase that …"

"I know what you mean. I think he's taking the long way back and kind of looking around. He might be a while."

Lucy was stuck in a corner again, and a middle-aged orderly was turning her around. A lot of new hires in white roamed the common area. Some nurses were new too. This was the most people Sophie could ever remember seeing here. "Grand Central Station here, huh?"

"Yeah. And more cameras on the walls. I wonder who's watching."

"It's almost as if Dr. Hollis is getting paranoid. Do you really think Parker's here?"

He leaned toward her. "If Danny says she's here, then she's here. I know you don't always like him, Soph, but he's always right about these things. He's got a knack."

A little redheaded girl ran past her and hugged an old lady's leg. "Grammie! Grammie!"

Sophie couldn't remember the woman's name. It was maybe Mary or Jane. One of the old-time names. The old lady stared at the child and smiled as if she recognized her. Then the connection was lost, and she walked away. A woman, probably the girl's mother, chased after her. The little girl sat at a table and waited. She didn't cry.

Sophie took Freddie's hand. "Tell me about the dream."

"I'm not sure we need to talk about it right now."

"We're not doing anything else. Just waiting for Danny."

He sighed. "It was a little scarier than in the past."

"How so?"

Freddie clutched the collar of his Patriots sweatshirt, stretching the fabric. "Well, the old lady wants me to turn around. You know that part."

"Right. What do you see when you turn?"

He frowned. "It's weird. It's a real struggle to move, like I'm fighting someone, but in slow motion."

A gray-haired man approached them wearing a nice shirt buttoned all wrong and an open pant zipper. He knocked on the table and walked away.

"Maybe he's saying hello," Freddie said.

"Maybe."

"Anyway, when I do turn around, I see me."

"You see you?"

He nodded. "But it's in black and white, and it's kind of distorted, and I look sort of wild."

"That's weird."

Danny approached them eating a brownie.

"Anyway, the old lady starts yelling at me. No surprise."

Sophie was wide-eyed. She loved listening to his dream adventures. "What did she say?"

"She says, '*No escuches.*'"

Danny sat down. "What's it mean?"

"I think it means *Don't listen.* Like, *Don't listen to that guy, he's a liar.*"

"You *think* that's what it means? You didn't ask Richard?"

Freddie looked at her then at Danny. "That was weird too. I know I dream in Spanish a lot. This time, I felt like I remembered the language when I woke up. It's sort of faded, but I'm pretty sure I'm right about *No escuches.*"

Bobby Bones walked by the table. Sophie thought the table shook as he passed, and she trembled a little. He nodded at Freddie, but he wouldn't look at her. He looked at Danny though, and his mouth tightened a little.

Danny watched him as he disappeared into the back. "He knows where she is."

Freddie shook his head. "You don't know that, Danny."

Danny didn't answer.

"Did you manage to look around some?" Sophie asked.

"Well, the laundry room is locked, with a big sign that says *Do not enter.* And cameras are everywhere."

Sophie eyed him. "What are you saying?"

He shrugged. "We can't get in this way. We have to find another entrance outside."

"I guess you're right, Danny," Sophie said. "Anyway, too many people are in here at any given time. We couldn't sneak past them."

"I'm going outside to look around. Give me a few minutes, okay?"

When he left, he headed toward the kitchen first.

Sophie couldn't help but smile. "Yep, his appetite's back."

"Yeah, and he's got a little more energy. He's still kind of slow though."

Lucy walked by, oblivious to them, and headed toward a wall. A nurse took her arm and led her to the couch. Her clothes were more stained than usual, and she only had on one slipper. Sophie guessed she'd be bedridden soon. That was usually the next step. And then she'd be gone—like Nancy.

She looked at Freddie. His eyes were so kind.

He smiled back at her. "We'll get her. Soon."

She nodded. "Do you think we should just tell the cops about the charm?"

"I don't think it's enough to get their interest. Anyway, they might ask how we found it."

"You're right, I guess. But we'll have to call them eventually."

Freddie squeezed her hand. "We can probably leave a note or something with my dad. Maybe put the charm in it, just in case things go screwy."

"I hope it doesn't go screwy."

"Danny knows what he's doing. It's crazy to say, I know, but he does."

Sophie remembered the scruffy loser kid who got busted for shoplifting and took pills to escape from life, the kid Freddie didn't care the least about and tried to avoid. When did he become this man of mystery leading their rescue mission, this kid with the biggest heart? And here she was, helping him. *Believing in him*. What exactly happened to *old* Danny?

She realized she didn't care. Sophie preferred *new* Danny.

Freddie said, "Come on. Let's go see if Danny's found anything."

CHAPTER THIRTY

A Questionable Plan

"Next time, buy a car with a little more leg room," Mick said. "I'm practically stuck in my seat."

A snow-and-rain hybrid splattered across the Chevrolet's windshield then ran down the glass in random directions. The wipers occasionally scraped their half-circle clearing pattern, but it wasn't enough for a clear view of the hospital. They saw enough to know constant traffic flowed in and out of the building, even at this late hour.

Paul Nault fiddled with his camera. It was his sister's and had cost her a mint, but it was light years better than anything the department had in stock. "I got a deal."

Mickey Roberts scoffed. "That's you. Always buying on the cheap."

"It gets me where I need to go."

The Chevy was parked almost blatantly across the street from Lakeside Residence's main entrance. A few cars were in the lot, including Dr. Hollis's sporty BMW. A running white security vehicle with a light on top was parked near the entrance.

I've had too much coffee, Paul thought. *And not enough sleep.*

"Somebody's pulling in," Mick said. "I think it's the Stevens kid."

The pickup coasted into a spot near the building. The truck bounced as the giant stepped onto the pavement wearing white pants and a white shirt with no jacket. Paul wondered if he was wearing boots but couldn't quite tell. The kid approached the main door and tapped something. Then he vanished into the building.

"What time is it?" Mick asked

"Around midnight."

"He has some weird hours. He just left around ten or so."

"Yeah, that's weird, but the patients wander around like zombies all night long. They probably do have to work some odd hours to keep up in there."

He took a shot of the BMW, still parked under a light. The car hadn't moved in a week, and an inch or so of powder covered it. Stevens or Matthews would come out and brush it off in the morning. The doctor wasn't coming out. He was making his stand.

"Where do you think he sleeps in there?" Mick asked.

"I don't know. The rooms are almost always full. As soon as they roll out one patient, another one takes their spot. Business is booming."

"Maybe his office couch pulls out into a bed."

Something smacked Paul's window and shook the car. He dropped the camera, and Mick spilled some coffee onto his lap. Both men swore as they reached for the weapons. The rear door behind Paul opened, and Officer Davies jumped in, laughing. "You should have seen your face."

Paul felt himself blushing. A grown man and a detective in the Camden Police Department was blushing because a girl jump-scared him. "I wasn't scared, Melissa."

She wore a dark sweater and some jeans. Her curly brown hair danced over her brown eyes. Her smile was broad, and he felt the blood rushing back to his cheeks. Thank God it was too dark for her to see. At least he hoped it was.

"You made me spill my coffee, Officer Davies," Mick said.

Her tone changed. "I'm sorry, sir. I didn't know you were with Detective Nault."

He found a napkin and dabbed at the stain on his pants. "When did you two get on a first-name basis, anyway? Are you two on some sort of a date?"

"That's ridiculous," Paul said. "We've been working together for weeks. You didn't know her first name?"

Mick looked at her. "Nope."

Paul shook his head. "What have you got?"

She smiled at him again. "I heard back from the guy at Drexel. It was them who sent her a letter, just like the mailman said. He said it's policy to not divulge the contents of their official conversations with student applicants."

"Did you explain what's happening?" Paul asked.

"Yeah. He wants to help. He said he has to talk to somebody, and he'll call me in the morning. I don't think he's yanking me around like the last three people I talked to down there. It's just a bunch of bullshit red tape."

Mick said, "If we don't hear from them or they keep jerking us around, we need a warrant," Mick said. "We're running out of time."

She nodded. "Any sign of the doc?"

"Nope," Paul said. "His two teenage henchmen keep popping in and out though."

"It's so weird," Davies said. "I've gone to Doc Hollis since I was a kid. He's seen me naked."

Neither man had a response.

After a minute, Paul said, "He's the *Big Bad*, I guarantee it. The other two doctors have lawyered up, even though I don't think they're involved, and anyone else who works there doesn't seem to know anything. Only that he's spending a lot of time there, and his two little friends come and go as they please."

"Dr. Hale hasn't been here in weeks, and Dr. Wyatt is in and out," Mick added. "They know something is going on, but they don't know what. They know it's bad though. Why else hire lawyers?"

The front door opened, and the substantial frame of Bobby Stevens stepped out. He walked to his truck and jumped in. The truck shook again. He drove out of the parking lot and regarded the cops as he drove by. Paul was sure he was smirking.

"That was quick," Mick said. "How's he get the run of a place like that?"

"I don't know," Paul said. "I think they're getting ready to run. The doctor's hiding. The kids are in and out. Sometimes they have packages. They know we're onto them, and we're currently powerless to stop them."

"You know who else is onto them?" Davies asked.

"Who?" Paul asked.

"Parker's friends. They were here yesterday."

Mick took a sip from his coffee cup. "They've volunteered before."

She shook her head. "They weren't here long. Sophie and Freddie stayed inside, but Parker's weird boyfriend came out and just kind of wandered around the building while it snowed. No jacket or anything. Just walked around, canvassing the building. He doesn't move fast anyway, and I swear he kept getting stuck in the snow. He scoped out the place for almost half an hour."

"That kid is determined," Paul said. "Weird, but determined."

Mick turned toward him. "I get this feeling when he's around. I can't explain it."

"It's an uncomfortable familiarity," Paul agreed. "I've met him in the past, but I can't square him with the kid he is now. But he still seems familiar."

"They're going to break in," Mick said. "They think Parker's in there, and they're going to break in."

"We'll have to stop them," Davies said.

"Maybe not," Mick said. "We could use this."

Paul raised an eyebrow at Melissa. She looked confused.

"We think they're getting ready to bolt, and we don't have enough to search that place."

Her eyes focused. "We'll have cause to look around if we see them break and enter."

"That's right, Melissa. We can look in every hidden corner of that building."

Paul tapped his finger on the steering wheel. This was pretty borderline policing—fruit of the poisonous tree and all that—and he enjoyed his career. A lot.

"What do you think, buddy?"

"I don't like it. But if those girls are alive …"

Melissa put her hand on his shoulder, and it felt good "They'll kill them, if they haven't already. Dr. Hollis knows we're onto him. That's why he's never there when we go to question him. Something bad is happening in that building. Something evil."

"If something that bad is in there, how can we let some teenagers walk right in?" Paul asked. "They'll be in danger. Real danger. It's a questionable plan."

"We'll be right behind them, pal."

They sat in silence for a moment. Paul noticed Melissa still had her hand on his shoulder, but he didn't say anything. It felt like it belonged there.

"I don't like it, Mick. But I'm in."

Mick nodded. "If the kids don't hit tonight, they will tomorrow. They know the stakes."

The silence returned. No one had anything cheery to fill the space. They weren't talking about it, but they all knew they were risking their careers and probably the kids' safety. And time was not on their side.

Paul's heart was pumping, the adrenaline flowing. He hadn't felt quite like this since Afghanistan. He kind of liked it.

"We'll have to park a little farther away," Mick said. "That damn kid will spot us if we're this close."

Paul agreed. "He sees just about everything."

CHAPTER THIRTY-ONE

FAMILY TIME

Freddie stood by the kitchen door, looking out onto the deck. The outside light was on, and it was bright enough to flood most of the porch. His father and Danny were leaning against the deck rail, laughing and gesturing. Both wore dockers and t-shirts. Jack's was white and sleeveless, and his big muscles popped whenever he waved his arms. Of course, Danny's skinny arms didn't pop much, and the pair looked funny together. They both looked full of life though.

Jack held his big cup in one hand and clapped Danny on the shoulder with the other. Danny's cup balanced on the railing, and it had to be hot chocolate. Freddie could see giant marshmallows overflowing. Their eyes were locked, and Freddie worried he was intruding just by watching them. He wasn't jealous or threatened, just happy the family was together.

"So, where are you boys off to tonight?" his mother asked.

He turned and saw her leaning against the doorframe. "Nowhere in particular. We're picking up Sophie in a while."

"*Hmm*, I like that girl."

Freddie was surprised. "She thinks you just tolerate her because she's my girlfriend."

Maureen wore a blue dress which made her look slimmer. Or maybe she *was* slimmer. His parents seemed a lot happier lately. Of course, she would always be the beautiful young woman who saved him from a life on the streets so long ago. Her face was his first clear memory. She'd said something to him then, but he didn't understand at the time. He knew now. She'd said, *Hello, I'm your mother.*

She smiled. "I know I'm a little cold to her, but I do like her. She has substance."

"Substance?"

"I admit that when I first met her with those fancy clothes and tight pants, I had a different opinion. But she looks out for people. Poor Jessica would be a wreck without her."

"Her pants aren't that tight."

"And I imagine she's taken some grief somewhere about dating a man with brown skin. That was inevitable."

Freddie contemplated that. "She's never really said anything."

He opened the refrigerator and grabbed a plastic water bottle then sat at the table. He thumbed through a small pile of mail to see if anything was for him. He placed the few letters from colleges aside. The rest were bills for his parents and a few bits of junk mail.

She sat across from him. "Aren't you going to open the letters?"

He shook his head. "Not until everything gets straightened out."

She looked concerned but kept quiet.

"Anyway, we know I'm accepted to UMO. That's good enough for me."

"Freddie, you have to look at all your options. We can survive without you for a few months at a time. You have to start … stretching."

He knew she wasn't mad, but her words stung. He took a sip from the bottle.

"I know you want to stay in the area and be part of the business, and I hope that's what you do. I really do. But you have to see the world to make sure Abbot Pond is the best place for you. I think it is, honestly, but you have to look for yourself."

"Does Dad feel the same way?"

His mother laughed. "I'm pretty much parroting his words. It took me a while to see he was right, but now I do."

His phone buzzed: *Can you come soon? Jessica is asking me a lot of questions. Almost as bad as my mom.*

"Speak of the Devil?" Maureen asked.

He nodded. "She's waiting for us."

The door opened, and his father and Danny entered, bringing the cold air with them. Their wet boots left a trail as they crossed the floor. Jack had Danny in a loose headlock, and Danny couldn't stop grinning. Freddie's smile stretched ear to ear.

"For God's sake, Jackie, let the poor boy go before you strangle him."

His father released the grip, and Danny pretended to fall to the ground, clutching his throat. He made a gurgling noise and pretended to shake.

His mother rolled her eyes. "Oh, Good Lord, you're as bad as your father."

Danny climbed to his feet, laughing. He smiled at her and hugged her weakly. Her eyes got misty, and she hugged him back hard enough to crack something.

That weird feeling crept into Freddie's mind again—the sense that something this good couldn't last. He pushed away the thought for now, but it was getting harder to do.

"You're crushing him harder than I was, Maureen. Let the poor boy go."

She let go and wiped at her eyes. "You boys should be leaving. Don't keep Sophie waiting."

"We can stay a little longer if you want, Mom," Freddie said.

She sighed. "Just go."

Danny opened the cupboard then closed it. "No more cookies."

"I'll get some tomorrow," Maureen said. "After work."

Danny smiled a weird smile. "Okay."

Freddie whipped out the phone and tapped a quick message. *Leaving in just a minute.*

"The Celts are playing tonight," Jack said. "If you get home early enough, you can watch the end of it with me."

"When did you learn how to work the remote?" Freddie asked.

"I didn't. I just don't change the channel."

Freddie laughed. "We have to go."

They walked through the living room and found their coats. Danny had a new black spring coat that fit comfortably. Freddie had a dark winter jacket from LL Bean that he didn't usually wear. He would probably have to take it off if they managed to get inside the hospital. Right now, he just wanted to look casual.

Jack called out from the living room, "Bring your keys. I'm locking up after ten."

Danny stepped into the living room. "See you."

Freddie couldn't hear his father's reply.

The boys headed to the black Mustang. Danny turned and stared at the white cottage and across the pond. He smiled and bobbed his head as though he was deciding something.

"Why don't you drive?" Freddie asked.

"What?"

"At least till we get to Parker's house. I don't know if Sophie, um, wants you driving after that."

Danny licked his lips. "Are you sure? The roads are wet, and I don't remember too much about driving."

"It'll come back to you. I'll talk you through it."

CHAPTER THIRTY-TWO

Last Supper?

Dr. Hollis was inside the doorframe with Bobby Bones standing ominously behind him. Bobby had a Wendy's bag in each hand. Parker could smell the fries, and her mouth watered at the thought of chomping on them two or three at a time. Did they have burgers too? She didn't like beef that much, but she was willing to make an exception. She was starving for real food.

"May we come in?" he asked tenderly.

Parker wore baggy jeans and a green shirt dotted with dark stains. She wished she had on more clothes when Dr. Hollis was around. He made her feel so weak, so defenseless. That would change soon, she hoped.

She didn't say anything. Dr. Hollis would come in whether she wanted him to or not.

The doctor entered the room and looked around. "You're keeping the place quite tidy, Parker. I'm very pleased."

She nodded but said nothing.

He wore a dark suit with an oddly shaded blue tie. It made him look a bit younger.

"How is our patient doing?"

Ciara was laying on the couch. She wasn't talking, and the sight of Dr. Hollis made her tremble. She wore green hospital pants—the kind that looked like pajamas—and a white shirt that read *Sexy Grandma* in big red letters. She rolled over so she wouldn't have to look at him.

"Our patient needs more time. She can't make it through a day without crying."

"Robert, could you put those bags on the table please?"

Bobby did as instructed. He wouldn't even look at her as he passed, and he was sweating through his white hospital clothes. The boy might as well have had the word *guilt* tattooed across his forehead.

Is this my last meal? she wondered. *Is this it?*

"Dr. Hollis, why have you done all this? We just want to go home."

He turned to Bobby and whispered something.

Bobby nodded and left, closing the door behind him—probably grateful to leave.

Pulling a chair out from the table, Dr, Hollis sat in front of Parker. He smiled weakly and gave her his compassionate doctor look. It was oddly convincing. His voice was cool and relaxed. "This will all be over soon, Parker. I'm sorry you got mixed up in this. I really am."

That was when she knew for sure he was going to kill her. He wouldn't do it himself; she knew he had no taste for that kind of violence. Ciara knew the type of violence the doctor liked. No, one of his minions would handle it—probably Derek, he had the experience. Bobby might be unable to complete the mission. Somewhere deep in his tiny little brain, he had a conscience. It wasn't enough for him to do the right thing, but it was probably enough that Dr. Hollis wouldn't expect him to do the deed. Derek would be happy to do it. He probably dreamed every night of different ways to kill her. He was the sickest one of all of them.

"I realize it's just a matter of time now. The police have been *staking out the place*, as they say in the movies."

"If that's true," she said, "it will look better for you if you let us go."

He nodded. "Very soon. I just need to get my affairs in order first."

Her stomach turned, and her appetite faded. "How soon, Dr. Hollis?"

"Soon enough, Parker. You know, the school was right about me."

Oh God, she thought. *He's confessing.*

He dramatically wiped his brow. "Bill Hollis was a friend of mine and a good doctor. We went to school together, Parker. I really did go to Drexel. That part was always true. He died young, suddenly, and I just sort of took over for him."

Parker didn't want to ask, but she couldn't help herself. "Why would you take over for him, Dr. Hollis?"

He smiled. "I honestly didn't think anyone at Drexel was aware of his death. He had no family, really, and he was just starting his career when he passed. I would never have given you that recommendation if I'd known. Again, I'm sorry you were drawn into this."

"Me too," she whispered. "Me too."

He stood and headed for the door. "But it's almost over, and soon, you'll be home with your mother and spending time with that interesting young man of yours. They all miss you."

He banged on the door, and Bobby opened it. He waved goodbye as he stepped out. Bobby stared at the floor and closed the door. He looked like he'd lost a puppy.

Ciara sat back up and began to speak.

Parker shook her head and put a finger to her lips. No one could know she was moving around now. They needed to think she was practically in a coma and unable to defend herself. Parker wheeled herself to the door and listened for nearly a minute. Nobody was there.

Ciara opened one of the bags on the table. "At least we got lunch. I'm starving."

"I wouldn't eat that if I were you."

"You think they put something in it?"

Parker shrugged. "I think it's time we get out of here."

"He said he was going to let us go. You don't believe him?"

"What do you think?"

Ciara's hair kept falling across her cheek. She kept trying to sweep it back, but it wouldn't stay. Her cheeks were sunken, and she was way skinnier than in the picture Parker had seen of her from Thanksgiving. She had lines around her eyes, like Parker's mother, but these weren't from aging. They were from surviving.

Parker rolled over to the table. "Are there any drinks in there?"

Ciara looked in the second bag. "Two Frosties. Chocolate, I think. Can't we at least have them?"

"No. Please tell me we have spoons."

Her friend rummaged through the bag and pulled out two plastic spoons. "I hope Danny was right."

Ciara knew who Danny was. "Right about what?"

"He says there's always a way out. If he was here, we'd be home studying for midterms right now. He can open anything."

Parker wheeled across the room and into the bathroom. She was pretty sure Dr. Hollis and the others weren't paying attention to it. As far as they knew, Ciara was still practically catatonic, and Parker could never wheel through the rubble. The door was useless, as far as they knew. But Parker and Ciara had their secrets. Hollis and the boys probably didn't even have a key for it themselves.

Parker glanced at the shower. "That's the first thing I'm doing when I get home. Taking a real shower, not a quick one with you standing in front of the door."

"I know it sounds weird, Parker, but I'm glad we at least had each other. I trust you."

"I know what you mean. Me too."

Parker stuck the long end between the doorframe and the heavy metal door and poked at the latch. She couldn't get it to work right, and it got stuck. She wiggled the spoon around so it got loose, and she pulled it out. She wrinkled her nose and tried to look at the latch, but she couldn't see it very well. She knew where it was though and poked the spoon back in and tried to gently push the latch enough for her to pull open the door. Instead, she heard the spoon snap. When she pulled it back out, it was broken in half.

"Damn it," Ciara said. "It won't work."

Parker shook her head. "Give me the other spoon."

Ciara handed it to her, and Parker tried again. She didn't really do anything different, but it worked, and she could pull open the door. Of course, it squeaked, but she couldn't do anything about that. She stuck her head into the adjoining room, which was dark. She'd gotten a look at the hallway entrance on her *date* with Bobby, and she knew the door was mostly off its hinges.

The room was probably full of clutter though, and she didn't have any sneakers. Neither did Ciara.

Parker said, "Put something down to hold the door open."

Ciara stuck a roll of toilet paper on the floor to gently prop the door. "How's this?"

"Good. Come with me."

They returned to the main room.

"We need something to block the door," Parker said. "To make them think we're still here and we won't let them in. If something was in the food, they might think we're dead in here."

"The bed doesn't have wheels, and it's heavy."

Parker considered the couch, but she knew her limits. They hadn't eaten well in a long time, and neither of them were up for moving heavy furniture. There was only one thing to do.

"Okay, don't freak out." Parker rolled the chair backward under the door latch and locked the brakes.

"What are you doing, Parker?"

Parker stood. Her legs wouldn't run a marathon, but they might be strong enough to get out of this prison. They needed to be.

"Parker, how are you doing that?"

"We're leaving now. We're not staying another minute."

CHAPTER THIRTY-THREE

THE DOOR

"Where are you kids going tonight?" Jessica asked. She was wiping the dinner table with a wet towel, like a waitress would do. Parker's mom was becoming a bit OCD lately, probably to compensate for all the thoughts bouncing around in her brain since the disappearance. Sophie could usually talk her back to reality, except when she got on a certain topic.

Sophie went with honesty. "We're heading over to the Lakeside tonight. We thought we'd visit a few of the patients."

Jessica scrunched her face. "Is that boy joining you tonight?"

Sophie sighed. "If you mean Danny, then yes, he's going with us."

"I know you've suddenly grown fond of him, but just remember all the trouble he's been in before. He could be pulling the wool over your eyes."

"Maybe. But I don't think so. He's not that same boy."

Jessica made a *pffft* noise and went upstairs.

Sophie wore a brand of ankle skinny jeans called Joe's Jeans that she'd ordered online. They were a color called forest floor and were surprisingly comfortable. She had no trouble turning and bending. She also wore a black football jersey Freddie had given her before all the craziness and chose comfortable sneakers. She wanted to be able to run if she had to.

She looked at her phone and saw a message from Freddie. *Be there in a few.*

Was he texting and driving? She hoped not. She wrote back, *Be careful.*

She waited a few minutes and saw a black Mustang sail by. Brake lights came on, and it backed up in something of a straight line and stopped in front of the driveway. Two figures—one stout and the other lean—jumped out of the car and switched seats. Somebody beeped the horn.

What were they up to? She wouldn't ask.

"I'm leaving," she called out. "Goodbye."

Jessica didn't say anything. Maybe she was in the upstairs bathroom, or maybe she was playing her 90s station a little too loud again.

Sophie whispered, "It'll be over soon."

She threw on her black-diamond quilted jacket from L.L. Bean. It was light but insulated. *I guess I'm really doing this.* The door stuck, and she had to throw her shoulder into it for it to open. She looked back inside at the gloominess and then closed the door. In a hurry, she scrambled down the steps, slid on an icy spot on the walkway and approached the car. Both boys sat in the front, so she climbed in back.

Freddie was behind the wheel, and he smiled at her as she fastened her seat belt. He accelerated the Mustang past all the happy homes. Jessica's was the only house without Christmas lights, and the cheer of the neighborhood lights brightened her mood a little. She handed Danny a brownie she'd baked with Jessica earlier.

He grinned as he chewed.

"Are you sure we have to park so far away?" Sophie asked. "Snow will get in my sneakers."

"Paul and Mick have been watching the hospital every night," Danny said. "During the day, some other cops are staking it out. I think they're waiting for Doc Hollis."

"How do you know?"

Danny smirked. "I've been staking *them* out. They're so busy watching what's in front of them, they don't see me standing in the trees by the embankment."

"And you've been *staking out* the hospital with him, Freddie?"

He didn't answer.

"You boys make quite a team."

"The embankment is the key," Freddie said. "If we keep down and stay on the other side of the iron fence, we can make our way to the other side of the hospital. We hop the fence and book it to Danny's invisible door."

They were parked in a driveway about ten houses past the hospital. The house was seasonal, and Freddie knew the owners. They weren't returning from Florida until at least May. The driveway was plowed though, and the cops wouldn't notice them parked under the carport. The house was dark and without Christmas lights.

"You should wait here," Freddie said. "Keep the car running, and hope-fully, we'll bring her out."

Sophie shook her head. "We've talked about this. I'm going."

"Your parents will be pissed at me if I let you, Soph."

"*Let me?* When did you get put in charge of me?"

"Sophie, he doesn't mean anything by it," Danny said. "He just means you should stay here because you're a girl."

Her brain began to sizzle before she saw his grin. She smiled and said, "Very funny, Danny." Even in the dark, she saw the worried look on Freddie's face. "I'm going."

Freddie turned off the interior lights, and they each climbed from the car. Sophie felt the chill from the lake and zipped her jacket; it didn't seem to make a difference. She suddenly realized she had forgotten to bring gloves.

"Follow me," Danny said.

They weren't at the embankment yet, and the road was a nonstarter, so they marched through the snow. Only a couple houses had residents, and they didn't have much in the way of decorations. Sophie's feet burned from the snow seeping into her sneakers, but she wouldn't complain. None of it mattered. Right now, all that mattered was getting into the building.

A few cars passed, and they ducked. No one saw them squatting in the darkness. No one cared.

The last house before the hospital was the tough one—a smaller cottage with no dock and no bushes. They could see the parking lot of the Lakeside diagonally across the street, and a Chevy Malibu was parked in the road across from it. The streetlight above them wasn't too bright, but it was a problem as well.

"Malibus are terrible in this weather," Freddie said.

"We'll have to run across the street and get in the ditch fast," Danny said. "Then we can kind of keep low along that embankment."

"Are you sure you can run?" Freddie asked. "I mean, walking isn't that easy for you in the snow."

Sophie thought he'd say something brave about how he could do it, how he had it in him. Instead, he said, "You'll have to help me. Just kinda pull me along, okay?"

She looked down the street at the innocent-looking car. "Are you sure it's them?"

Danny sounded a little frustrated. "My eyes still work, Sophie. I can see them. They're drinking coffee."

"Okay, so how do we know when to run?"

Freddie wrapped an arm around her. She felt flush with excitement. Was it from his touch or from their predicament?

"Get ready," Danny said. "Alright … go!"

Running was harder than she had expected after kneeling in the snow, but her legs grew stronger with every step. Freddie was ahead of her, dragging Danny through the snow like he was an empty sack. The poor kid's arms jerked around, and he might have been moaning, but that could have been the wind from the pond.

The narrow embankment shielded them from the car's view. Danny brushed snow from his pants and jacket. He caught his breath and peeked his head past the edge of the bank and crawled back to them. "They didn't see us."

They half-walked and half-crawled along the edge of the pond. The ice glowed from the full moon, and the weird pond fog wrapped around their ankles. She kept thinking she would step into the water and fall under the ice. That never happened, and they wormed to the edge of the fence. It felt like it took forever though.

She and Danny were panting, so they took a break in between the trimmed bushes that ran parallel with the fence. The pines were gone, but the shadows from the hospital made them mostly invisible. At least that's what she hoped.

Freddie whispered, "Can you climb over the fence, Danny?"

Sophie judged the four-foot-tall, plain wrought-iron fence—high enough to keep the patients from wandering into the pond but not enough to obstruct their view of the pond. She knew she could jump it.

Danny shook his head. "You're gonna have to toss me over it."

Freddie nodded. "When do we go?"

"There's somebody in that car in the parking lot. I think he's that security guard we ran into the other day."

"Is he looking?" Sophie asked.

"No. He's on his phone. I think he's playing Words with Friends."

"How about the cops?"

"They're looking."

Freddie took her hand. "Are you sure you want to do this? I don't want you to get hurt."

"Parker gets out tonight. No matter what."

Freddie frowned, then he repeated her words. "She gets out tonight."

A truck pulled into the lot. Bobby Boots climbed out and stared at the cops.

Sophie thought he was grinning. "So, he just strolls into this place any time he wants?"

Bobby banged on the security guard's window. He approached the door, framed with blinking Christmas lights, and typed something onto the keypad. The door didn't open, and he had to try again. This time, it opened, and he disappeared inside.

The security guy went back to his game.

Danny said, "Paul and Mick are talking. Let's go."

Sophie didn't hesitate. She put her hand on the non-spiky part of the fence and jumped over, looking like the athlete she used to be. She laid flat in the snow and watched Danny soar past her, landing on his butt. Freddie hopped over it like it was the smallest fence in the world. He was a big guy, but he was light on his feet.

"Let's go," Freddie said.

They scrambled to the edge of the building. Sophie heard "Silent Night" softly escaping from the building. She wondered what the residents thought of the music. Did they even know Christmas was coming?

"Look behind this bush," Danny said.

It all looked like snow to Sophie. "What are we looking at?"

Danny stumbled closer to the building and scraped the snow.

She saw something dark under his hands. She crawled over and helped him dig. She didn't have much feeling in her feet, and her hands felt like needles were pricking at them.

"A cellar door?" Freddie asked.

"The place has been rebuilt a couple of times, you told me that," Danny said. "This must be left over from way back."

Sophie knew a couple had owned the property long before it was a hospital. "How do you know the doors don't open into a concrete wall?"

Freddie grabbed a rusty handle and tried to lift. "It's locked."

"Do you still have the thing?" Danny asked.

Freddie reached for his inside pocket. He had trouble unzipping the jacket, his hands probably frozen. After a few seconds, he removed a six-inch piece of steel.

"What's that?" she asked.

"Pry bar."

"The door's more rust than metal now. It can't keep us out," Danny said.

Freddie jammed it between the doors by the handles and tried to force one of the doors open. He mumbled something, shimmied the bar and lifted again. Something snapped, and a small cloud of rusty powder mushroomed across his face. He pulled the handle, and the door creaked open a little.

Sophie heard something metal skittering across the concrete inside.

Freddie opened the door about halfway, and Danny climbed in. Freddie looked at her. "Last chance."

About ninety percent of her wanted to stay outside. It wanted her to go back to the car and wait in the warmth. She could listen to one of Freddie's country stations and learn about rowdy honkytonks and unfaithful wives. That would be the smart thing to do but not the right thing. She knew what she had to do.

Sophie followed Danny into the darkness.

CHAPTER THIRTY-FOUR

STARTING AT THE BOTTOM

"Where are we?" Sophie asked. She couldn't see anything, and the air seemed thin and stale.

"In front of a concrete wall, like you said," Danny replied.

Her heart sank. "Really?"

"There's a door though."

She heard Freddie futzing around until she saw the beam of light from his flashlight. It started at the wooden ceiling and slowly traced down the wall and hit upon an old wooden door.

"Where does this door go?" Freddie asked.

Danny stood in front of the door, his fingers circling the knob. "I bet they were going to clear the earth around the foundation but just never got around to it."

"Maybe they were trying to keep some of the original building," Sophie said. "Like for historical reasons?"

Freddie's light moved to the ground. The floor was an uneven mix of dirt, cement, and what looked like tree branches. She couldn't quite tell, and Freddie kept swinging the light around, like he was conducting an orchestra.

"Can you hold the light in one place, Freddie? You're making me dizzy."

"Sorry."

"This door's wicked old too, Freddie," Danny said. "If you kicked it right by the door handle, it should give in."

Freddie handed the light to Sophie, and she shined it on the door handle. He moved his feet around—she guessed for balance—and suddenly, shockingly, booted the door. Wood splinters seemed to go everywhere, and the door came loose not only at the latch, but the top hinge came off too. The door fell sort of diagonally, mostly landing on the ground and partly hanging from the bottom hinge. Freddie stepped backward then stomped on the door, and it came free from the hinge.

She knew he was smiling at the destruction he had caused, though she couldn't really see his face. Boys like breaking things.

"Great job, Freddie," Danny said, his voice full of pride. "That was awesome."

Freddie pointed the light through the doorway into what looked like an extra-long basement with a high ceiling. "What's this?"

"No one's down here," Danny said. "Let's start looking."

Nobody asked him how he knew no one was around.

Freddie pointed the light forward, and they walked across the concrete, their steps sounding unnaturally loud. Danny held them back with his shuffling, but she didn't mind taking a slow approach. Her biggest fear was that they would have to run from something—something very bad.

"What do you suppose that is?" Sophie pointed toward a pile of bags by the far wall. They were heavy-looking, at least in the dark, and seemed out of place. A pile of rocks or something sat beside the bags.

"I'll go look." Freddie trotted over and flashed his light around like it was a Star Wars sword.

Danny put his hand around her arm, calming her. He probably already knew whatever Freddie knew. Her boyfriend was in sight again, rubbing his hands together, walking back to her. It didn't seem that he was in any hurry.

"What is it?"

The light wasn't on his face, but she could still see it a little. He looked freaked. "It's about three feet deep. There's tools, and someone's dug a big hole."

A queasy feeling settled in her stomach. "And the bags?"

"Cement. I guess to fill the hole."

No one said anything more about the hole.

Sophie briefly stared at the excavation site as Freddie tugged her away. It didn't take much for her to guess what would fill that hole. Parker. And maybe Ciara, if she was in here.

Danny's voice echoed in the empty chamber. "There's a room up there, to the left."

Sophie hoped it wasn't a crematorium or something else worse than the hole. She put her hand over her nose. "It smells like pee and Clorox."

It was a big room with metal tables of varying lengths. Some were counters, and they had sinks. Plastic was taped around the back of the room, and she noticed what looked like glass bottles with rubber tubing. Glasses and bottles of varying sizes were everywhere.

Sophie stepped closer, past a series of neatly stacked boxes, and studied the odd setup. It looked like a mad scientist's laboratory in an old black and white movie. It occurred to her again that it wasn't too late to leave. She sighed because she knew she couldn't. "Freddie, flash the light over here."

"I hear footsteps," Danny said. "Someone's coming."

"We need to hide," Freddie said. "Is there a spot?"

Danny grabbed Sophie's hand and shuffled them past the glassware and into the far corner. A sheet, probably filthy, hung over the side of a table. Freddie extinguished the light and squeezed beside them, breathing on her neck, and they all kept quiet. The odor was much worse in what must have been the work area of the lab, and Sophie pulled up the top of her sweatshirt to cover her nose and mouth. Was this a meth lab? Would she get stoned just kneeling here? Could she become addicted just breathing the stuff?

A dim light turned on, and she heard cardboard ripping.

Danny whispered in her ear, "It's Derek. He's going through one of those boxes."

She could hear Derek humming, like he didn't have a care in the world.

The light went off, and she heard footsteps. She wanted to get up and get away from the smell, but Danny had a surprisingly strong grip on her wrist, and Freddie had his arm around her waist. Something like claustrophobia attacked her thoughts, and she struggled to hold it back. Sophie did not want to be kneeling in a corner with the drug smell overwhelming her and the darkness pushing at her like a current. She wanted to get up. She wanted to run.

"He's still there," Danny said.

The light came back on, and she heard Derek mumbling and swearing as he fumbled through the box again. After a minute, he said, "Finally."

She heard the footsteps again, but the light stayed on.

"He's gone," Danny said. "He just forgot the light."

They all stood and hurried from the makeshift lab. She nearly tripped over a flipped-over propane tank but stepped across it at the last minute. A few more of them were stacked against a wall. *I should have stayed in the car. This is horrible.*

Freddie rifled through the open box of dozens of prescription bottles. "Jesus."

Sophie picked one up. "Vicodin."

"This one is Percocet, and it's for Nancy," Freddie said, rummaging. "What's Lexapro for?"

"I'm not sure, but my mom used to take it."

Freddie looked at her. "This is not good."

Sophie said, "Maybe they dispose of old drugs down here somewhere?"

He shook his head. "It's brand new. They just keep refilling prescriptions after the patients die. Maybe they don't give the drugs to the patients when they're alive."

"Derek's a drug dealer. The old me probably knew that," Danny said.

"If he is, he's not the brains of the operation, that's for sure," Sophie said. "This has got to be Dr. Hollis's deal."

Freddie looked glum. "I'm always making excuses for Derek. You've always known though. "

She didn't answer.

Danny started shuffling away.

"Where are you going?" Sophie asked.

"This is all interesting, but we're here to get Parker. Mick and Paul can deal with this when the time comes."

Sophie knew the detectives made weird faces when Danny called them by their first names. They never corrected him though. She liked Officer Davies, but she never called her *Melissa*. It just didn't seem right.

"What's down the hall?" Freddie asked.

Danny's voice was choppy, as though he was already out of breath. "Stairs. We have to start working our way up."

Freddie turned his light back on, and they started toward the stairway. Their steps sounded heavy, and Sophie was worried someone would hear them. She wondered if Freddie and Danny were as nervous as she was. Danny was too obsessed with finding Parker to be scared, plus he was weird. Freddie, though, had to be feeling it. He covered it well and only looked slightly more serious than usual—like he was getting ready for a job interview.

Sophie looked back at the lab. "I bet that used to be a morgue. You know, back when this place was a regular hospital, before it burned down."

"It kind of still is," Danny said.

She was confused. "Still is what?"

"A morgue … It's *still* a morgue."

CHAPTER THIRTY-FIVE

A Breakthrough and a Break In

Mick was in the back seat, slurping his Dunkin' Donuts coffee. "You know, you can ask her out if you want."

"What?" Paul asked, turning off the radio. He sipped from his own cup, savoring the caffeine blast that made his fingers tremble. *Good coffee makes good policework.* That should be the nationwide police motto.

"There's no conflict involved. She doesn't technically work for you—you're just visiting."

Paul tilted his head. "Are you talking about Melissa? We're just—"

The car rocked, and he flinched, thankfully not spilling his drink this time. The passenger door opened, and Davies jumped in, laughing.

She wore jeans and a parka and held a big manila envelope. "Got you again."

"Nice of you to stop by, Officer," Mick said. "Do you have anything for us?"

She looked at Detective Roberts and nodded. "School's still giving me the runaround."

"I already talked to my boss about a subpoena. Sounds like that's what they want."

She nodded. "But my guy down there is annoyed too. He wants to tell me something, but he can't."

"Like what?" Paul asked. He worried he was staring at her a little too hard, but he was having trouble looking away. Instead, he tried a serious look—respect among equals.

She lowered her voice, as if people were eavesdropping. "When I speak to him, he's all apologetic and everything, and he's definitely been looking into Doc Hollis. Then he mentions it should be easy enough to get Doc Hollis' yearbook online. He says Hollis had a lot of friends."

Mick seemed interested. "Did you find it online?"

She shook her head. "I found another student, an unrelated one. She copied some pages and sent them to me. She had to rummage through her basement, I think, but she sent me some pictures."

Paul was impressed. "You've been busy."

She dug through her envelope and handed Paul a picture. "This is William Hollis in seventy-nine, his last year at Drexel."

Paul turned on the interior light and inspected the picture. A happy-looking guy with a mop of dark hair covering his head smiled at him. He handed it to Mick and waited to see what he thought. His friend stared at the picture for a minute then shook his head. He had to be thinking the same thing as Paul.

"That's not him," Mick said. "I mean, it was forty years ago, and people change, but I don't think it's him. Are you sure this lady sent you the right photos?"

Melissa looked excited. Her lips kept trying to curl into a smile, but she was holding it back. Her hands were shaking. "I looked at all of his classmates and about the billionth one was this guy." She peeled another photo from the envelope and handed it to Paul.

Mick grabbed it and, after a second, gave it to Paul. The guy in the photo was smiling back at Paul, and his heart jumped. This guy was *their* William Hollis. He looked almost the same, except the younger version had more hair, and his glasses were different. The name under his picture was Martin Bennet.

A car passed by, and everybody jumped just a little.

"You're telling me that the guy hiding out in that building, our number one suspect, isn't even a real doctor?" Mick asked.

"Oh, he's a real doctor. Bennet and the real Hollis were roommates for a while and classmates."

Mick grinned, enjoying the adventure of the moment. "Tell me more, Davies."

"It looks like Hollis just kind of graduated and moved back to Iowa. He got run over when he was changing a tire in the rain soon after. By the way, that's why I have Triple-A."

"What about Martin Bennet?" Paul asked.

She reached forward and turned down the heat. "Well, Dr. Bennet started a practice just outside of Atlanta. He got investigated for overprescribing. Nothing came of that, but then he got popped for inappropriate behavior with an underage patient. He might have talked his way out of that too, but several other girls came out of the woodwork with similar claims."

Paul remembered what she had said about Hollis being her doctor and seeing her naked. "Jeez, when was this?"

"Early eighties."

Another vehicle passed them and pulled into the hospital parking lot. The truck looked familiar.

"He do any time?" Mick asked.

She shook her head. "He bolted. Hasn't been spotted since."

Paul watched the dark pickup. "And then Doc Hollis pops up around Abbot Pond, and everybody loves him. He's everybody's favorite doctor."

Melissa stroked her hair. "I think she somehow mentioned Doc Hollis to Drexel in her application, and they got back to her that he was dead. She calls him, and he pops over with his boys and grabs her and the letter. Probably kills her."

Paul didn't like the theory. Not because it sounded wrong, but because he didn't like the ending. "Why wouldn't the school just tell us?"

"They got rules," Mick said. "Same as us. They can't disclose personal information. Her application's private."

A familiar figure climbed down from the cab and sprinted toward the door. He appeared to bang on it. It was Jack Morgan.

"Hello ..." Mick said. "Isn't that your buddy Jack?"

"Yep."

The security guy put down something—probably his phone—and exited his vehicle. He straightened his belt and strode to Jack. They looked like they were exchanging words. Apparently, this guy was unaware of Jack and his reputation. The big guy was being too aggressive.

"We should probably intervene," Mick said.

The rent-a-cop was burly, and he seemed to tower over Jack. Jack was talking with his hands and pointing at the big guy.

"Security's not deescalating the situation properly," Paul said.

Mick nodded. "He appears overconfident and unreceptive to what Mr. Morgan has to say."

"Aren't we going to do anything before he hurts that guy?" Melissa asked. "You guys seem to be enjoying this."

The men laughed.

The security guy pushed Jack backward. Jack said something, and the big guy reached for his shoulder.

"That's a mistake," Mick muttered.

Jack moved quickly, and the not-really-a-cop was on his hands and knees, looking up. To his credit, he climbed to his feet before a decent right hook knocked him back down for good. He napped right between two flashing reindeer. Jack returned to the door and pounded again.

"Best barroom brawler in the county in his day," Mick said. "Looks like he's still got it."

"We should get over there," Melissa said. "He might hurt someone."

The door opened, and he pushed his way inside.

"Well, looks like we have an illegal entry happening right before our eyes," Mick said. "I think we'll have to investigate."

Paul turned on his lights and pulled into the hospital entrance. *Thank God for Jack Morgan*, he thought.

CHAPTER THIRTY-SIX

Looking for the Doc Hollis

"What's going on, Jack?" Paul asked.

Jack was slightly off the rails. He was pacing, and the poor, middle-aged woman who opened the door was backing away from him. A softball-sized yellow stain smeared the right shoulder of her white nurse outfit. She said, "He wants to see Dr. Hollis, but I don't know where he is."

Paul was standing by the front desk, and Mick was beside him. Melissa was still outside checking on the security guy. He was on his feet, but his legs were Jell-O.

"Why do you need to see the doctor at this time of night, Jack?" Paul asked.

His face was crimson, and he looked like his wires were about to burn out. "Stay out of this, Paulie."

"You know I can't do that, Jack."

Jack eyed Mick. "Can I talk to you alone?"

Paul smiled. "Let's go to that table over there. We can talk."

He led the guy to the conference table and sat. A flier in the center of the table featured a picture of the Lakeside and some quotes detailing people's positive experiences at the residence.

Jack's eyes danced from adrenaline and beer. "My boys are here."

"Why do you think that, Jack?"

He removed a sheet of paper and handed it to Paul. "The boys were acting weird when they left the house, so I looked in their rooms. This was on Freddie's desk."

Paul read it.

Dad, Danny and I have gone to the Lakeside Residence. Danny believes Parker is there, and we are doing something you and Mom will be mad about. We think Doc Hollis took Parker. Danny says he found a way in (you know he's good at that), and we'll find her if she's there. Sophie is with us too. I am trying to talk her out of going with us, but she is pretty stubborn. Don't tell her I said that.

If you don't hear from us, call the cops. I know you like Detective Nault.

I'm sorry if I let you down.

Freddie

He looked up at Jack. "We've been staking out this place all night, Jack. We haven't seen them. Maybe they went to a movie instead."

The blood vessels around Jack's temples pulsated. "Jesus Christ, Paulie. No offense, but if Danny wanted to sneak past you, he could do it, no problem."

Mick was talking to the nurse when Paul motioned for him to come over. "Jack, Detective Roberts is my friend. He knew Ryan too. He'll help me find your boys, okay?"

He nodded. "If you say so, Paulie."

When Mick reached the table, Paul handed him the paper. Mick read it. "We've been watching this place all night, Mr. Morgan."

Jack looked at Paul and rolled his eyes.

Paul stood and grabbed Mick's arm. He spoke softly, "I think we've got enough to search this place. Suspected drug activity, evidence that this doctor is a fraud, and now we have missing teenagers. What do you think?"

"We gotta go with our guts."

A small crowd of nurses and orderlies had gathered.

"Alright," Paul said. "We need your help, people. Has anybody seen Dr. Hollis? He seems to be living here now."

There was a lot of headshaking.

Paul sighed. "Officer Davies, stay by the door, and don't let anyone out. No one leaves."

"Yes, sir. No one leaves."

He looked at the nurse who had let in Jack. "What's your name?"

"Mary. Mary Anderson."

"Show us around, Mary."

"I'm going with you," Jack said. "They're my boys."

"You stay here. Let us do our job," Mick said.

They didn't wait for Jack to answer. They followed Mary through the security door and into the much-too-warm main room. The television was on, and "Rudolph the Red-Nosed Reindeer" played over a speaker. They checked the kitchen to see if anyone was hiding behind the refrigerator. The main room was a horror show in Paul's mind. Patients shuffled around, not seeing him— not really seeing anything. An old man was sleeping on a couch. Somebody somewhere was crying that they couldn't find something. It had to be at least eighty degrees in here, and it was slowing him down. They probably cranked it up to put the patients to sleep.

"Why are they all still up?" Mick asked. "It's the middle of the night."

"They don't know that," Mary answered. "They're all on their own schedule."

"Jingle Bells" came on, and an old lady with a Mickey Mouse shirt sang along. She didn't sound half-bad.

Mick scanned the room. "What's with all the cameras?"

"It's all new. They installed all this stuff just a few weeks ago."

It all fit. Hollis was up to something bad, and he was getting a little paranoid about it.

"Mary, where does Dr. Hollis usually hang out during the night?" Paul asked. "Does he sleep in his office? I know he hasn't left the building in quite a while."

She looked worried. "I don't want to get him in trouble, Officer. He's a wonderful man."

"I'm a detective," Paul said. "And I'll let you in on a secret. He's already in trouble. I'm thinking he's a bad man, and he's about to do something terrible."

Mary looked like she didn't believe him. "He might be in his office."

"Bring us there."

She steered him there and opened the door.

Mick passed them and looked around. It resembled any other doctor's office.

Paul wondered if the diplomas hanging on the wall were fake or if he had somehow gotten the originals. No pictures on the desk, which was unusual in Paul's experience.

Mick started digging through the drawers.

"Don't you need a warrant?" Mary asked.

Mick looked annoyed. "There's nothing to see in the desk."

Paul took Mary's arm. "Where else does he like to go?"

She thought for a moment. "He talks alone with his boys in the laundry room sometimes."

"His boys?"

"Derek and Bobby. He's taken them under his wing."

The laundry room was next door, but it was locked.

Mary said, "I know we have a key somewhere. I'll go get it."

Paul jiggled the handle, but that didn't stop the door from being locked. He looked inside and saw a few industrial-size washers and dryers and a table in the center of the room. Directly across from him, Paul noticed an old metal door that looked pretty sturdy.

"I wonder where that leads us?" Mick asked. "Maybe Wonderland?"

"Hey," Paul said. "The door's opening."

He watched the door creak open—at least he imagined it creaked—and saw a little girl enter the room. She might have been five years old, but it was hard to guess through the window. Her hair was dark, and she wore a little red skirt and an unzipped jacket. The girl seemed to be crying. Paul felt like he should know her.

Dr. Hollis stood behind her, talking, and pointing at her.

"Who the hell is that?" Mick asked.

Paul looked at Hollis, and their eyes met.

The doctor seemed to shake when he recognized the detectives, and he froze. He grabbed the girl's hand, yanked her back through the doorway and slammed the door loud enough for Paul to hear it.

Paul pulled at the door in front of him and swore as it resisted.

"Where is that damn key?" he shouted. "I need the key!"

CHAPTER THIRTY-SEVEN

A Surprise

The stairs were concrete, and the dust they kicked up swam in his lungs. Their steps weren't noisy, but Danny's heavy huffing and puffing sure were. Occasionally, he whooped a big hacking cough and had to clear his throat. It sounded like he was being strangled. Danny was in even worse shape than Freddie had thought. He flashed his light at his friend and saw Sophie holding his arm, gently tugging him along. She looked at Freddie and frowned.

"Do you need a break, Danny?" he asked.

Danny shook his head. "We're almost at the next floor. Let's wait till then."

Freddie turned and climbed the steps. The staircase was built in a basic 180-degree design, which his father called switchback stairs. He wanted to bounce double steps to the top and get a quick look around, but he had the only flashlight. Not that Danny needed one, but Sophie wasn't handling the dark as well as he'd expected, and he needed her calm. She had freaked out in the meth lab.

Finally, they reached the landing.

Freddie shook the metal door's handle. "Locked."

"Can you open it, Danny?" Sophie asked.

Freddie and Sophie both helped him to the door. "This works better if no one's looking."

"Why?" Sophie asked.

Danny caught his breath a little and said, "A magician never reveals his secrets."

Freddie turned the light toward the next flight of stairs. He unzipped his LL Bean jacket, revealing an old sweater that felt two sizes too tight. "Only one more floor is left from the old hospital. After that, I bet the stairs lead to the laundry room."

He realized Sophie was holding his hand. It felt good. Comforting.

"I got it," Danny said. "It was just stuck."

Of course, it was, Freddie thought. *It was just stuck.*

Freddie pushed open the door and pointed the light down the hallway. He heard the humming of electric current and wondered if it was the original wiring. Freddie was pretty good at running wires, but he knew when to call the electrician. Doc Hollis probably had to do it himself. He wouldn't want to bring an outsider into his chamber of horrors.

"What's that?" Sophie asked.

Much of the ceiling had collapsed into a pile of steel and mortar. Dim light grazed the top of the pile but not enough to give Freddie hope that he could maneuver over the obstruction. He pointed his light up at the origin of the mass and saw what looked like wooden patchwork. "Someone filled the hole."

"We'll have to go up and circle around," Sophie said. "We can check the next floor on the way."

Danny didn't look convinced. "I think I can climb over. The pile doesn't go all the way to the top. Light is shining through from the other side."

Freddie shook his head. "You can't even climb the stairs. You should stay."

"I can make it, Freddie. I'm just worn down from the heat."

The hallway was hot, no doubt, and his face was sweaty, but Freddie didn't think that was why his friend was having such a hard time. Danny was just out of gas. Pure and simple.

"Why don't I look ahead, and you two stay here?" Freddie suggested. "This seems like a great place to hide."

Sophie's voice was sharp. "I didn't come all this way to hide by a pile of junk, Freddie Morgan. I came here to get Parker. I'm going with you."

He wanted to argue, but he knew Sophie. Anyway, he didn't know how much time they had, so he had to get going. "Okay. But stick with me."

Danny leaned against the wall then sat and rubbed his legs. "I need to catch my breath."

Freddie said, "If you want her back, Danny, you should let me go ahead."

"I'm slowing you down," Danny said. "I know it."

"You're the one who found the cellar door in the first place, Danny," Freddie said. "You brought us this far."

The light wasn't on Danny's face, so Freddie couldn't see the disappointment. He felt it though.

Danny said, "Go. If I get my legs back, I'll catch up with you."

Sophie took Danny's hand. "We'll be right back, Danny. Hopefully with Parker."

Freddie squatted beside him and patted his shoulder. "I'll find her, Danny. If she's down here, I'll find her."

All Danny could say was, "Okay."

"I'll bang on the floor up there when I'm above you. Try to make some noise back."

Sophie followed him as he stepped onto the landing. He aimed his light at the center of the stairs in front of him, and they began climbing. She gripped his arm, and he held the rusty railing. It took a minute to reach the next landing and the next metal door. Freddie tried the door, and it was locked.

"What do we do?" she asked.

Freddie fished around in his pocket for the pry bar. He handed the light to Sophie. "This works better if you shine a light on the door."

She smiled and aimed the light. He slammed it on the metal knob, and it crashed to the floor and rolled away. He poked the bar into the hole and knocked out the knob on the other side. Freddie reached two fingers into the hole and pulled open the door. Breaking in is easy if you're not worried about making a mess.

"I guess this one was just stuck too," he said.

The hallway was long and had some jerry-rigged lighting—still dim but enough for him to turn off his light. The walls were yellowed, but Freddie imagined they had been white long ago. The patchwork on the floor looked like double plywood nailed to the floor. He tapped on the wood with his foot. There was no tap back from underneath. Hopefully, Danny just didn't hear him.

The ceiling was demolished too, replaced by what looked like solid concrete.

"They just built the new hospital over the old one," Freddie said.

"Can they do that?"

He shrugged. "I don't think they're supposed to. My dad says sometimes builders don't want to see what's under the site, because it might be something important, like a historic site or an Indian burial ground."

The floor felt secure, but Freddie knew he was a heavy guy. He placed one foot on the plywood, feeling it sink a little, and jumped the rest of the way onto the solid floor. He reached over and said, "Come on."

Sophie stepped onto the plywood and then took another step. "It's holding my weight just fine, Freddie."

"Are you saying I'm fat, Sophie?"

"No …" She took his hand. "I'm saying there's more of you than there is of me."

He shook his head. "That's definitely not true."

They came upon a long official-looking desk—maybe a sign-in area—and continued down the hallway. A broken window to their left stretched down the hallway, and Freddie shined his light through it. It was empty. Freddie thought of every zombie movie he'd ever seen. This was how they always started.

"I think this was a nursery back in the fifties," Sophie said.

"I bet a lot of the older folks in town were born here."

Next, they found two doorless rooms that had once held patients. One of them still sported a bed, but it was folded. They shared a bathroom. He turned the faucet, and cold water came out. *Plumbing works*, he thought. Freddie tried the hot water, and, after a minute, it worked. He thought about flushing the toilet, but he didn't want to make any more noise.

"Why is the water still on?" she asked.

"I'd have to check the plumbing. Either it just never got turned off and no one noticed, or the pipes from the Lakeside were just hooked into the pipes from the old hospital. Kind of shoddy, either way."

They approached another desk, this one broken in the middle but still standing. A big clock hung over it, its black hands gone. The red seconds hand still revolved dutifully. Freddie pictured guys pacing the hallway, like in old movies, handing out cigars and waiting for babies to appear. Occasionally, someone would faint when the doctor told him it was twins.

A janitor's closet was open, and a bright yellow bucket was inside, along with cleaning supplies.

"Janitor still comes down here?" Freddie asked.

"Probably Bobby. Derek wouldn't use a mop."

He heard a banging sound and pulled Sophie into the closet.

It was Derek's voice, and it sounded slurred. "Step back."

Freddie snuck a look and saw his old friend tapping on a door at the end of the hallway. Derek was sipping from a can of something, and Freddie wondered if he was mixing booze with those pills he had earlier. Maybe Derek was more than just a dealer; maybe he was a junkie too. He kind of hoped that was the case. It would help explain why Derek seemed so different. Freddie didn't want to believe he'd been wrong about his friend. But, deep down, he knew the truth, and he was beginning to resent Derek more every time he thought about him.

"Derek's paying somebody a visit?" Sophie asked.

Freddie looked again, and Derek was gone. He handed her the pry bar. "Stay here. I'll see what he's doing."

His blood was pumping, and he was in no mood to creep. He wanted to confront Derek, to find out what he was up to. He sprinted down the hallway and stopped at the mystery room. Bright light spilled into the dim hallway. When he looked in, the light burned his eyes, and he had to squint away the pain.

The room was bright and painted pink. The furniture seemed nice, and pictures decorated the wall. A table had a vase filled with pink roses. Derek stood with his back to Freddie. He wore a white orderly outfit and was yelling at somebody, not really making sense.

"You were supposed to eat the Wendy's. We got it especially for you."

"You eat it then." Freddie didn't recognize the voice. It was a girl's voice. Maybe Ciara? Definitely not Parker.

Still unaware that Freddie was behind him, Derek reached over and screamed some more. Freddie couldn't understand him. Derek was lost in the fog of alcohol and drugs.

"Let go of me, you lunatic," the girl said.

"Let her go, Derek," Freddie said. "Let her go now."

Derek shuddered at Freddie's intrusion then turned, shaking his head when he saw Freddie. He put his can of beer on the floor. "Can my day get any worse? How did you get in here?"

"What's going on here, Derek?"

"You're not supposed to be here, Freddie."

Freddie's arms shook in anticipation. A fight was imminent; he could feel it coming. He always knew when a fight was coming. His body would tremble, probably from adrenaline, and his body would shift around, like a boxer warming up before a match. His mind always stayed clear, looking for a way out, a way not to have to hurt somebody. But not this time. This time, he hoped to fight.

Derek's eyes were bloodshot, and he was smiling like a crazy person. "You were never as tough as everybody thought, Freddie. Everyone was so scared of you because you're kind of a Mexican badass. But I'm not scared."

"Yes, you are. You've always been afraid of me. That's why you pretended to be my friend."

"I was a better friend than that Cole kid, that's for sure. I don't see him with you now. A friend always has your back, Freddie."

"He's more than a friend to me. He's my brother. You're just a guy I used to hang out with—a guy I always knew I couldn't really trust."

Derek swung a crazy hook at him, most of it absorbed by Freddie's big forearm and the padding of his heavy jacket. He stepped backward then tackled Freddie, taking him off his feet. Derek wasn't as big as Freddie, but he was strong, and he was out-of-his-mind stoned. They rolled around, knocking over the beer can and bumping their heads into furniture. Freddie got to his feet and stomped on Derek's back like he had stomped the door off its hinges less than an hour ago. Derek groaned but still tried to stand. Freddie helped him, only to punch him in the gut. Derek coughed blood, but that didn't stop Freddie.

He knew rage was taking over, a pent-up anger he'd kept in a compartment in the back of his head for months now. Freddie always knew Derek was dirty, but he didn't want to believe it. Now, here he was pushing some girl around, threatening her. He was calling Freddie a *Mexican* when he knew he was Columbian and trashing Danny. His anger rose again, and he threw an elbow into Derek's temple. Derek crumpled to the floor again, and Freddie went to beat him some more.

Someone tugged his arm, though he barely felt it. The touch was familiar. It was Sophie. He couldn't quite understand what she was saying. Whatever it was, it was calming him down. He stepped away from Derek, who was twitching on the floor.

Her hands were on his cheeks. "You have to calm down, Freddie. You don't want to do something you'll regret."

"No," he said. "You're right. I was just so angry at him, but I don't want to kill him."

Someone said, "I do. Keep hitting him."

It was the girl Derek had been pushing around. She wasn't Parker, and she wasn't Ciara Clark.

He knew the face. He'd seen it in photos a hundred times. She was a few years older in real life, but she looked almost the same. Maybe a little paler. A lot sadder.

"Oh my God," Sophie said. "You're Rachel. Rachel Randall."

CHAPTER THIRTY-EIGHT

CORNERED

Parker stepped on something soft and hoped it wasn't a rat. A dead one had been under the couch back in the room, and part of her was convinced there was an infestation. It didn't move, whatever it was, so she and Ciara teetered on toward the dim hallway. They held each other's arms for balance and comfort and somehow managed to keep on their feet. By the time they reached the doorway, Parker was struggling for air. She felt like she'd just run a marathon. How would she do this?

"Which way do we go?" Ciara asked.

"Going right brings us to that cafeteria I told you about. I don't know where left goes. Maybe an exit?"

Ciara's face expressed a contrast of fear and fortitude. She was terrified of the doctor and his little helpers, but she wanted to escape even more than Parker did. Dr. Hollis had treated her a lot rougher than Parker wanted to think about, and she was still pretty damaged. Ciara was tough, probably tougher than she had been a few weeks ago.

"Left. If the boys are around, they'll be hanging out in the cafe. We should avoid them."

"I don't know which one of them is worse. Derek for being a creep or Bobby for always going along with him."

Ciara frowned. "Derek's the worst. He seemed nice, and he wanted to party."

Parker knew where she was going.

"He went to the basement with that nice boy, and he was the only one who came up. Then he grabbed me by the hair and told me I was next if I didn't do what he said."

Parker had heard the story before. "I'm sorry, Ciara."

Ciara's eyes were misty. "I just don't want him to find me. We should avoid the cafe."

"Okay, let's go. Take my arm."

The hallway was smoother than she'd expected, but she still stepped on small pieces of debris, and it slowed her down. Her bare feet weren't used to this kind of a workout, and her brain wasn't recognizing every sensation. She felt like she was typing with the lights out, with her feet.

"How long have you been walking again? I mean, I'm glad for you, but I had no idea."

"It's been coming on for a while now, Ciara, since before we wound up here. I guess I just felt ready."

Ciara looked suspicious. "Well, I'm glad. We'd never have made it even this far with you in your wheelchair."

Parker looked down at her wobbly legs. *I hope they last.*

"It's getting darker. Maybe the lights don't work as well on this end of the hallway."

Parker was okay with the dark. If she couldn't see them, they couldn't see her.

They passed a few offices, the doors still locked. One door was open, but the room was gone, leaving only a wall of dirt. The hallway was quiet except for the humming of the overhead lights. Parker tried to picture the place as it had been—candy stripers hurrying through the halls, children following their parents to visit aunts or uncles, every now and then a nurse would page a doctor over the intercom because he was needed for an emergency. The place was probably *alive* back then. Now, it was some kind of a murder house.

"Oh, no," Ciara said, releasing her arm. "The ceiling must have collapsed."

A ten-foot-high pile of steel and concrete towered in front of them. Wires and sharp metal bits protruded from the rubble, seemingly threatening them. A crazy amount of dirt and roots mixed with the debris. It was impossible to climb around, and Parker doubted she could climb over it, not in her current state. Rat images reentered her head. Would they nest in there? She shook her head, hoping the crazy thoughts would fly away. "We'll have to go back the other way."

They stopped and leaned against the dusty wall. Parker was sweating.

"It's okay. It's just a setback."

Parker nodded. "We can't panic."

"Let's go."

Walking was a little more of a strain, and Parker worried that her new legs might give out. She didn't stop though, because that wouldn't fix anything. Maybe she'd need the wheelchair again after she got out of the building, but it would be worth it. Some things were worse than her damn chair. She knew that now.

Someone left the cafeteria. Someone wearing white pants and a white shirt. Someone very large.

"Bobby Boots," Ciara whispered as though he were the villain in a horror movie.

Bobby looked in their direction but didn't seem to see them pressed to the wall of the dim hallway. It seemed like they were a mile away from him, and the lights sucked. Parker stopped breathing as she stared at him. He turned to walk away from them. Maybe he was off the clock for the night. *Just keep walking, Bobby.*

But then he turned around, scratching his head and looking at them.

"Don't move," Parker said.

"Where could I go?"

His first few steps were slow and innocent, but he looked in their direction. He saw something. Then he accelerated faster than she expected, considering his size and the fact he was wearing work boots. Parker imagined the walls shook as he ran toward them, good china falling from cabinets and smashing on the floor. Her heart beat like a Recycled Percussion concert. There was nowhere to go. Neither girl moved.

He slowed when he got near. "Parker?"

She trembled. "Just pretend you don't see us, Bobby. Just go wherever you were going."

Bobby looked back down the hallway. "I can't do that. Dr. Hollis—"

"Forget him, Bobby."

Bobby Boots was not a handsome kid. His face looked like it had been patched together with pieces of three or four other kids' faces. Ugly kids. But she could see the confusion, the trauma of his thoughts. His eyes, the only normal parts of his body, squinted sadly at her. "You have to go back to your room, Parker."

Did he even see Ciara? Did he notice she was walking?

"It's not my room. It's a prison."

He slammed his palm into the wall beside her and left a hole in the sheet rock.

Parker winced.

"You have to go back. Doctor Hollis will be mad."

Parker's eyes narrowed. "Screw him, Bobby. Look what he's done to us. You know what he did to Ciara."

Shaking his head, he reached for her arm. She stumbled backward, and Ciara grabbed her, keeping her from falling. Ciara didn't let go, and her grip pinched Parker's side. "Bobby, don't do this. I don't want to die."

Tears dripped down his monster face.

"Let us go, Bobby. Do the right thing."

"I can't," he said, lunging for her. Both arms wrapped around her frail form.

Ciara screamed something and scratched at his cheek.

Bobby, finally aware of Ciara, let go of Parker and swung a haymaker at her. She ducked and fell onto the floor. He grabbed Parker's hair and pulled her as he stepped toward Ciara. Parker held onto his leg and bit into his calf, but he didn't seem to notice. Was he on drugs?

Then a soft voice came from the darkness. "Leave them alone, Bobby Boots."

She knew who it was.

Danny shuffled from the darkness, brushing dust and dirt from his face and hair. He coughed a little, and his jacket was ripped, probably from climbing over the big pile of rubble. His eyes locked onto her, and the goofy smile was there, like they weren't currently in mortal danger. In her mind, they were the only ones there; even Ciara was out of her thoughts. Finally, they were together again.

"I had to find you," he said.

Bobby let go of her hair. His voice was full of rage as he screamed at Danny. His words made no sense, either because of his anger or because she was only listening to Danny. It didn't really matter what he was saying. Not now.

He looked down at her. "Why do you love him and not me?"

The answer was easy. "I just do."

Bobby lunged at Danny, but he stepped out of the way. Bobby grabbed him and slammed him into the wall. The expression on Danny's face never changed. Danny reached for Bobby's head, slowly placing a hand on either side of his titanic skull. Bobby tried to pull away, but he just couldn't. He was a fly caught in a spider web.

"What are you doing, weirdo?"

Danny didn't say anything, but something was happening. Bobby struggled but only briefly. His eyes seemed to spark dimly at first then brighter and brighter. Then it stopped, and Bobby fell to the floor. He looked up at Parker but didn't seem to recognize her. The weirdest thing was that he was smiling. It was a sweet smile, like that of a child.

"He's not going to hurt anyone. Not anymore," Danny said.

"What did you do to him?" Ciara asked, stepping away from them and probably considering running as far away from Danny as possible.

Parker knew she couldn't explain any of this to her friend. It would take too long, and honestly, she didn't understand all of it either. She just didn't care.

Parker smiled at him. "Are you okay?"

Danny grinned. "I'm fine. I see you are too."

She hugged him as hard as she could.

He reached into his pocket. "I think this belongs to you."

It was her memory charm.

"I knew you'd find it. I knew you'd come."

CHAPTER THIRTY-NINE

Behind the Metal Door

Mary returned with a key ring and opened the laundry door. The room was warm and smelled like old underwear. One of the big dryers was running, making a dramatic thump-thump sound with every spin of its drum.

"Does one of these keys open that big metal door over there?" Paul asked.

"I don't know. Maybe."

Mick looked pale—not scared pale but excited pale. "Mary, who is that little girl we just saw?"

The nurse frowned. "What little girl?"

His voice was shaky, a rarity for Mick. "We just saw old Doc Hollis with a four-year-old brunette in a red dress. He has no children that we know of, and we should know. So, who is she?"

She shrugged. "His little niece visits him occasionally."

"He's got no goddamned niece," he spat. "Who is she?"

Shaking, Mary said, "Her name is Daisy. She's his niece."

"Hold on," Paul said. He retraced his steps to the doctor's office and opened the glass door leading to the main entrance.

Melissa stood by the front desk talking to the security guard and Jack. The big guy looked a little foggy, but he seemed to be smiling and listening to Jack tell a story.

Looks like there's no hard feelings, Paul thought. It was easy to forgive Jack Morgan. "Officer Davies, I need you here. Jack, don't let anyone leave until more officers arrive."

Jack frowned, but he nodded. "Now I'm a volunteer cop? I'll do it, but you find the kids."

A grey-haired lady stood at attention outside the laundry room when he returned. She wore pajamas with pictures from a Disney movie Paul had never seen. Her face was lined, and she had that confused look that was so common at the Lakeside. Yellow splotches graffitied her sleeves. She said, "Good, you're here."

Paul didn't know what to do. He saluted. "As you were."

Mick smiled behind her. "We have some backup now, I guess. Her name's Lucy."

"Did you deputize any other residents?" Paul asked. "Or just her?"

"She seems harmless."

Melissa followed him into the laundry room, glancing curiously at Lucy.

"This is big, Melissa. Way bigger than we thought."

"What do you mean?"

He told her about the doctor's *niece*.

"Oh, my God. Who is she?"

He shrugged. "Maybe another kidnap victim. I don't know. This guy's full of secrets, and none of them look good."

"Paul," Mick said. "She found the key."

The metal door opened a crack. When Mick pulled on it, the hinges creaked loud enough to wake up half the residents.

Paul looked into the darkness and saw stairs. He glanced at Mary, "Where do these steps lead?"

Mary shook her head.

"We've got officers on the way," Mick said. "We could wait for them."

Paul didn't want to wait. The mystery girl was down there somewhere, not to mention Freddie and his Scooby Squad were probably wandering around and trampling evidence. And Hollis was trying to bolt, no doubt. Waiting seemed like a mistake.

"What do you think?"

Mick snorted. "You know what I'm thinking. Let's go."

That was what he wanted to hear. "Officer Davies, stop anyone who comes out this door that isn't us, got it? And make sure our guys set up a perimeter around the building when they get here. The doctor's looking for an exit."

Melissa didn't seem herself. She tapped her hand against her belt, and her breathing seemed irregular. This whole case was going to be a shitstorm for the ages—lots of press, lots of second guessing. The case of a lifetime probably, and she was feeling it. The next few hours could make or break her career.

"I guess the old lady's keeping an eye on the door for us over there," Paul said. "You just do what you've been trained to do here."

Melissa smiled at him, but she looked nervous.

Paul took his flashlight from his belt and stepped onto the landing. He flashed the light down the steps and started walking as he massaged his holstered service weapon. He could hear the *tap-tap* of his partner's duty boots and looked back.

Mick was a few steps behind him on the other side of the stairs. His light was examining the walls and the ceiling. "Let's roll."

CHAPTER FORTY

The Room with a Treadmill

Rachel's hair was darker than in pictures—not black but really brown. And her skin was white as porcelain, probably from being inside for all these years. She wore Lee jeans, a tight blue sweater, and dark socks without shoes. The clothes made her look a little older than she was. More than anything, Rachel just looked tired. She was still alive though, and Sophie couldn't believe it.

"Who are you?" she asked.

Sophie tried to smile, but she was in too much shock. "I'm Sophie. This is Freddie."

"What are you doing here?"

"We're looking for a friend of ours," Freddie answered. "We think Doc Hollis took her."

"Oh, no. William's been acting ... weird, even for him. Sleeping over every night, eating with us."

"*Us?*" Sophie asked.

Rachel nodded toward the wall, and Sophie saw a door that didn't match the rest of the room. It was hung crooked, and she knew Freddie was judging the craftsmanship. He could do so much better.

He opened the door and looked in.

"What is it, Freddie?"

"It's a kid's room. A girl, I guess."

The walls were pink, and Disney posters hung everywhere. A bed with a bright, fluffy comforter consumed much of the space. A glowing plastic moon decorated the wall, and coloring books covered the floor. It reminded her of Belle's room.

Derek groaned and started to get up.

Freddie kicked him in the shoulder. "Stay down until I tell you to get up."

"Where is your daughter?" Sophie asked.

"He has her."

"Doc Hollis?" Freddie asked.

Rachel nodded.

The main room was a mix of bedroom and living room. An old-time stereo sat on a shelf mounted to the wall. A treadmill was on the other side of the room near the bathroom. The room was painted yellow, and an unopened Wendy's bag sat on her bed. With all of that, it still looked like a lonely hospital room. How long had Rachel been here?

"Where did he take her?" Freddie asked.

"He takes her upstairs sometimes. William tells everyone she's his niece. She has to call him *Uncle Bill.*"

Sophie's heart skipped. "And everybody believes him?"

She shrugged.

The room was starting to swallow Sophie up, and she wanted to leave. "Have you been down here all this time? I mean, you've been missing for six years."

"Only six years? God, it seems so much longer."

Her pale face was lined, and purple bags hung under her eyes. She didn't seem sad exactly—maybe melancholy, if Sophie understood the word right, like her will had been broken, but she couldn't quite give up on her past. She wasn't rushing to leave the room she'd been locked in for so long. Maybe Rachel had just grown accustomed to it all.

"We're getting you out of here, Rachel," Sophie said. "He's gonna pay."

"I need to find Daisy. He brought her a jacket. Why would she need a jacket?"

"The cops are watching the entrance," Freddie said. "He's not going anywhere."

Sophie grabbed Freddie's arm and nodded toward Derek. "Get him up. We need to find out what he knows."

She didn't have to ask him twice. He grabbed Derek's collar and yanked him to his feet then pushed him against the wall.

Derek's eyes were more red than white, and he slurred, "Let go of me."

"I have two questions … no, three questions, Derek," Sophie said. "First, where's her little girl? Where's Daisy?"

Derek shook his head and half-grinned. "I'm not saying anything."

We don't have time for this, she thought.

Freddie was reading her mind. He slammed Derek against the wall, ripping a hole in the dry wall. "Tell us now, or—"

"He has her. He's leaving."

"That's impossible," Sophie said. "The cops are outside."

"How'd you get in then?"

Sophie thought about it. If they could find a way in, Doc Hollis could certainly find a way out—probably not the same way though. The cellar door had been locked from the outside. "How's he getting out?"

A stream of blood ran from the side of Derek's mouth to his jaw. She wondered if it was just from a loose tooth or if he had internal damage from Freddie's gut punch. Was she bad for hoping it was the worst injury? This kid really needed to suffer.

"Derek," Freddie said. "We're not asking again."

"The office at the end of the hall after the nursery."

"What about it?" Sophie asked.

"There's a window that's above ground. It's behind the bushes and the glass is all dirty. He's climbing out."

Rachel's frail face tightened. "Where's he taking her?"

"I don't know. He's collecting some stuff upstairs, then he's taking off. He said he'll send for us."

Sophie looked at Freddie. "What do we do?"

"We go upstairs and call the cops. He won't get far."

"First, we find Parker," Sophie said. "She's here. Isn't she, Derek?"

He tucked his head and pushed Freddie back, bolting for the door.

Freddie grabbed his neck and pulled him back, throwing him to the tile floor. Freddie's face was tight, and he looked wicked mad again.

"Don't hit me, Freddie. Please."

Sophie put her arm around Freddie's waist. "We have to find Parker."

He didn't say anything. Instead, he stomped to the doorway and stood there, arms crossed.

"Derek, I don't know if I can stop him again. Honestly, I don't know if I *want* to stop him. How could you get involved in something this bad?"

Derek glanced at Freddie then looked away quickly. He lowered his voice. "Doc Hollis understands me."

Sadly, that was probably true. "Is Parker down here? Is Ciara?"

Rachel almost sounded jealous. "*Two* girls?"

"They were downstairs."

"*Were?*" Sophie repeated.

He tilted his head so Freddie couldn't see his smirk. "We got Wendy's for them too."

Sophie didn't understand. "What's that mean?"

"He was yelling at Rachel when I got here, pushing her," Freddie said. "He was really mad because she didn't eat her Wendy's."

Sophie flashed back to the hole in the basement. "You freak! What did you put in their food?"

"I don't know. Doc gave it to us."

She slapped him across his cheek, the palm of her hand burning from the blow. "Parker's my best friend!"

"If they're dead, I'm feeding *you* the Frosty. You got that?" Freddie added.

Derek nodded.

"Where are they?"

No smirk this time. "Downstairs, about halfway down the hallway."

"Is Bobby Boots with them?" Freddie asked.

Derek couldn't resist. "Are you afraid of Bobby?"

"No. He's just another bully."

If Freddie was afraid of anyone, it was his mother. Bobby Boots and Derek and probably even Doc Hollis didn't scare him. He wasn't wired that way. That's why she loved him.

"Let's go get my friends," Sophie said. "Then we'll get Daisy."

"Give Sophie the keys. And your phone," Freddie said.

Her phone didn't work in the basement, but maybe he had a different plan that worked in underground prisons. Sophie wasn't taking any chances.

They entered the hallway and closed the door behind them, making sure it was secure. Derek whined about being locked up, which made it feel good to close the door. He would be locked up somewhere else when this was over.

Rachel looked around. "Wow."

"Have you been in the hallway before?" Sophie asked. "I mean, recently?"

"I got the door open once, and Daisy and I made it to the top of the steps. There was a locked door, and we banged on it until some confused orderly found us. William told the kid we were special patients and he'd take care of us."

"Did the kid have red hair?" Sophie asked.

Rachel nodded. "Do you know him?"

Sophie looked down.

"Anyway, that's when Derek and his friend started helping out. I guess William decided he needed backup."

"We have to go," Freddie said.

Rachel was lost in her memories. "William said he wouldn't have caught me if I wasn't so fat. He said my ass was too big to get up the stairs and no woman of his was going to have a fat ass. That's when he got the treadmill. I have to run for at least an hour every day. Sometimes, it makes me lightheaded."

Sophie's heart broke, but Freddie was right. Parker and Ciara's lives were on the line. She used her gentlest voice, "Let's get going, Rachel. We'll talk about your butt later, okay?"

Rachel smiled. "Okay."

Freddie stared down the hallway past the janitor's closet and the nursery. Two figures stood in the hallway—one an adult, the other a child. It was Doc Hollis and Daisy; it had to be. The taller one grabbed the smaller one and disappeared into an office. He was making a run for it.

"I have to get Daisy," Rachel said.

Sophie held her slim arm. "You're in no shape to climb out windows and crawl through three feet of snow in your stockings. Freddie, you have to do something."

"What do I do?"
"Go get her, Freddie. She's a little girl."
"But what about you and Rachel?"
She gave him her angry look. "Go frickin' get her!"

CHAPTER FORTY-ONE

REUNIONS

"Freddie will find her," Sophie said. "He won't fail."

Rachel leaned against the wall, crying softly. "She's my daughter."

They were still outside Rachel's old room, and they could hear Derek screaming.

Sophie banged on the door. "Be quiet in there, or I'm sending Freddie back in."

He stopped.

Sophie said, "Let's go downstairs and try to find my friend."

Rachel shook her head. "I should wait."

"They're not coming back this way, Rachel. We need to find my friends then get the cops."

"I don't know."

Sophie was trying to be thoughtful, but she had to get to Parker. "I can't leave you here, Rachel. Daisy needs you to be strong."

Rachel nodded. "I guess you're right. I'm her only family besides William. Isn't that just terrible?"

"You have family, Rachel, and they miss you. They'll love Daisy too."

Sadness washed across her face. "My family's gone. It's just us now."

"What are you talking about? I've met your parents. They haven't given up on you."

"My parents are alive?"

Sophie smiled. "Of course."

"But William told me that my father died right after I … I came here. He had a heart attack. And my mother died soon after in a car accident. He was lying?"

"Oh my God, Rachel. Doc Hollis is such an *asshole*."

It was like somebody had turned on a light. Rachel's smile was wide.

"Freddie and Danny know your dad. Danny told him you weren't dead."

She looked confused. "Who's Danny?"

That was such a good question.

Sophie took her hand and led her toward the stairs. "We have to find Parker and, hopefully, Ciara. That's why we came here in the first place. You're a bonus."

Rachel laughed. "A bonus. I'm a bonus."

"Come on."

The stairs were dark, but Sophie didn't want to use her light. Bobby Boots might be patrolling the hallways, and she didn't want to deal with him. Freddie wasn't afraid of the monster, but she sure was. She'd had nightmares about him chasing her around the church after Sammy's funeral service. She would run as fast as she could, but he always caught her, like the killer in *Halloween*.

A door at the landing was propped open. The hallway was brighter than she expected, and that made her nervous. Less light meant less chance of Bobby seeing them. "I'll just peek down the hallway. You wait here."

She felt Rachel's grip tighten. "I'm going with you."

They tiptoed across the landing until they stood just outside the doorframe. Something sticky on the floor made her sneakers squeak with each step. It must have been worse for Rachel, who was only in her socks. The stairway was warm, and the stale air carried a rusty taste. The claustrophobia that almost got her in the meth lab was bubbling back up. She shook her head to clear away the crazy thoughts. This wasn't the time to be weak.

Sophie dipped her head and looked down the hallway. Someone sat near the pile of crap that had blocked their way earlier. She thought it might be Danny, but she realized it was somebody much larger. It was Bobby.

Sophie yanked back her head. Her heart was beating almost enough to rip a hole in her chest.

"What is it?"

"Bobby Boots."

Rachel's face grew even paler.

"Do you hear someone talking?"

A murmur mixed with laughter came from somewhere.

Sophie looked at Rachel. "How many people does *William* have helping him?"

"Bobby and Derek. That's it, as far as I know."

She looked down the hallway again. Bobby hadn't moved much. The noise came from a room near them. A light was on, and she definitely heard laughter—familiar laughter.

"I'm going to see who's in there."

Rachel said, "Maybe we should go. If Bobby see us—"

"If he sees us, we can outrun him. You run an hour a day on your treadmill."

Rachel didn't look convinced.

"He's not looking this way. Come on."

"Listen, I should be the one leading the way. I'm the grownup."

She yanked her new friend's arm, and they tripped into the hallway.

Bobby didn't look at them; he sat still and occasionally moved his hands around. Maybe he was meditating? Sophie rolled her eyes at the thought. He was probably high, like Derek. That's the only way those two creeps could get themselves to bury their victims. Maybe Bobby was liquoring up because he'd just disposed of Parker. Maybe it was too late.

The voices were louder and more familiar.

Sophie pulled Rachel's hand again and sprinted toward the room. The floor was rough, like upstairs, and she kicked a piece of metal that skittered almost all the way to Bobby. He didn't seem to notice. The laughter stopped though. Somebody had heard it.

After some excited whispering, she heard footsteps. Sliding footsteps.

Before she took a step, she saw the grin and the crazy hair shuffling from the room. His jacket was torn, and his face and hands were dirty. Despite that, Danny looked happier than he had in weeks. For the first time ever, she realized he was kind of cute, in his own way. He was eating something, of course—a strawberry Pop Tart. He could find food anywhere.

She released Rachel's hand and ran to hug him, not caring if he got dirt or crumbs on her nice jacket.

His voice sounded kind of British. "Very nice to see you, madam."

"What are you? A butler?"

He laughed. "I'm Mr. Belvedere."

She didn't know who that was. "How did you get here?"

He grinned. "Climbed. I've got something for you in the cafeteria I think you'll be happy to see. An early Christmas present."

"What's wrong with Bobby Boots down there?"

He glanced down the hallway. Bobby flailed his hands and seemed to be arguing with shadows. "He's reflecting."

Reflecting, she thought. *He's reflecting.* "Okay."

Danny looked past her. "You found Rachel."

"We did. What did you find?"

The cafeteria was bigger than she expected. The bright lights didn't flicker, like in the hallway, and the refrigerator hummed loudly. Parker sat at one of the tables, along with a pretty blonde girl who had to be Ciara. The girl was smiling, but she seemed sad. Sophie didn't want to ask her why. She could guess.

"Sophie!" Parker cried out.

She ran to greet her friend.

Parker stood and hugged her, and they both cried.

"I'm so sorry for making you mad, Parker. I'm so sorry."

Parker laughed. "Danny says you've more than made up for it. Thanks for looking after Jessica."

When they hugged again, Sophie remembered that her friend shouldn't be standing. "How are you walking?"

"You know how."

Sophie looked back at Danny, who was walking in with Rachel. She remembered the time he had touched Parker's back at the bowling alley.

Her feet had been twitching after that. Doc Hollis had made it seem like it had been nothing, just nerves. Boy, was he wrong.

"Is that her?" Parker asked.

"It's Rachel Randall."

"Holy cow."

Sophie snorted. "I know. And she has a daughter."

"Holy something else."

Rachel looked at them and smiled. Her gaze shifted to Ciara. She looked like she would cry again.

Sophie took a step toward her. "Are you okay?"

Rachel shook her head. "I should have stopped him."

"It's not your fault, Rachel. None of this is."

She leaned in. "William has told me over and over again that he loves me, that he took me because he had to have me. Part of me always thought, at least he's not hurting somebody else, just me. I never really believed him about the loving-me crap, but it didn't occur to me he wanted to start a harem."

"He's not hurting anyone else now," Sophie said. "He's done."

Danny shuffled into the hallway. "There's soda in the fridge and a bunch of snacks. You guys should eat something before we get going."

Rachel said, "I could eat. Just smelling those French fries was making me hungry." She walked into the café, and the girls rose to help her. *They should get to know each other, because they'll all be testifying at Doc Hollis' trial.*

"Sophie, where's Freddie?" Danny asked.

CHAPTER FORTY-TWO

SAVING DAISY

The light in the room didn't work, and he'd left his big flashlight with Sophie. Freddie still had his cellphone though, so he pressed the bright light app and navigated through the small room. It was tight and had no bathroom, and the floor didn't have a bunch of debris everywhere, like most of the other rooms he'd seen. It looked like it had once been somebody's office—maybe an administrator or the head of neurosurgery. It didn't matter to Freddie. He was just passing through.

He heard the wind whistle through the window before he saw it. It must have been stuck, and Doc Hollis had been in a hurry, because the glass was busted. Freddie didn't know what the doctor had used, but he had cleared away most of the shards. Dark liquid drops dotted the window frame, and he guessed either Doc Hollis or Daisy had cut themselves climbing out. It didn't seem like enough blood to be anything serious.

The window was narrow too, but he could squeeze through if he held his breath. He pushed a sideways metal cabinet to the window. The metal was rusty and wobbly under his weight, but he pushed off and climbed through the smashed window and landed face first into a snowbank. His legs angled weirdly, and he had to twist around before he could pull them out. Then he stood. The snow was to his waist; he was outside, staring at Lakeside's parking lot.

His head was wet from pushing it through a snowbank, and his fingers burned from the cold. He wiped at his face and hair until it felt partially dry then put his hands in his pockets. The cold pond wind stabbed him with little razors until he pulled up the hood from his parka. It helped a little, and he wished he'd thought to have it on when he had climbed out.

The parking lot was a little fuller than when he and his friends had arrived. The cops' white Malibu was in the parking lot now, right near the entrance. The security car was still running, but the driver-side door was open, and it was empty. A truck resembling his father's Silverado was parked near Doc Hollis' car. What was his dad doing here?

He saw flashing lights coming down the street, the howling wind muting their sirens. Somehow the cops had an idea of what was happening. They were inside looking around. He wondered if one of the detectives had recognized the Mustang and had called his house. Or maybe his dad had found the note he'd left on his desk.

Though the wind whipped everything around, the sky was quiet and peaceful. The moon was about three-quarters full, and the stars were bright. The pond was glowing under the cloudless sky. Freddie noticed his house lights were on. Was his mother up? She was probably sitting in her chair, knitting and worrying.

Somebody was tugging a smaller person through the parking lot. Freddie knew it had to be Doc Hollis making his getaway. He hollered for someone to stop them, but he couldn't hear his own voice in the wind.

Doc opened his BMW's driver-side door and tossed in his daughter. The interior light came on, giving Freddie a glimpse of a terrified little girl squirming in the back seat. Doc Hollis was pointing at her and fiddling with her seatbelt. Freddie realized the poor girl had probably never been in a car, let alone put on a seatbelt. She had to be scared. The light went off, and the car moved. Doc Hollis didn't put on the headlights as he pulled away.

Freddie ran toward the parking lot, hoping to get somebody's attention. He screamed loud enough to hurt his throat, but the wind was still too loud. He cursed at Doc Hollis with words he'd learned from his father.

The Beamer stopped at the entrance and started to turn right. Freddie saw police lights coming from that direction. Doc Hollis backed into the parking lot and stopped. Freddie changed direction and bounced through the snow toward the parking lot. Maybe it wasn't too late to stop him.

The BMW turned left toward the pond. The doctor was taking the back route along the edge of the pond—the same way Freddie had taken to get to Lakeside. Freddie wondered if he could reach his Mustang in time to chase after the BMW. Maybe he would find out who had the faster car after all.

The car stopped again, and Freddie saw more flashing lights approaching. Hollis was cornered, it seemed. The BMW moved forward then backed up and pulled into the nearest plowed driveway. The cottage was small and didn't even have a carport. He inched forward until it was at the edge of the driveway then floored it and bounced through some bushes and onto the ice.

"No, no, no," Freddie said. "Stop!"

Freddie thought about waiting for the cop cars and flagging them down, but he didn't think there was enough time. That ice wouldn't hold a car for long—not even a light one, like the BMW. The weather had been too weird lately, and the temperatures had been all over the place the last few weeks. Doc Hollis, of all people, should have known better.

He sprinted through the lot, slipping on black ice once, and followed them to the edge of the driveway. He looked across the pond and saw the tiny car spinning, ice clouds exploding around its wheels as it tried to find traction. It was already a quarter of the way across the pond, but it was stuck. The car would back up a little and then spin some more.

He remembered following Danny onto the ice just a few weeks back. They had been lucky to make it back to shore. Following Doc Hollis and Daisy onto the frozen pond seemed like a dangerous idea. But what else could he do?

He took a step onto the ice, and then another. It seemed solid.

The BMW sputtered toward him, and Freddie hoped Doc Hollis had come to his senses and was coming back. The headlights came on and froze Freddie in his tracks. He knew Doc Hollis was looking at him and thinking.

Freddie took his hands from his pockets and gestured for the doctor to come back. "You can't make it that way! Come back!"

The car suddenly reversed at a dangerous clip. Freddie shook his head.

He tried to slide rather than run across the ice, but it was hard and jagged, not smooth, so he ran, falling twice and scraping his knees. Both times, he got up and hustled after them. Freddie didn't really care much about Doc Hollis at this point, but he couldn't let the little girl down. She deserved a happy ending—or something close to it.

The car stopped abruptly, and he couldn't see the headlights anymore. Freddie knew that wasn't because the doctor had turned them off. The ice was giving out, and they were sinking. The taillights were high in the air, and he thought of the movie *Titanic*. The ship had raised up before crashing down. And then most everyone died. Freddie didn't want to be Leonard DiCaprio, hanging onto that piece of debris.

When he reached the car, the front end was underwater. Daisy's face was pressed against the glass, and she looked terrified.

He banged on the window. "Roll it down, roll it down."

The poor girl had no idea.

"Tell your father to roll down your window!"

She must have heard him, or at least understood him, because she turned her head and said something. The window began to go down.

"Help me," the girl said. "I'm stuck."

The window stopped at the halfway mark.

"Roll it down more, Doctor Hollis! Roll it all the way down!"

The dome light came on, and Freddie saw Doc Hollis' face. The doctor could barely look him in the eye. "I'm pressing the button! It won't go down any farther. I can't get the doors to unlock either! Freddie, save my little girl."

Freddie carefully placed one hand on top of the car and put the other through the window. "I'll pull you out."

"I'm stuck," she said. "Uncle Bill put me in these ropes."

She meant the seatbelt.

"You have to find the release button. It's down by your hip. Press the button, and the belt will come loose."

The car shifted, and the front sank deeper into the water. Daisy screamed.

Freddie tried to sound calm. "Don't be afraid, Daisy. Just press the button, and then I can pull you out."

"I'm trying."

He nodded. "You're doing great, but you have to hurry."

He felt the ice bursting apart beneath his feet. The little German car spilled into the water, and Freddie fell in with it. He reached for the ice to pull himself up, but he couldn't find anything to grab. His pants were soaked, and his legs felt numb already. His parka was only half underwater, but it was getting wetter and heavier. Freddie twisted around and pulled one arm from its sleeve and then the other. It slowly floated to the other side of the hole.

I am screwed, he thought. *Screwed royally.*

He knew what he had to do.

Freddie took in a breath and went under. The water was pitch black, but that was useful. He could see the BMW's interior lights below him in the dark. He kicked off his shoes and swam slowly toward the light. It felt like the water was crushing him, and he had to fight the panic that screamed at him to turn back. His heart was racing, even in the bitter cold.

Freddie knew the water was close to twenty feet deep, and it was a tough swim. His fingers weren't numb enough yet, so he felt the needles stabbing at them. The wet clothes kept trying to pull him in the wrong direction, and course correction drained his struggling lungs. Somehow, he wriggled off his sweater, and that helped a little. His head felt a weird kind of cloudy, and he didn't know if he could trust his thoughts. He almost felt drunk.

Still, he reached the bumper and pulled himself toward the rear door. When he looked in, he saw the car filled with water. Daisy looked at him again, but she had this foggy look, like she was ready to take a nap.

He tried the door handle—locked. Freddie reached in and struggled to find the seatbelt, but he didn't have a good enough grasp on the car, and he started to float away. His fingers caught the half-open window, and he pulled himself back. He reached in with his other hand and found the top of the seatbelt. Tracing it to her side, he found the button and pressed. The seatbelt came loose.

Freddie grabbed her shoulder and pulled her to the window. She was small, and he yanked her through the opening with ease. Weird thoughts wormed through his brain. He thought about letting her go and swimming for it. Nobody would ever know. After shaking off that idea, he considered giving up. The needles were gone now, though his lungs still burned, and he felt kind of good—almost euphoric. Maybe he could just go to sleep and see what happened. That wouldn't be so bad.

The interior lights suddenly turned off and snapped Freddie back to reality. He wrapped one arm around the girl and kicked toward the surface. The pond was well-lit from his vantage point. His legs weren't kicking much, even though his brain was ordering them to. Freddie's arm still worked, so he paddled until his head bumped the ice. It was solid, and he saw someone looking at him, someone with dark skin and a terrified look on his face. He knew it was his reflection, but it was more than that. It was an image from a dream.

The water pulled him down again, but he fought it and forced his way up. This time the ice was gone. He gulped in air and coughed and gulped in some more. He was right in the middle of the hole the BMW had created. Freddie kicked to the edge of the water and tried to lift Daisy. She must have weighed a thousand pounds, because he couldn't move her. He wrapped a frozen hand around the edge of the ice and lifted her with the other hand. This time, he was moving her. When she was out of the water, she felt lighter. He lifted her straight up then dropped her onto the ice. The ice didn't crack. Daisy might be okay if somebody got to her quickly.

He tried to pull himself onto the ice beside her, but he knew he didn't have the strength. He was spent.

Freddie sank back into the black water that had taken Ryan all those years ago.

CHAPTER FORTY-THREE

A Bird Under the Blue Moonlight

It wasn't so bad.

Freddie couldn't move his arms or his legs anymore, and the weight of his pants and shirt pulled him downward but not all the way to the bottom. He floated at about the halfway point, enjoying the view. The moonlight through the thick ice was bright and seemed a light shade of blue. It was beautiful.

Occasionally, his lungs ordered him to gasp for air, but he fought the urge. Freddie wasn't sure why. He knew would die, and that was alright. The little girl wasn't drowning, and Doc Hollis wasn't going anywhere. Overall, it was a victory. He was going to miss his friends, but he knew they'd remember him.

It would be hard on Sophie. He knew how he felt about her and was sure she felt the same. Maybe they would have been one of the few couples who got married young and stayed together, like in a George Strait song. God, he was going to miss George too. He could really carry a song. No autotune for that guy.

Above the ice, a bird flew in silhouette under the moon. It was hard to watch it, because his body spun from the pond current, and his eyes, which refused to blink, had trouble focusing. The bird's wings flapped as it glided back and forth, perhaps hunting prey. It turned and dove at him. He hoped the poor thing didn't smash into the ice.

The ice never even slowed it, and it sped toward him. Maybe it was an angel come to take him home. He'd never thought much about religion until recently, and he still didn't really have an opinion. It didn't seem likely that angels flew from the sky and grabbed people, but that would be cool. He was alright with it. *Come and get me.*

It wasn't an angel.

It was Danny. His cheeks were puffed out, like he was holding extra air in them, and his oversized t-shirt flapped in the current. Danny's crazy hair stood up in all directions. He looked like a peacock. Freddie laughed a little and choked on some water.

His friend grabbed his collar and looked into his eyes. Danny seemed scared and tried to pull Freddie's shirt, but he wasn't strong enough. Honestly, it was a miracle he'd made it all the way out onto the pond, considering how frail he was.

Freddie smiled at his friend and tried to shake his head. It didn't move at all, but it did feel warm. And cloudy.

Danny snaked around until he floated above him. Freddie wanted to warn him away, to tell him to save himself. The look of desperation on Danny's face told Freddie that he wasn't going anywhere. His lungs screamed at him again, and he considered gulping in the water. That might make Danny leave.

Placing a hand on Freddie's chest, Danny grabbed one of Freddie's hands with the other. He felt something like a squeeze, but all sensation was fading. Danny looked frustrated and seemed to squeeze harder. That was when Freddie felt the shock.

It was like the time he'd reached into an aquarium to grab a light that had fallen in. He was only a kid, six or seven, and he didn't know anything about electricity. He was in class, and his teacher yanked his arm out of the water. Mrs. Morton asked him if he was okay. He was, though the fish kept swimming into the glass after. It was like that but times a thousand.

His arms lurched forward, and his legs kicked, hitting Danny. He kept squeezing.

Freddie's mind was clear, and his eyes were sharp. Boy, were they sharp. He looked down and saw the BMW sticking out from the pond sand. The lights were out now, but he could see Doc Hollis locked in by his seatbelt, his eyes open, dead. Freddie saw the giant rocks that jutted up from the beneath, some of them large enough to pierce the surface. He realized he was nowhere near the opening the BMW had made, but it was easy enough to spot. Right now, he could see just about everything.

He looked for Danny and saw him floating away. Freddie kicked toward him, amazed at how strong his arms felt. It took only a few seconds to grab his friend and paddle for the surface. That was harder because of Danny's weight. It seemed impossible at first, but he wouldn't let the water take Danny this time. No way.

They probably needed to cover ten feet, but it felt like a hundred. Freddie's arms were felt crazy strong, but his lungs burned. They didn't have much time. Danny wasn't moving; he wasn't doing anything. That thought scared him enough to kick harder and will them to the surface.

It seemed like forever, but his head broke through the top of the water. His throat made a hacking noise as his lungs desperately gasped at the air. Danny was still underwater, so he pulled him up with both arms until his head was on the right side of the pond. He didn't make the same noise Freddie had made, but he looked like he was breathing. Freddie trusted his eyes and gave himself hope.

Tossing Danny onto the ice wasn't as easy as it had been with Daisy. He did it in steps, pushing him farther onto the ice each time. He heard Daisy ask, "Is he all right?"

Freddie could only see her head; Danny's jacket was wrapped around the rest of her. She stood beside Danny, looking down at him.

"Move back, Daisy. I have to climb out."

He saw a piece of ice jutting up enough to be a hand hold, and he grabbed it with his right arm. It wasn't easy, but he pulled most of his body from the pool and jerked the rest of it onto the ice. Sitting on the ice on his butt and soaked with freezing pond water, Freddie still felt warm. He still felt good.

"How are you, Daisy?"

"I feel warm."

"We have to get off the ice. You have to stay close to me, okay?"

"Okay."

Freddie noticed a crowd forming at the cottage with no dock. One of the detectives was inching onto the ice. The other was holding back Rachel Randall.

She was in a panic, but Freddie knew he'd get Daisy to her soon enough. He could see the ice like he was looking at a blueprint. It looked funny but made complete sense to him.

Sophie and Parker stood near the water's edge, holding hands. How was Parker standing? Ciara Clark was behind them, a blanket draped over her shoulders. His father ran across the parking lot and appeared to be swearing. Some of the hospital staff peered into the darkness from outside the entrance as an orderly smoked a cigarette. Police lights were everywhere. Not your normal December night on Abbot Pond.

He gripped Daisy's hand then grabbed Danny's collar just behind his head and dragged him across the ice. They moved quickly toward land, but they weren't worried about soft spots; Freddie saw them all. So did Daisy.

When he reached land, Sophie ran to him and hugged him. He didn't hug her back; he was too busy pulling Danny onto the plowed driveway. "Somebody get him a blanket!"

Lights flooded the driveway, and Danny feebly raised his arms to shield his eyes.

Freddie looked back and saw a police car with its high beams and blue lights activated behind him. Christmas was coming early.

Danny grabbed his arm. "Freddie …"

Sophie still held him from the hug. She hadn't let go, and he hadn't noticed. "He doesn't look good, Freddie."

Danny looked *small* somehow, and his eyes were almost blank. A puddle of water had formed all around him, like a liquid chalk mark for a dead man.

Daisy fiercely held onto Freddie's leg and didn't look like she had any intention of letting go.

Rachel put her arm on her daughter's shoulder but didn't pull her away.

"Hold on, Danny," Freddie said. "Help is on its way."

Parker pushed past him, sat by Danny's side and took his hand.

Freddie whispered, "Don't do this, Danny. Don't do it."

"Parker …" Danny said. "Parker …"

"Danny, I'm here. I came for you."

He smiled. "Do you remember what I told you that night in my room on Thanksgiving?"

Parker looked down then back up again and nodded. "I remember."

"I promise," he said.

She squeezed his hand.

"I promise."

Parker sobbed. "Don't go."

He whispered, "You know I was only here for a visit."

Freddie's dad ran up and stopped a few feet away, breathing heavy. He glanced away for a second then back at Danny. "No …!"

Freddie kneeled beside Parker. "You'll be okay, Danny. Help is coming."

Danny turned his head slightly. "Freddie, you're my brother. We have the same parents. You'll always be my brother. You have to believe that."

Tears streamed down Freddie's cheeks. "Don't do this, Danny."

But Danny was done. He had no more light to give.

CHAPTER FORTY-FOUR

Friends Forever

Freddie stood just outside the church by the kitchen entrance, watching the crowd of reporters parked across the street. A building was behind them—a small one, where the mortuary was storing Sammy's casket until spring warmup. Danny's casket was going to be left there too after everybody left. When the ground unfroze, he was going into the family plot—not the Cole family but the Morgan family, where he belonged.

Snow fell at a good clip. The weatherman had predicted six to eight inches, but it felt like more. The cars in the lot already had an inch or so covering them, and the storm was just beginning. Freddie looked up at the grey clouds and wished he could see the sun. There had been enough snow this winter.

Sophie came out and stood beside him. She wore a tight-fitting blue dress. They had spent two hours at the mall looking for just the right outfit. It took him about fifteen minutes to find his nice charcoal-colored suit. He didn't mind shopping with her. It cleared his head.

"Your mom's looking for you," she said. "She wants you to meet someone she went to high school with."

He nodded. "I just need a minute."

"Jessica apologized to me again. I'm kind of tired of it."

"Richard told me he'd been wrong, that Danny wasn't an idiot. I know it sounds funny, but I cried when he said it."

"I'm so glad I changed my mind about him."

He took her hand and kissed her forehead. "He liked that you were watching out for Parker."

The door flung open, and Daisy came running out, wearing an unzipped heavy winter jacket with mittens spilling out from her pockets and a cute red dress. She threw open her arms, and he wrapped her in his arms. "I love you, Freddie."

He teared up. "Right back at you, little girl."

"And Danny too. He helped me."

Vince and Rachel followed her out, and Rachel hugged him too. She was still pale, but her cheeks were fuller, and her hair was shorter, with new blonde streaks. Freddie thought she looked better. Better and stronger.

"We have to get going, Freddie," Rachel said. "The traffic's going to be rough in this snow."

"You're welcome to stay with us," he said. "We have room."

She smiled. "I know you love this town, but …"

He just nodded.

Rachel hugged Sophie then said, "Come on, Daisy. We have to get going."

"When will I see you again, Freddie?" Daisy asked.

He messed her hair a little. "We'll be down in the spring, I promise."

She took a few steps with her mother then turned. "Friends forever, right?"

He nodded.

Vince Randall grabbed Freddie's hand and shook it firmly. "I can never thank you enough. And Danny, he was a great kid. So are you."

Freddie watched them weave through the parking lot. Reporters shouted obnoxious questions at them and took pictures. If Rachel noticed, she covered it well and never looked at them. Vince was driving a new SUV, and Rachel put Daisy in the back, carefully strapping her into a car seat. Daisy waved.

Sophie tugged on his arm. "Your mother …"

He shook his head. "Why don't you go get Parker, and we'll go do something. Maybe go bowling again. It's been a while."

She cocked her head and made a funny face. "Dressed like this?"

He smiled. "You look great."

Sophie shook her head. "Your mother will blame me, you know. You should really talk to her first."

"I think she'll understand, Sophie. I really do."

"Parker will want to bring Ciara."

"That's okay. I like her."

"Can we bring Belle? She held my hand all through the service."

"We can squeeze her in. I like her too."

Sophie disappeared into the church, and Freddie walked toward his Mustang. It was covered in snow; he would need to brush it off. He hoped the roads were okay. The bowling alley was across town, and some black ice was probably still hiding in the snowy streets. Maybe he should start looking at colleges in warm-weather states. That wouldn't be bad.

He'd had enough of winter.

Acknowledgements

ABBOT POND was a little more challenging to write than the others, but well worth the effort. I couldn't have pulled this off without my wife and partner, Jennifer, who gets things done.

Shout out to Emily, Colby and Zack. Your support means everything to me.

I'd like to thank Anita Haskell and Lynn Vadnais for their assistance. Apparently, I am capable of making grammatical mistakes.

Thanks always to Teresa Tucker, who still motivates me.

Many thanks to Brian Paone.

Finally, I'd like to mention Fred Peavey, who is a good guy and looks out for his mom and dad.

About the Author

Steve Hobbs is a Maine native still residing in New England. He is a graduate of Southern New Hampshire University and lives a quiet, normal life. Steve likes to write about normal people involved in somewhat abnormal circumstances. He never guarantees a happy ending but sometimes comes close. To learn more about Steve, visit www.hobbspond.com.